I0760805

LOST IN SPACE FOR CENTURIES

"Even if this container is just full of wood, it's a win," Quinn said. "Real wood is worth serious money." Quinn peered at the screen over Carter's shoulder as the drone began to move through the crowded aisle. Often the pilot had to maneuver the drone sideways to get past obstacles.

"We have something," Quinn reported. On the screen, the aisle opened to an area of about three meters cubed. The fan of light from the small drone revealed a single console and an occupied chair in front of it.

Reclined in the chair was a body in an ancient emergency pressure suit. The desiccated head leaned back inside the helmet. The toothy mouth was wide open as if it was screaming at its maker. Empty eye sockets stared at the ceiling.

"Look at this," Pope said.

In the standard name block on the helmet, right above the visor, was the word, "Curator."

Anthologies from the Hourlings

The Curator
Reliquary
Tranquility and Other Myths

Other Tannhauser Press Anthologies

Fantastic Defenders
Silence of the Apoc
Whispers of the Apoc
The Witness Paradox

Forthcoming Anthologies

Outsiders: Tales of Outlaws, Lone Wolves and Drifters
Tales from the Forever House

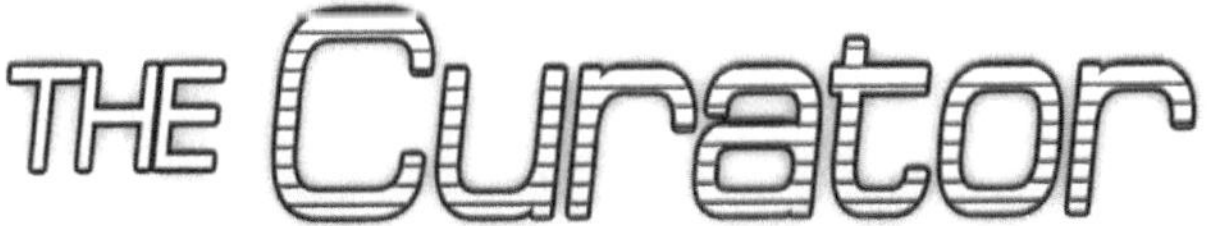

the

HOURLINGS

T

Tannhauser Press

The Curator

V1.0

Published by Tannhauser Press (tannhauserpress.com)

Tannhauser Press
9141 Dartford Place, Suite 110
Bristow, VA 29136

ISBN: 978-1-945994-36-4

Packaging by Worlds Enough LLC
Cover Art by Luca Oleastri
Cover Design by Don Anderson
Copyediting by Donna Royston

For Ronald Balfour and Walter Huchthausen, two of the Monuments Men from World War II, who gave their lives in the service of protecting priceless works of art for future generations.

CONTENTS

	Salvage Mission	Martin Wilsey	1
1	**First Use of Magic**	Elizabeth Hayes	11
	Salvage Mission		25
2	**Dry Bones**	Donna Royston	27
	Salvage Mission		39
3	**Land of the Blind**	TR Dillon	41
	Salvage Mission		89
4	**Paris in the Rain**	S. C. Megale	91
	Salvage Mission		103
5	**Trompe l'Oeil**	Erica Rue	105
	Salvage Mission		129
6	**The Arctanthropist**	Jeffrey C. Jacobs	131
	Salvage Mission		179
7	**The Little Cottage**	Peter Dube Jr.	181
	Salvage Mission		187
8	**Clash by Night**	David Keener	189
	Salvage Mission		333
	About the Authors		335
	Acknowledgments		339
	Artwork Credits		340

SALVAGE MISSION, PART 1

Martin Wilsey

"This has got to be the ugliest spaceship I have ever seen," Ron Carter laughed. "But it now has the sweetest long-range, multi-spectrum sensor array I have ever installed." Carter was putting away the last of his tools. All the access panels on the bridge of the *Oxcart* had been returned to their proper place.

"Don't you bad mouth this beautiful girl," Owen Quinn said from the captain's chair in the center of the bridge. "She may be old, but we have upgraded the hell outta her." Quinn was the team's data salvage specialist and the captain of the *Oxcart*. He had pioneered new methods to find salvage using massive data analytics on old logs and other data that he would cross-correlate.

"I can't remember the last time I was on a bridge

with actual windows." Carter shook his head. "Didn't anyone tell you that windows are dangerous in space? We are one layer from vacuum. On Earth Defense Force ships, regs say we should be wearing vac suits."

Quinn laughed. "EDFs are cupcakes."

The colossal bridge of the salvage ship was seven meters wide and ten meters long. It had floor-to-ceiling transparent walls on three sides, giving it a full 270-degree vista for the command crew. It was clean but well worn. Decades of use showed. The newest consoles filled the middle of the bridge. The captain's chair was in the center.

"I don't know if I told you," Quinn said. "It was once a heavy deep-space tug. This baby can push an Embassy class colony ship. As modified, it can hold one hundred eighteen cargo containers or other salvage. The new series of dorsal cargo arms can secure either containers or derelict ships." Quinn bragged like a proud parent of an ugly but talented child.

"The dish and new antenna arrays don't help the looks." Carter laughed. "The ass is all engines and the ax-head shape has no style. Some new paint couldn't hurt, either."

"If you are done insulting the *Oxcart*, I'd like to begin testing the new sensor array." Quinn laughed, covering his mouth and shaking his head. The bridge hatch slid open and a woman with long black hair entered.

"Carter, this is Tressa Pope. Everyone just calls her Pope."

"Thanks for your help, Carter. I need this baby to

put money in my pockets!" Pope said, as she gave Carter a firm handshake and a bright broad smile. Tressa Pope was about thirty years old and wore a form-fitting black flight suit that showed off her extreme level of fitness.

Pope sat down at the navigator's station as Quinn rose from the captain's seat to take the primary science and sensor station.

"How'd it go, Carter?" Pope asked. "Are you finished with the final diagnostics?"

"Diagnostics complete," Carter confirmed. "All individual unit tests complete. The new array is standing by."

Screens showed the view of the maintenance drones that were used for external views of the array.

"Jesus, it looks like the *Oxcart* has teeth now around the primary dish," Pope said. "And here I thought our girl could not get any uglier."

"Powering up the array," Carter announced.

Quinn literally gasped.

The room fell silent.

"Holy shit," Pope said, examining the flood of data to her console.

The fidelity and range of the sensor array had increased exponentially.

Quinn stared at the raw flood as Carter began populating a tactical visualization of the newly mapped data.

"How did you select that vector for the sensor?" Rob Carter asked. "At this setting the field of view is tiny. That's a debris field. Did you know it was there already?"

"Mr. Carter, I'd like to take this opportunity to thank you for the excellent work installing the new array." Quinn paused. "I'd also like to remind you about your non-disclosure agreement. It includes details about the system you installed AND any incidental data you may have seen."

"Quinn, the new algorithms you developed were spot on," Pope gushed. "The new sensors are better than we could have hoped. Even the optical sensor is amazing." She studied the data, then said urgently, "I think it's the debris field of an old colony ship. The one from the old log data we salvaged last year."

"Correct." Quinn punched up coordinates that revealed a slowly tumbling object. "We'll start there."

Carter had apparently been waiting to speak. "Quinn, the fidelity on this debris field is so good that it's hard to grasp the size of the field. It must be at least 200,000 kilometers across."

"Most of the debris is just fist-sized," Quinn said. "We could have flown through the middle of it and never seen a thing."

"Plotting a course," Pope said.

"I think that's a small shuttle engine," Carter said. "The bell is still attached. This level of destruction is crazy. They must have had a main reactor core breach… Jesus."

"I would like to draw your attention over here," Quinn said, as the main display highlighted something on the edge of the debris field. "It looks like a cargo container. An intact one."

"Pope?" Quinn said, in well-practiced shorthand, indicating their first destination.

"On it," she said. "Way ahead of you."

***

"How can this be the only cargo container that has remained intact?" Pope asked as the *Oxcart* approached the solitary container an hour later.

"They must have known they were going to breach," Quinn said. "Colony ships were so big that they had no core ejection systems. They were supposed to be safe. Too many safeguards."

The *Oxcart* settled in next to the container. Pope extended two cargo arms and a standard docking collar.

"Carter, feel like you want to suit up and head for Bay 2?" Quinn asked.

Carter nodded.

"Quinn, you remember that container of pig carcasses that were all desiccated and mummified?" Pope laughed.

"Yeah. What a letdown." Quinn said, as the collar clamped on and the arms began to draw the container in.

"Umbilicals are attached. Old type-one channel interfaces. We have power and atmosphere. Seriously cold in there though," Pope said. "Close your visors up. I'll send in a drone first to make sure no virals are active."

***

Quinn and Carter stood in Airlock 2, with Carter holding the drone controls. The hatch closed behind them. Pope had them up on four camera angles, plus the grapefruit-sized drone so the bridge could follow.

The hatches to the container opened. The drone slid into the dark, with its floodlights and cameras rolling.

The container was packed with crates, crowding the single aisle that went the length of the container down the center. "These crates are made of wood. Actual dead-tree kind of wood," Pope reported. "Air is stale. -34 degrees Celsius."

"Well, even if this is just full of wood, it's a win," Quinn said. "Real wood is worth serious money." The drone began to move down the crowded aisle. Often Carter had to turn the drone sideways.

"We have something," Quinn reported. On the screen, the aisle opened to an area about three meters cubed. The fan of light from the small drone revealed a single console and an occupied chair in front of it.

Reclined in the chair was a body in an ancient emergency pressure suit. The desiccated head leaned back inside the helmet. The toothy mouth was wide open as if it was screaming at its maker. Empty eye sockets stared at the ceiling.

"Look at this," Pope said.

In the standard name block space on the helmet, it said, "Curator."

Propped above the console was a painting in an ornate frame.

"Is that what I think it is?" Quinn asked.

"It's *On a Lee Shore*, by Winslow Homer," Pope replied over the radio. "It's listed in the database as lost."

"The console is powering up," Quinn said, as he watched the old initialization sequences scroll by. "Last boot was almost two hundred and three years ago. Wow. These old colony systems were made to last."

"They had to be made that way. No replacements were expected," Pope said, as the drone floated over the console. "It's loading a Lexington 1.1 AI," Pope added.

Quinn groaned. "Lex 1.1 AIs are pedantic pains in the ass. But maybe there is a manifest or inventory in there."

They watched as the initialization completed. They waited for the standard Lexington 1.1 greeting, but it never came. A red light came on over the console camera.

"Who are you and where is Kate Walton?" The Lexington said into the room.

"My name is Quinn. Who is Kate Walton? Is she the Curator?" Quinn asked.

Carter stood there staring at the mummified face of the dead body.

"Yes… Yes, she is the Curator. Was the Curator." The Lex 1.1 sounded despondent. Quinn raised an eyebrow at its tone. "Has it been so long?"

"Your clock should have already synced," Quinn said from the drone. "What is all this?"

"The Curator saved all she could," the Lex 1.1 said in sad tones. "She knew she was going to die. She wanted me to give a message to whoever found these works of art." Lex 1.1 began a recording playback.

An image of a woman in a pressure suit came up on a screen over the console just to the right of the painting.

"The Havero Colony Transport knew it was doomed," said the woman who was the Curator. "They couldn't stop it. We are too far away from any planet. Lifeboats launched but most people stayed. Quick death over starvation or suffocation." She swallowed hard. "I could not allow these works of art to be destroyed when the reactor overloaded."

She reached up and touched the painting with a gloved hand. "I have the water recycler in my suit. So…I've lasted a while. I decided to write stories about some of my favorite paintings in the collection. Just to keep my mind off…well, you know… The Curator, signing off…"

"She wanted me you read you these stories." Lex 1.1 began.

On a Lee Shore, by Winslow Homer, 1900.
Oil on canvas.

Havero Colony Transport, Catalog #: 42

1. FIRST USE OF MAGIC

Elizabeth Hayes

A great bank of clouds towered in the West, their edges yellow-gold in the late afternoon sun. From the height of the aft deck, Prince Kirandûr scanned the endless line where the sea met the sky. A swell rolled beneath the ship and lifted it high in the air. There it was, a roughness on the horizon, barely noticeable but definitely there. He stepped up on the stern rail for a better look, holding the backstay for balance. Tolan, the old helmsman, shot him a warning look. *Have a care, young princeling.*

Above the irregular spot, the undersides of the clouds were tinged with green, a reflection of the green of the fields and forests beneath them before the land itself could be seen.

The swell rolled on, and the ship dropped into the

trough between waves. The prow dipped below the water, dunking the lavender and rosemary tied to the bowsprit, an offering to the sea gods.

When the ship rose on the next swell, he saw it again. It could be a triangle of sail, but it could be an undiscovered island, too far west to be recorded on the charts.

He would hold this course just long enough to get a better look.

He glanced over his shoulder in the direction of home. A small bump, the peak of the highest mountain on Armelos, interrupted the otherwise unbroken horizon. The cities hugging the coast had long since disappeared from sight, but as long as he could see any part of Armelos, at least intermittently, he'd still be able to find his way home.

They continued sailing west. When they slipped into the troughs, he lost sight of the tip of the mountain. He sent Wynn, the lookout, into the rigging to keep an eye on it.

"I can't … oh wait, I can still see it," the slender boy called from his perch just below the tip of the mainmast. Their pennant, a white ship against a dark blue background, snapped in the breeze above his head.

He chafed under the constraint to keep land in sight, and every time he sailed West, he pushed the limits a little harder.

Someday, if wind and tides allowed, he would walk on the shores of the undiscovered island. The people of Armelos had outgrown their island home and desperately needed more land. A wall of squalls was moving in from the north. The ugly clouds danced with lightning, and a low rumble reached him from across the waves. If the squalls continued on their current course and speed, his view of the peak would be cut off behind diagonal curtains of rain.

Kirandûr took a last look to the West, at the billowing white clouds reflecting green underneath, which might be the only look he would ever have of the undiscovered land. Reluctantly, he gave the order to turn around.

"Jibe ho." The stern swung around, and the sails filled with wind.

The course back to Armelos led them directly into the path of the squall. If they were lucky, they'd outrun it, but if it caught them, they'd be in no real danger. They would shorten sail, drop the sea anchor, and wait out the storm below decks. There was nothing to run into out here. They were sailing through blue water, unimaginably deep, with no rocks or shoals.

The great mass of cloud lit up from within, revealing the enormous height of the waves. The water was pockmarked from rain, and wisps of spume raced across its surface.

The wind freshened. The deck tipped until it dipped into the water, and the sea hissed along the gunwales. The sky turned black. When the rain hit, it was stinging hard and cold as ice, startling compared to the warm water sloshing over his feet.

A gust blew out one of the sails, leaving ribbons of canvas flapping in the gale. The bow drifted off the line of swells, and a wave broke over the bow.

"Helmsman, I relieve you." The exhausted man shot him a look of gratitude, and Kirandûr took over the tiller.

"Shorten sail." His words were torn away by the shriek of the wind—even he couldn't hear them. He put his fingers in his mouth and blew ear-splitting blasts, two short and one long. A sailor at the bow nodded and took down the larger of the two remaining jibs. There was almost no canvas left to take in. They were flying a jib the size of a snot rag, and nothing else.

Hours past dark, the squall showed no signs of letting up. The stars were hidden behind the clouds. Without them, Kirandûr lost his bearings. It didn't matter; in a storm like this, he had to abandon his course and steer directly into the waves.

The bow of the ship lifted on the next crest, and the hull slid down the side of a mountain of a wave. They landed wrong, and the keel shivered as if it would snap. Kirandûr gripped the rail and struggled to keep his footing on the slippery deck. He stood upright, his face still. It wouldn't do for the men see him afraid.

A bolt of lightning struck, too close, and the crack of thunder came at almost the same moment. The lookout on the prow gestured wildly and pointed to something off the port quarter. Kirandûr saw his lips move but couldn't hear anything above the shriek of the storm and the ringing in his ears.

He looked where the man was pointing. The light from the next strike revealed a line of breakers, the boiling foam pale against the black water. Rocks, where there should be only blue water of unplumbed depths.

He threw his whole weight against the tiller. "Ready about!" The jib swung from one side to the other, and the ship began to turn. The waves hit them abeam, driving the ship closer to the rocks. He cringed at the drawn-out scraping of wood against stone.

"The sea gods, spare us and I will raise a temple to you."

Assuming the sea gods wanted another temple.. Armelos was a seafaring nation. It was lousy with roadside shrines and temples to the sea gods, probably one for every person on the island.

He ordered the mainsail raised, and the canvas filled with a snap. The deadly breakers passed alongside them, and soon, they left the fangs of rocks in their wake. Kirandûr put a hand to his chest and held it there until his pulse dropped to normal.

Sometime past midnight, when the storm had died down to a heavy rain, he told Sevrann, his first officer, "Set a double watch. We'll update the charts as soon as it's light."

He went below into the low-ceilinged cabin, barely large enough for the six bunks shared by a twelve-man crew. He collapsed into the nearest one fully clothed, too tired to care that he was dripping onto the sheets. When he closed his eyes, he felt like he was falling. He clutched the edges of the pallet for support.

There was shouting on deck, and the sound of running feet. Someone screamed. He struggled from deepest sleep, as if swimming toward the surface from a great depth.

"Hard a lee," ordered the first officer. The ship wallowed through its turn, and canvas flapped.

A blow struck the vessel. It flung him from his bunk and resonated through the hull like a drumbeat. He was on his feet in an instant, but the next blow knocked him to the floor. Pain shot from his wrist to his elbow.

The ship was lifted and dropped, lifted and dropped, and each time, the vessel rolled further onto its side. There was the scrape of wood against rock, and the sound of timbers splintering. The blows sounded flat and dull, as if they came from a drum with a split skin. At that moment, he knew the hull had been breached.

He crawled through seawater a foot deep and reached the hatch. The deck was canted at an unnatural angle, but he could keep his footing by hanging onto the roof of the cabin.

"Captain, there was another rock." His first officer looked terrified, either of being shipwrecked or of his own Captain. Kirandûr couldn't tell.

The ship rolled in the surf and seemed to twist, and the timbers groaned like whales. The ship started to break apart.

"Abandon ship," he said. The order no captain ever wants to give.

The hull had been driven so high up on the rocks that they could step from the deck and wade through the foaming surf.

Judging from the height above which no mussels or barnacles clung, the rock would keep them above water at high tide. However, no plants grew here, and as far as he could tell, there was no water.

He stood among the rocks, breathing hard and staring out to sea.

No one knows where we are.

It was his own fault. Kirandûr hadn't told anyone he was planning to sail so far into uncharted waters.

If his brother Atelic failed to return on time, they'd search for him right away. Unlike Kirandûr, Atelic did what he was told. But if Kirandûr were late, his father would assume he'd gone off exploring, and wouldn't worry.

Some captains always kept a silver mirror used for signaling on their person at all times against this very possibility. He felt for the cord around his neck, at the same moment he remembered when he'd taken it off and where he'd put it. By all the sea gods! They might be here for a long time.

But there was no time to brood. The more food and water they could recover from the disintegrating ship, the longer they could hold out. The men made trip after trip over the razor-sharp rocks, moving the wounded, carrying water kegs, and bringing out whatever tools and equipment they could carry, taking care not to fall in the darkness and the swirling water.

Some of the men refused to go below decks, now in pitch darkness and tilted at an unfamiliar angle. Kirandûr could have ordered them below; they needed to retrieve the kegs of water in the hold, but there was only so much he could ask of the terrified men, so he did it himself.

After that, Kirandûr carried armloads of wet canvas from the wreck until his limbs trembled from exertion. His left arm was almost unusable. He could grip with his hand, but it hurt to lift any weight.

The hull rocked in the waves. It could crush a hand or foot if a sailor was unlucky. Timbers cracked. Something snapped, and the mainmast came down. Hempen ropes trailed in its wake. However badly they needed supplies, it was no longer safe to collect them.

"All ashore. We've done enough for tonight."

He went to the makeshift tent where they were treating the wounded, jury-rigged from a sail draped over a spar across two boulders. He lifted the edge of the canvas and crawled beneath it. There was enough sand between the rocks to lay a man on, but it was soaking wet.

Tolan, the old helmsman knelt over a still form. "It's Sevrann, Captain. He's bad hurt."

The fabric of his legging had been cut away to above the knee, and pieces of wood were bound the length of his shin with strips of cloth. Kirandûr hoped the bone splinters hadn't pierced the skin. If they had, it would be a death sentence.

Kirandûr knelt beside the wounded man and

asked, "How's the leg?" His first officer bit his lip and grimaced. He turned to the helmsman. "Was there any wine among the water barrels we managed to save? Give it to him." He couldn't do anything more for the man.

Outside, he stood in the rain, the cold water running in rivulets down the side of his face, down his neck. This was his fault. He looked around to be sure he was unobserved, then fell to his knees and punched the sand over and over. Remorse hit him like a punch in the gut, and he couldn't seem to catch his breath.

Recovering his composure, he joined the others and counted those who remained. Two were in the tent and the rest were salvaging things from the ship. That made ten. No, eleven, he'd forgotten to count himself. They had been a crew of twelve. Wynn, the lookout, was missing. Kirandûr punched the sand again.

The rain was still coming down, icy cold. It didn't rain often in this part of the world. He tasked two sailors with catching rainwater in a square of canvas, and told another to find a cask or pot, anything that would hold water.

Sometime in the small hours, the moon began to show through broken clouds. The rain had stopped, but mist continued to soak his hair and clothing. Kirandûr sat in the sand with his knees pulled up to his chin, his thoughts swirling.

The helmsman came over and sat beside him. "Sevrann's sleeping now." Kirandûr nodded. "And now for you. That's blood on your leg. Do you want me to patch you up?"

Kirandûr looked down. A dark stain spread across the outside of his thigh. He touched it, and his hand came away sticky. Something protruded from the fabric. He tugged, and eased out a splinter the size of a writing pen. It must have been four or five inches deep, just under the skin. Ugly, but not serious.

The helmsman tore a strip of linen from the tail of his shirt and passed it over. Kirandûr knotted the ends, then dropped it over his head. With the weight of his arm supported by the loop of fabric, the sudden stabbing gave way to a dull ache. Much better.

"Thanks," he said, and he meant it.

Nearby, two men bent over the collection of driftwood and broken timber, striking a stone against the blade of a knife over and over. Every once in a while, a spark landed in the shavings cupped in the second man's hands. Once, it glowed for a moment under his breath, but it didn't catch.

It would be better to have a signal fire at night, it could be seen for much further away. He wouldn't want to lure a ship up onto the rocks, but experienced mariners would know not to approach until daylight.

Kirandûr looked from one face to another. "Did anyone rescue the tinderbox?" The men looked at each other. In the dark, with the waves threatening to drag them over rocks as sharp as knives, while thinking of more important things, like rescuing the drinking water. "It must have been lost with the ship."

Once, Kirandûr had seen one of the court astrologers light a candle with his will alone. It took a long time, and seemed to take a lot of effort, but finally there was a curl of smoke, and a yellow flame leapt up from the wick.

Kirandûr had assumed it was a street conjurer's trick, something with flammable oils and a rough surface to his fingertips, but the man didn't seem the type. He was a serious scholar, and not one to draw attention to himself.

"How did you do that"? the young prince had asked him.

"Keep your mind still, and focus the whole of your attention upon the wick. Be patient, and expect to have to work at it."

Kirandûr had tried a couple of times. He'd stared for what seemed like long minutes, and had punched the wall when nothing happened. But once, just once, he managed to produce the smallest wisp of smoke. When he touched the wick, it was warm.

Kirandûr knelt beside the makeshift fire circle. "Let me try."

The sailors had arranged a bundle of driftwood twigs into a miniature tent, and put shaved curls of wood under it.

Kirandûr knelt in the wet sand by the edge of the fire ring and sat back on his heels. He rested his hands on his thighs, to the extent the sling would allow it. His left wrist was twice the size it should be, the wrist bone and tendons had disappeared under puffy flesh.

"Give me some room." The sailors withdrew by two or three paces, but he still felt crowded. Maybe the secret to magic is getting past the fear of looking stupid.

Kirandûr focused on the shavings. He drew a breath, held it, let it go. The stones on the shingle beach clattered as the waves lifted them and then drained back. His wrist hurt. He ignored it. The ankle he was sitting on started to go numb, and he shifted his weight. Focus. He closed his eyes. Breath in, breath out.

The swell of the ocean all around him was like a living thing. The power of it seemed to fill him. Breath in, breathe out. Send with it all the power from the surf, from the ocean, the storm.

It took what seemed like hours, but finally, a curl of smoke rose from the shaving. A spark glowed orange, and the tangle of shavings burst into flame, which ignited the tip of a driftwood twig. Soon the whole structure was burning, the wet wood popping in the heat. Kirandûr hung his head, exhausted.

"How did you do that?" The sailor's voice was awe-stricken.

"He's a sorcerer, that's how. Don't ask stupid questions," said his shipmate.

Kirandûr was as amazed as the sailors. Was he a sorcerer? Or, as the court astrologer had said, did you just need to be patient and work extremely hard?

The men fed timbers from the ship into the blaze. Someone slapped him on the back. The flame shot up four or five feet high, burning hotter than a natural fire, the soaked wood popping and hissing with steam.

Kirandûr unfolded himself from the sand and brushed off his knees. "Get some rope and an oar."

They wrapped the rope around the blade of the oar and wedged it between two rocks, a fiery beacon high in the air. It was impossible to tell if anyone was out there, all they could do was wait.

All night they fed the fire, keeping it alive in the drizzle and damp. Even standing on his feet, Kirandûr's head kept falling forward and snapping him awake.

The day dawned under a cloudless sky with glassy calm seas. What was left of the ship were strewn up and down the shore. Debris floated on the water.

"Captain! There's a ship on the horizon. We need to fashion a smoke signal, right quick."

There were no plants on the rock, and everything from the ship: timber, fabric, or rope, was soaking wet.

"Bring some more tarred rope," Kirandûr told the nearest sailor.

A sailor came back with a coil of rope over one shoulder and dumped it into the fire. Resinous smoke billowed from the twisted hemp, forcing Kirandûr back, his eyes burning.

An oily black column rose hundreds of feet in the air, as thick as the trunk of a tree. On the horizon, the ship tacked, and tacked again, the white triangle of sail growing larger as it drew near.

A pennant floated from the top of the mainmast, unreadable against the sun. The rock on which they were marooned was to the west of Armelos, far from the normal trading routes. Reputable vessels didn't come this way.

"Captain, what if they're pirates?" The young sailor's face turned pale.

Kirandûr kept his face still. *Worse than that, what if*

they're slavers?

He lifted the sling over his head and let it drop to the ground. The newcomers needn't know he was injured. He stepped to the edge of the surf, motioning his men to stay back. His good hand tightened around the hilt of his dagger.

The vessel completed another tack, bringing it closer. Its lines were slender and graceful, like an elvish ship. Ordinary merchant seamen had no trading routes west of Armelos, but it was said that those evading the law, pirates and smugglers, passed this way all the time. Kirandûr chewed his lip, waiting.

The breeze freshened and lifted the pennant, revealing a blue background arrayed with a host of stars. Kirandûr's knees almost buckled with relief.

"Captain, it's one of ours," said Tolan.

SALVAGE MISSION, PART 2

In one corner of the container, Carter stirred. "How many stories did she have time to create?"

"Not so many," Lex 1.1 replied, the sadness returning to the AI's voice. Do you want to hear the next one? You'll find the artwork just there."

It was warmer in the container now. Quinn and Carter were comfortable in zero-G. Quinn lifted the next artwork up to examine it. It was very different than the first. An etching, in black and white.

"We have to. It's like a…play the next one," Pope said over the comms.

Calavera de la Catrina, by Jose Guadalupe Posada, 1912. Zinc etching.

Havero Colony Transport, Catalog #: 75

2. DRY BONES

Donna Royston

La Catrina woke in the morning, saw the brightness in the window, and stretched her old bones luxuriously. "Too beautiful to lie in bed," she told herself. She rose and put on her elegant bustled gown. Looking in the mirror, she noticed with approval the smallness of her waist. She put on her hat, its large brim edged with lace and trimmed with flowers and two ostrich plumes. She made an adjustment to get it perfect and admired her reflection, turning slightly to get the most flattering view of her empty eye sockets and white gleaming skull. She looked quite fine today!—in fact, she probably had not looked finer in all her dead days.

At last she turned from the mirror and picked up her little lace purse and went out for her morning walk. She stopped at her favorite coffee shop and sat at one of the outdoor tables, because the day was so fine. She didn't drink any coffee—nor did the shop have any to offer—but she took a fan from her purse and fanned herself in a ladylike fashion.

There were two skeletons sitting at a table near her, one of them tapping with a purposeful manner at a smartphone, studying what he saw—or didn't see—then tapping again rapidly, his index fingerbone making a sharp staccato sound, an ostentatious gold ring rattling on another fingerbone. The other sat, resting his arm bone on a folded, yellowing newspaper, looking warily around at whoever was near. She tried to catch their eye sockets, but the first was too intent, and the other continued to scan his surroundings. Expensive suits and silk ties hung sadly on their bony shoulders and ribcages.

"I can't find out anything," said the first skeleton. "Something went wrong."

"El Blanco betrayed us," said the other, in a low voice.

La Catrina coughed delicately and the two skulls turned in her direction. Coyly, she raised the fan to hide her lower jaw and fluttered it slightly. "Good morning, señores. A fine morning."

They rose to their feet, stepped close to her table, and gave her a glare. "What do you know about this?" said the first skeleton.

"I am pleased that you have joined us here."

"Don't waste my time," said the skeleton. "Maybe you don't know who I am—"

"No one is important here," she said.

The skeleton gave a look at his companion, who apparently understood it to mean to take a gun out from his jacket, which he did. He held it to La Catrina's skull.

"Ready to answer?" he said.

La Catrina fluttered her fan coquettishly.

The second skeleton pulled the trigger. There was a sharp crack, and the shot reverberated dully in the distance. The bullet fell to the ground like a stone, but there was a black powder burn on La Catrina's skull.

"You are mine now," said La Catrina. "Whatever questions I wish to answer, I will answer this evening. You will find me at the mission. Now, until then, go and enjoy yourselves. You might look for a movie." She waved them off with her fan. "Shoo."

They turned and walked down the street, their shoes loose and wobbly around their footbones.

La Catrina opened her purse, took out a mirror and a handkerchief, and wiped away the black powder. A few moments later, she rose and resumed her stroll under the pitiless and blank sky. She had not gone far when there was a roar from down the street, and a truck carrying several skeletons, who were wearing ski masks and holding AR-15s, accelerated toward her. When they got close, the truck skidded to a stop and the skeletons pointed their guns at her. "Stop!" they shouted. "You're fucked, old lady!"

"Who shall I surrender to?" asked La Catrina.

One skeleton emerged from the truck, wearing a black military uniform, bulletproof vest, and pistol belt, and walked up to her. His rifle was slung across his back.

"The soldiers came on us without warning," he said. "What happened to our informant, that he failed to call us?"

"No one informs here," she said. "I will see you at the square in the evening."

La Catrina turned and walked away. She heard gunshots, and bullets pattered to the ground around her like lead raindrops, but she paid no heed.

She saw two skeletons standing at the corner of a boarded-up building that displayed the faded sign of a real estate dealer, and walked toward them. One was the skeleton of a teenage girl. The other was the skeleton of a dog. Each had a single bullet hole in its skull. The dog skeleton wagged its tail rapidly when it saw La Catrina coming, making a tat-tat-tat sound against its owner's fibula. The skeleton of the girl shrank away, as though she might turn and run.

"Good morning!" La Catrina greeted her. "Are you lost? Do you need directions?"

For a moment the girl skeleton said nothing. Then— "I saw the guys in the truck. Narcos."

"Oh, them," said La Catrina.

The girl skeleton evaluated this uncertainly. "I…was on a bus…going north to my mother," she whispered. "The narcos stopped the bus and made us all get off…"

"*Chula*, they are nothing."

"Even Benito, they shot him. I'm afraid…"

"No one is afraid here," said La Catrina. She leaned over and scratched the top of the dog's skull. "Come to the mission this evening."

The girl skeleton stared at her as La Catrina strolled away.

***

She walked all day, greeting the new arrivals. As evening was falling she went back to the center of town through the many skeletons that were coming from different directions, assembling in the square.

When she had their attention, La Catrina, imperious, held out her bony hand. "Where is the music?"

Two guitar players, who had approached when they saw her arrive, started playing "Perfidia."

The skeleton with the large gold ring, still clutching his phone, pushed through the crowd as though he had some urgent business. "I only did what I had to do, I did it to support my family," he said.

"There are no excuses here," said La Catrina.

The other skeletons pressed closer, as though intent on hearing what La Catrina said, all gazing at her with their vacant sockets.

"Today is your day, every one of you. It is your wedding day, your funeral day, your birth day. Today you are wedded to the void, you are buried in eternity, you are born out of a sheath of flesh; therefore we dance and celebrate your liberation." She reached out her hand to the skeleton with the gold ring.

The skeleton thought about this, and then he nodded, and reached out and grasped La Catrina's hand. "That's right!" he said, sounding cheerier. "I hadn't thought of that."

"We will dance," said La Catrina.

One after another, all the skeletons joined hands, except that those next to either of the guitar players, not wanting to disrupt the music, took hold of a rib.

But the teenage girl refused to take anyone's hand. "No!" she said.

"Make her dance!" the other skeletons cried out.

"I want to be alive," she said.

The other skeletons heaped scorn on her. "We have left that ball of dirt behind us," said one, angrily.

"We are better than alive," said another. "We have transcended."

She knelt on the ground, her arms around the dog skeleton, refusing to look at them, and then she jumped up, eluding hands that would grasp her, and started to run away. The dog skeleton ran beside her. But the skeleton with the pistol caught her and dragged her back by her armbone, struggling and screaming. The dog skeleton leaped up, then hung from his arm, biting down hard and growling.

"Release her," said La Catrina, stern.

He obeyed. "What about me?" he complained, trying to shake the dog skeleton loose.

The girl skeleton took the dog skeleton in her arms and backed away, and the dog finally released the armbone.

"*Cariña*," said La Catrina to her, "what to do with you? I will send you to my sister."

She said nothing, trembling.

"First, though, we will dance." The guitar players played a new tune, and the skeletons began to murmur, hum, and then sing the tune with whatever words they thought of. The sound spread outward from La Catrina in an ever-widening circle. Then she took the hand of the skeleton nearest her, who wore a tank top and jeans, and began to lead in a large circle around the plaza. Others joined hands and followed. When a full circle had been made, she led the line so that it spiraled inward, around and around, while they sang. At the small center, after many circlings, a grayish, misty gateway appeared. La Catrina stepped aside while the line moved slowly into the gate and disappeared, one skeleton after another, singing. Some leaped forward into the mist. Some hesitated, but were pushed from behind. Some stepped gravely.

One by one they went. The throng of dancing skeletons diminished, and contracted; the plaza in front of the mission was emptying, and the voices grew thinner, the rattle of footbones diminished to a soft clicking, and still they went. Then the singing was only two voices, which became one voice, silenced mid-word. The music went last, but it too ceased, and two abandoned guitars lay on the ground. The gate dissolved away.

And all that were left, besides La Catrina herself, were the girl skeleton, her dog, and the skeleton with the gold ring.

"I'm not going," he said, forcefully. "If there's a way out, and she gets it, then I do, too."

"If that is your choice," said La Catrina. "Come

with me."

They walked down the main street, which became a dusty road, leaving the town and going into an empty land, under the dull gray sky.

"What is this place?" asked the girl skeleton, after they had been walking a long time.

"This is the threshold," said La Catrina. "The no-place between one place and another."

"How long have you been here?" she asked, after a timid pause.

"There is no time here."

"Your sister," said the skeleton with the gold ring to La Catrina, with the importance of one who has figured out what needs to be done, "she is the one with the say-so."

"She is La Brecha. Address her by name and then give your name."

They could see, ahead, a small house; the road led dimly up to it and beyond. As they drew closer, it seemed there was something smaller beside the house. When they were almost upon it, this became the figure of a woman sitting in a chair by the roadside.

And she was a *woman*. She had flesh on her bones. The girl skeleton shivered with terror.

The skeleton with the gold ring was not terrified, however. He strode forward. "Doña Brecha, my name is…is… I know it, but it has slipped my mind."

"What do you want of me?"

"I want to live! I want to go on… doing what I have been doing."

"Have you not yet done enough? My sister's

doorway will still open for you."

"I refuse!"

She smiled coldly. "Then pass by, and follow the road, and may you be happy with your choice."

"This is the road to go back?"

"Don't you remember?"

"Yes...yes...this is how I arrived."

"Then it is the way back."

After a moment's thought, the skeleton with the gold ring sauntered past with a "Thanks, I owe you!"

But before they stopped watching him, he paused, looked confused, and wandered off the road.

La Brecha sat quietly, not looking, and not speaking.

La Catrina gave the girl skeleton a little nudge. She stepped forward. "Señora Doña Brecha?"

"Yes."

The girl skeleton realized that La Brecha was blind. Her eyes were white, and they did not move. "I want to live. And Benito, also."

The dog skeleton's tail moved tentatively.

She could still see the skeleton with the gold ring in the distance, wandering in a circle.

She remembered that La Catrina had told her to give her name. "I'm Maria Castillo."

"What do you want to do, if you live, Maria?"

"I want to see my mother again, and my sisters and brothers."

"That is possible, if you walk and stay on the road."

***

As Maria walked forward, it seemed that the road, everything around her, grew hazy and indistinct. All had been gray when she had arrived, and between then and now the sky had slowly become darker and darker, and now she couldn't see where she was… but she could hear raised voices that sounded desperate. And then gunshots. "Señora Doña Brecha," she murmured, but there was no reply.

She opened her eyes. Her mind was moving slowly, and all she could do for a long time was stare at the dead girl beside her, lying in a sprawl on the ground in the half-light of the building where everyone from the bus had been taken.

After a while, she was able to move, and she turned her head. Everyone from the bus was dead, all around, lying still as stones. Men, women, children…then something breathed on her ear, and she flinched before realizing—"Benito!" she whispered, and touched his fur with two fingertips. "We have to get out of here… I want us to live."

She crawled slowly between the bodies, away from the men who were at the other side of the building, intent on firing their guns outside. Who were they shooting at? Maybe police had come at last, but if so, they were very late.

She crouched behind some boxes, moving one slightly to make a larger space that hid her on all sides but one, and held Benito beside her through the storming of the building, and more bullets, and new voices. It became quiet and she wondered what the men who had shot their way in were doing. She heard footsteps, and they were talking in hushed tones, but she could not understand the words.

At last she had to look, and there were soldiers, moving among the dead, checking each person for life and finding none. One of the soldiers suddenly saw her, and exclaimed, and moved toward her.

He made her lie down, and she told him her name.

"You will be all right," he said.

***

The gunmen moved closer to the bullet-riddled man, and one nudged him with a toe. He was not quite dead. "Doña Brecha…"

"What'd he say? Hey! Fucker! Do you know who you are?"

The man's lips moved, with hardly any breath, and his words were faint, indistinct. "My name is…is… I know it, but it has slipped my mind."

The gunman laughed. "I think your name is Don Perdedor. Now there is a new boss in town! Anything you have to say to that?"

The man clenched a fist weakly, sticky with blood. "I want to live…"

"Not going to happen." The gunman pointed his rifle downward, carelessly. "Why don't you point us toward the valuables?"

"I refuse!"

"OK." The man pulled the trigger, and laughed. "Adios."

***

La Catrina stood by La Brecha in the empty land, watching.

"So much for that one, sister," said La Catrina.

"El Grito will find him," said La Brecha.

"No one is overlooked here," said La Catrina.

SALVAGE MISSION, PART 3

Pope spoke over the comms. "Quinn, both of these works of art once hung in the Metropolitan Museum of Art, in New York City, on Earth. Everyone thought they were destroyed during the war in 2631."

Carter looked back into the container. There were perhaps a thousand crates there.

"Are you ready for the next story?" Lex 1.1 asked politely.

"Yes, please," Quinn answered. "Before you begin, can you send Tressa Pope the manifest for this container as well as the stories?"

"Yes, sir. It's done," the AI replied.

"Please continue."

Madame de Brayer, by Gustave Courbet, 1858.
Oil on canvas.

Havero Colony Transport, Catalog #: 7

3. LAND OF THE BLIND

TR Dillon

Leopold's consciousness returned like scattered balloons popping. A few moments here. A few moments there. To him, lost for so long in the clutches of a dreamless night, it felt like months passing. Perhaps years. Even eons. Time was so elusive without sun and air and tactile sensations.

Without Edna.

Seeing Leopold's eyes open, the Seph nurses assumed he could hear them as he lay there bound and naked and motionless in his dirty glass-topped cage.

So after they cured him, the Seph nurses regaled him with the story of how their space trawler tethered to his cryohull, the Elusive Destiny. How they remotely surveiled his ship to find, as expected, thousands of floating skulls, the desiccated remnants of Earth's last survivors. How they discovered a single operational cryotank, a sarcophagus really, the way a stethoscope seeks a heartbeat. How they donned their ragtag spacesuits and boarded the disintegrating cryohull, zapping skulls like a video game, to retrieve the cryotank. How they pried open the lid and found the miracle they'd been seeking for years — an intact vitrified human male, perfectly preserved and, most important of all, fully functional.

And how Leopold clutched to his bosom, like his life depended on it, the portrait of a woman.

But Leopold didn't comprehend a word the Sephs said. His eyes were open, but his ears were stuck in cryo. And he didn't speak the Sephs' language anyway. If Leopold heard anything, it was mere babble. Background noise.

Leopold's mind instead was driven by a single thought, a single image—a single concept—as he battled to surface from forty years of cryogenic storage.

Edna!

***

Leopold was slammed into awareness when his cage overturned and slid screeching, metal on metal, for several seconds. His first sight was the filthy floor. His body tipped but, tied tightly to the mattress, did not fall out. It just hung there. Instantly, he sensed the gurgling tubes taped into his nose and down his mouth. The wraps penetrating his wrists and ankles and neck.

In shock, Leopold surveyed his room upside down.

The pock-marked ceiling sagged, and the walls were scuffed and scarred. A jumble of equipment, some in makeshift stacks three layers high, rested on a dangerously slanted counter. Other machines sat on the floor, some sideways. The tubes running into his body were held high by a piece of wire nailed to the ceiling. Bags of unidentified liquid swayed from bent clothes hangers. Sirens blared, and red and white lights flashed.

He saw several pairs of feet. One wore mismatched socks with no shoes. Another wore no socks at all. *One, two, three,* and then they hoisted his cage back upright.

A breathless woman with stubbly gray hair, wearing a stained white tee shirt, burst into the room. Waving a weapon Leopold did not recognize, the woman yelled commands at the nurses, who raised their hands as if to say, *I know, I know.* The nurses wore masks but no uniforms, and their unwashed clothes were rags. The breathless woman glanced at Leopold, tilted her head, grimaced, then departed as fast as she had come. Eyes upward, the nurses stood still, as if waiting for something terrible to happen.

Something that would ruin everything.

And in that moment of fearful intensity, Leopold remembered who he was. Unleashed, the memories slammed into each other, like too many people at the bottom of a down escalator.

He was a postal worker from Des Moines. Married for forty-five years, no children. He and Edna had wanted children, but when they gave up trying they gave up on parenting as well. So they'd settled for nieces and nephews and other people's kids. They had each other, and they told themselves that was enough. Then came the awful day they received his test results. *We can cure so much these days,* the doctors said, *but we can't cure this. Maybe in ten years. Maybe sooner, depending on research and drug trials. But not yet. Not in time to save you.*

Edna came up with the idea of cryogenic storage. But only until they found a cure, of course. They reassured themselves it was a temporary measure. *Interim*, Edna liked saying. She was healthy. Her parents had lived into their nineties. She would wait for Leopold. Then they could die in each other's arms like they'd always planned. Edna volunteered all their savings, and Leopold had nothing to lose except a few months of a rapidly declining quality of life.

The cryo facility was outside Red Hook. A new-fangled underground vault. Leopold reviewed the blueprint with the engineers. He was reassured even though he didn't understand a word they said. But Edna rejected one cryotank after another. This one was too small, that one too flimsy, and so on. Finally they rolled in their deluxe model. The self-powered version. It could, they said, withstand a nuclear attack and last for decades. Edna nodded, and that was that.

To Leopold, it felt like only yesterday he and Edna had driven to Red Hook. They had clung to each other and said tearful goodbyes. He could still feel her warm skin on his fingertips.

But it wasn't the day after yesterday, and Leopold wasn't in Red Hook. He stared at the Seph nurses, who exchanged worried glances and tried not to hyperventilate. Leopold strained to hear their low garbled talk. Their language sounded like a guttural mash of German and Chinese, maybe with a touch of Russian and Spanish thrown in. Leopold had awakened into a strange and terrifying future. A distant future.

Which meant, he thought, that Edna was almost certainly dead.

Leopold leaned back to cry, but his eyes could not yet produce tears. So he lay there, whimpering and trembling, a beaten animal in an unfamiliar world expecting a mortal blow. Instinctively, he bared his neck.

And then the cryo took over again, and Leopold went under.

***

Leopold startled awake. It felt like he'd slept for hours, though it was mere minutes.

Tensing, Leopold wondered what had happened. For long moments—nothing. The nurses were gone. The lights strobed, but the siren had stopped. His room was empty and still, the equipment strewn like litter. Then the floor heaved, as if for a second or third time, and everything jerked like a toy on a string.

Another tremor struck, and loudspeakers announced something he could not understand. One word was repeated with foreboding — *Titan*. The booming voice spat the word out, distinctly enunciating both t's. *Ti-tan*. Straining against his straps, Leopold saw a metal swag flap like a screen door caught in a twister. Then the room shuddered again, and the walls and floors screeched.

A thunderous metallic noise reverberated overhead. Then grating echoes and the clatter of boots, and Leopold realized the Sephs' vessel, *his* vessel, was being boarded.

The word *Titan* suggested size, so Leopold craned his head to see if giants would come lumbering down the corridor. Instead, a petite woman with a shaved head—still bristly like a man's five o'clock shadow—peered inside. Black circles shadowed her eyes, and she wore gleaming metal piercings in her ears and cheeks. She spied Leopold, let out a whoop, and vanished.

Minutes later, the most magnificent woman Leopold had ever seen sauntered through the door. She was tall and built like a gladiator. But what he noticed first were her hips. Firm and muscular, they swayed suggestively with her stride. Her face was Eastern European with a touch of Chinese, and ringlets of auburn hair brushed her broad shoulders. She wore a skin-tight black velour outfit, highlighting her every contour, with a saucy gold stripe running from her left collarbone to below her right breast. One look told Leopold she was in charge.

And one look was all he gave her. Her clothes were so tight Leopold felt like he was seeing her naked. And he had never seen a naked woman before. Not in person, anyway. When he and Edna had sex, it was always fumbling at night under the covers. And Leopold was embarrassed for himself, for his own nakedness there in his cage.

More uniforms, but without the gold stripe, entered the room. To Leopold they all seemed naked. One pushed a robot on a wheeled chair. It was missing its left leg, and its right arm was gone at the elbow. The robot was patched with tape in various places, and a wire mesh kept its head from falling off. As it was, the head lolled to the left, creating the appearance of being drunk. On its chest was scrawled in big letters, *L-OID.*

To Leopold's surprise, the L-OID spoke to him. He did not understand the language, but it sounded familiar. Like it came from Earth. Then the robot spoke in a different language, followed by a third and a fourth. One of them sounded like French. Another, Japanese. Leopold shook his head. He couldn't make out a word.

Then the robot spoke English. "Hello, I am a Language Droid. Please raise your hand or otherwise respond affirmatively if you can understand what I am saying to you."

Leopold's mouth was still taped over, and his arms and legs restrained, but he raised his head and nodded. He made muffled gurgling noises.

The L-OID tried turning its head inside the wire mesh, but succeeded primarily in rolling its bright yellow eyes. It spoke to the petite woman wearing kohl. The only word Leopold recognized was *English.* The woman produced a wristful of cloudy see-through necklaces with embedded chips. She synced them with the L-OID, then handed them to the other women. Finally, she raised Leopold's glass top and fastened one around his neck.

“Does this fukkin thing really work?” the leader barked, lifting her hair as an underling attached the necklace. “We’re all speaking the same verdammten gaijin language?”

“Yes, Kate,” the petite woman said.

“So the Dice can hear me?” she asked, staring skeptically at Leopold like he was an animal in a zoo. “I mean, understand me.”

“Yes,” the woman said, surveying Leopold from head to toe.

“Well, will wonders never fukkin cease? The Sephs find him, body and all, inside a German-designed cryohull made in Brazil with his own cryotank specked in Japan, built in France, and sold out of Russia. And the Dice speaks gaijin English?”

“Yes, Kate.”

Kate strode to Leopold’s module. He couldn’t take his eyes off her breasts. “Up here, Dice,” Kate snapped, two fingers to her eyes.

“You know why you lived, right?” she said. “When Earth died, everyone ran for the gaijin exits. The cryohulls only took skulls so they could jimmy more on board, and they dumped them in liquid nitrogen vats. But the launch G-force exploded the vats, so now all those useless verdammten cryohulls are filled with heads bouncing around like so many fukkin tennis balls. But you? Somehow you got your own private mausoleum. Someone must have paid a shit-ton to get you, body and all, inside that cryohull.”

Edna, Leopold thought, his eyes misting.

Kate turned brusquely to a different woman, this

one an older blonde. "The Dice seems so old and scrawny," she said. "All wing and no chicken. You're certain he works? I mean, absolutely verdammten fukkin certain."

The blonde smiled and nodded. "Yes, Kate. The Sephs tested and re-tested. And then tested again. He works."

A few more uniformed Titans—soldiers, he now assumed—sneaked into the room. There were at least fifteen. Leopold was surrounded by naked women staring at him. He tried not to stare back.

Kate frowned, then reached beneath his glass case to pull out a print. The one the Sephs had found Leopold clinging to. Kate stared at it, lifting her chin, judging it.

Leopold recognized it through the glass. Edna! They'd found the picture, a print of a Gustave Courbet painting, at the local library's rummage sale. It had looked remarkably like Edna, and she'd insisted he take the portrait with him into cryo. She had wanted to be the first thing he saw when he woke up.

Leopold tried speaking through the tape over his mouth, then nearly choked on the tubes draped down his throat. He struggled against his arm and leg restraints.

"Your wife?" Kate asked Leopold. Then she returned her gaze to the painting. "Well, not much to look at, is she? I bet you got a big fukkin discount when you brought *her* home from the wife store."

Leopold strained and gurgled and moaned.

"Take off his mouth tape!" Kate ordered, and the

petite woman complied. "Keep your hands off Edna!" Leopold spat, spittle dripping down his face.

Kate laughed. Not a small laugh, but one that made her bend over backwards a little. "You know she's gone, right? You've been in cryo for forty years, and Earth's a dead fukkin letter now."

"Even so," Leopold said in a strangled voice.

Then Leopold surveyed the room. An assemblage of Titan soldiers, all women. And the Seph nurses were women, too. Even the L-OID seemed vaguely female.

"Where are the men?" Leopold asked. The women fell silent.

"You really don't know shit, do you, Dice?" Kate said. "The men are dead. Have been for years. Our core generators baked their beans, and now they're gone. You, my scrawny fukkin friend, are the last of their gender. The last man."

Leopold gaped.

"And even if you are a runt, you're still *my* gaijin property," Kate said, beaming. Then everyone laughed. Everyone, that is, except Leopold and Edna.

***

The door burst open and two Titan soldiers dragged in a stumbling woman with her hands bound behind. Her face was bruised and bloodied, her tee shirt stained red. Leopold recognized her. The Seph, the one from before. Now a captive.

"We found her in an escape pod that misfired," one of the uniforms said. "She had a Grav-gun." The uniform held up the gun.

"How very like a Seph," Kate snarled. "Running from the fight. Hello, Lorelei."

"You won't get away with this, Kate," Lorelei said, tonguing the blood off her lower lip. "Helena and Hwee-Boon will talk. They'll sort things. They won't let you keep the Dice. He's ours."

The two Titan soldiers held Lorelei against the wall, and Kate strode closer. Lorelei couldn't help but cower.

"Lorelei, look at yourself!" Kate said softly, gesturing with one arm. "Look at this ship. It's a wreck. You're a wreck. When was the last time you had a good meal? Took a shower with real water? Your crew's in fukkin rags. You've been living in your own collective stink and filth and degra-fukkin-dation for six months. I could smell it when we boarded. Your whole gaijin operation is running on fumes."

"Our mission was a success," Lorelei said, her eyes flashing as she glanced at Leopold.

"And for that I fukkin thank you," Kate said, inclining her head in a mock bow.

"You must have hacked our transmissions," Lorelei said. "How else could you have known we found the Dice?"

"Didn't have to hack anything," Kate laughed. "Just had to listen. And think." She tapped her head. "Months of regular transmissions in regular lengths at regular intervals. Routine shit. Then all of a sudden massive excited fukkin gibberish. It could only mean one thing. You'd found the golden fleece. So we saddled up, and here we are."

Lorelei gulped. "So you didn't clear this with Helena?"

"Fukkin Crats," Kate snapped. "If I'd waited for clearance, we'd still be on Titus. Filling out forms. Holding hearings. Presenting to Council. Picking our asses."

"Then you'll need allies," Lorelei said, smiling weakly. "I can help. We're stronger together. Let's make a deal."

"I have leverage, and you have none," Kate said. "In our world, nothing else matters. You know that. No deal."

"Remember Hera," Lorelei said. "Things would have ended differently if she'd had allies."

In two quick steps Kate reached Lorelei, then grabbed her chin hard between two fingers. "I don't need a fukkin kunt like you to tell me about Hera. I was there. I saw it. I lived it. Her mistake wasn't too few allies. It was not enough fukkin leverage."

Kate glanced at Leopold, then back at Lorelei.

"And I've now got all the leverage I need, thank you very gaijin much."

Then Kate, grimacing, twirled a lock of Lorelei's graying hair around one finger, clenched it into a fist, and ripped it from her head. Lorelei screamed and dropped to one knee before the two uniforms pulled her back into a standing position. Cherry-red blood leaked down her forehead.

Kate pointed with her head to the blonde uniform. "Give me the Grav-gun," she ordered.

Sighing, the blonde complied. It was a block of black metal over a handle and trigger.

"Oh, how I love these verdammten things," Kate said, twirling a dial on the device. Then she wheeled to look at Leopold.

"I bet you've never seen a Grav-gun before, Dice. The science is complex, but the execution simple. It changes the gravitational field of what you shoot. Take Lorelei here. I'd say she weighs about 50 kilos. I dial the setting to twenty, fire it at her, and suddenly she weighs 1000 kilos. The results are so fukkin memorable."

Lorelei trembled against the wall as the two Titan uniforms edged away.

"Please don't do it, Kate," Lorelei pleaded. "There'll be hell to pay if I don't return from this mission."

Kate aimed and pulled the trigger. The gun buzzed, and the air between Kate and Lorelei undulated and glittered.

Lorelei crumpled, like all the bones in her body had snapped at the same time. She fell with such force her nose shattered on the floor and blood poured from her ears.

Kate sauntered to Lorelei's corpse. "Have hell send me the invoice, and I'll be sure to pay in full." Then she laughed, a big large throaty laugh, and stalked out of the room. Her hips were magnificent. The naked uniforms followed.

"Have the 'E' med-tech the Dice's tubes, then load him onto our ship," Kate said to one of the uniforms, her voice fading as she disappeared down the corridor.

"We need him de-vitrified and one hundred percent fukkin alive."

The room was empty and quiet. The dark pool of blood from Lorelei's head blossomed silently on the floor. Her pile of bones and organs and flesh did not move.

Edna, I'm so sorry you had to see that, Leopold thought.

***

Leopold almost didn't notice. A hooded, slumped blue form slipped into the room. Sidestepping Lorelei, it disconnected the Sephs' equipment, then rolled in replacements. Titan equipment.

Less banged up. Still shiny. Fewer pieces with more functionality.

Without warning, the blue figure appeared a hand's breadth from Leopold's face, lifted the glass case, and removed his restraints. Leopold relaxed for the first time in forty years.

The blue figure wore a necklace one of the uniforms had left behind. "Thank you," Leopold muttered. "I can't believe they thought I would run."

"They didn't," the figure murmured. "You were restrained for your own protection. You couldn't run even if you wanted to."

Leopold tried moving his muscles, and to his surprise he discovered they didn't respond.

At best, a mental command entailed herky-jerky spasms. He tested several times.

"It will take time, Leopold," the voice said, muffled.

"And practice. Be patient with yourself. Your muscles will recover, but cryo takes time. Devitrification takes time. Everything takes time."

"Who are you?" Leopold asked.

The blue figure shrugged off the hood, revealing a ghastly pallid hairless head with a belt strapped around and into its mouth. Carefully, the figure removed the belt, gobs of yellowed spit dripping heavily onto his cloak, then the mouthpiece, and Leopold realized it was a man.

"My name is Duncan Hillyer."

"Kate said all the men are dead."

"And so they are," Hillyer whispered. "I am a Eunuch. They call me the 'E.' They removed my testes to save my life, but at such cost. Such fearful cost."

"Are there others like you?" Leopold asked.

"Not on Titus, but perhaps at the Persephone Project. We call them Sephs. This is their trawler, and they're based on the moon's surface. Titus is a low orbiting station. I've heard the Sephs may have one or two like me."

"What happened to the men?"

"Cancer," Hillyer said. "Our energy cores leaked, and the radiation was lethal for testes. Every male quickly developed aggressive terminal cancer. They fixed the leak, but it was too late. Only a few survived more than a week or two after castration."

"So how do you make babies?"

"We don't. We tried cloning and gene solutions, but the experiments went horribly wrong. We just don't have the right tech out here. So we initiated missions to search surviving cryohulls for intact males. The needle in the haystack. But necessary to save our species. To save humankind."

"How many have they found?"

"You're the first, and it's been years. The Sephs and Titus once were close, but now they barely speak. I suspect Kate's play won't improve relations."

"Why does Kate call me the Dice?" Leopold asked.

"Because that's what you are. To them, I mean. The merchandise."

"And Earth?"

"It expired. Do not ask for details. It is forbidden to speak of it."

"So my wife, Edna, is dead."

"Yes. You must accept that. She saved you, didn't she? She's the reason you are here in this glass case?"

"Yes. She selected my cryotank, and she must have moved me to the cryohull when Earth failed. I owe her my life. I owe her everything."

Hillyer smiled strangely. "Don't be too quick to tally accounts," he said softly. "There is a saying on Titus. Over time all blessings are mixed. Life, especially."

"Why are you whispering?"

"On Titus, you must earn the right to speak." He held up the strap and mouthpiece. "The Silent must wear this as a sign of our low status. I should not be speaking to you now."

"What is Titus like?"

"There is a ruling caste divided into three factions. The Crats run the bureaucracy. That's Helena, who presides at Council. The Techs run the infrastructure, including medical. That's Zu and her assistant, Little Zu. And the Guardians, led by Kate, provide security. The politics of Titus are infinitely complex and enormously fragile. And also deadly. Everyone constantly maneuvers for more leverage, more power."

"So Kate was right. It's all about leverage."

"On Titus, nothing else matters."

"I guess someone named Hera found that out."

Hillyer smiled grimly. "Kate's predecessor. She wanted fewer masters, more slaves. She led an insurrection but misjudged the Techs, who ended up siding with the Crats. Hera died, and things simmered down. For the Silent, life remained as it was."

"So the factions survived?"

"Fully intact," Hillyer said. "But the compromise was to permit thralls. Women who voluntarily, quote unquote, pledge themselves to a Guardian. They wear white and cover their heads in public. You can tell a Guardian's status by how many thralls she has. Kate must have six or seven by now. A harem. Literally and figuratively."

While they spoke, Hillyer reconnected Leopold's tubes, replaced the patches, and administered injections. He covered Leopold with a blanket, then paused, looking at the door. To see if anyone was there. If anyone was listening.

"Leopold, if you like, I mean, if you want me to, I have something, here, in my pocket," Hillyer said, fumbling. "If you wish, you know, if you wish to take your own life," he continued, "this pill will do the trick. Quick, painless, forever."

Leopold frowned. "Why would I want to do that? I'm finally living again after forty years in cryo. My precious Edna's loving, lasting gift to me. It would be ungrateful to reject it. Why would you think I'd want to end things?"

Hillyer lowered his eyes, embarrassed. "So sorry," he mumbled. "I don't know what got into me." His eyes flickered up, then down again. "Just a random idea that popped into my head. There, now it's gone, and we shan't speak of it again."

Hillyer reinserted his mouthpiece and tied the strap. Quietly he pulled the blue hood back over his head. Then he leaned down to release the brakes on the wheels of Leopold's now- mobile cage. As he slowly steered Leopold and the Titan equipment out the door and down the corridor, he mumbled, barely loud enough even for Leopold to hear.

"Remember this, Leopold. On Titus, the primary rule is that anything without an approved use is discarded. Ruthlessly. Without remorse. Often violently."

"All right," Leopold said.

"And one other thing," Hillyer said.

"Yes?"

"There are no exceptions to the primary rule."

***

Leopold hated being wheeled down the hall. The helpless way he saw the ugly ceiling lights march past while he was flat on his back reminded him of his gurney ride at the hospital in Des Moines.

Leopold glimpsed the Seph crew huddled in their rags in a small room, the galley perhaps, some crossing their arms tightly, others staring hard at the floor, one rocking herself back and forth. Contemplating their future, no doubt—whether Kate would let them live.

At the end of the corridor, a hydraulic device elevated Leopold's cage, and he shivered as the temperature plummeted. Then a hatch opened and unseen hands lifted him into another vehicle. The Titan ship. Inside, the uniforms were strapping themselves into makeshift seats welded roughly to both sides of the fuselage. Leopold's cage and trailing equipment were secured by clamps and bound to corroded struts.

The pilot's door flew open and a wiry old woman with red-blinking goggles and a headset emerged. Her butch hair was so black it must have been dyed. She walked to Leopold's cage, then opened the glass top, tore off his blanket, and stared at his genitalia. Leopold winced as she grabbed them hard and shook. Shrugging, she returned the blanket, closed the top, and disappeared up front.

Kate sat in the seat nearest the pilot's door. Her face was a stone. The blonde uniform held her right hand and stroked it tenderly with her thumb.

"Don't do it," the blonde said, her eyes beseeching.

"Hera would kill them," Kate said stubbornly, staring straight ahead.

"You don't know that," the blonde said.

"Hera would kill them. No loose fukkin ends. That

was her motto."

"They aren't loose ends, Kate. They're Sephs. They're not the enemy."

"Mark my gaijin words, they'll come back to haunt us."

"Lorelei told her base we were boarding, so Hwee-boon already knows. The Sephs know, Kate."

"Then killing the crew won't make things worse."

"But sparing them might be an olive branch. Did you consider that?"

"Give me an olive branch, and I'll shove it up Hwee-boon's ass."

"You've already put Lorelei down. That's enough, Kate."

The two women continued speaking in animated murmurs, the blonde frantically stroking the back of Kate's right hand, talking reason, trying to calm her.

Trying to stop a war.

The Titan uniform with kohl-rimmed eyes jumped nimbly into the fuselage and twirled her right hand high over her head. Like someone at a rodeo. As if to say, it's time to go. She grabbed the door handle, waiting for Kate's order to secure stations and depart.

Kate leaned forward. "Anything to confiscate?"

The uniform grimaced. "A bare cupboard. Some power cells. A few medicines. That's about it. No food that's fit to eat."

"And the crew?"

"Up to you."

"Anything we can use?"

"They have a medtech. We can always use another

of those."

Kate paused, looking hard at the blonde, still holding her hand. Their eyes met for several long seconds. "All right," Kate said. "Take the medtech and leave the others."

The uniform returned minutes later with the Seph nurse, the one with mismatched socks. The nurse and Hillyer stepped through a hole in the floor to a dark, damp lower compartment, and the hatch slammed behind them. The uniform leapt into a seat and belted herself in.

Kate leaned back. "Tally ho," she said in a bored voice, twirling her right hand languorously.

Leopold expected some kind of blast-off, but instead their ship simply detached, like dentures from chapped gums. They drifted for several minutes before he felt the acceleration in his gut. Whatever was in his stomach gurgled into his esophagus. They were leaving the Sephs' trawler.

By then Hillyer's injections were taking effect. Leopold could barely keep his eyes open. "Sweet dreams, Dice," Kate called out. "By the time you wake up, we'll be on Titus. Home sweet fukkin home." Then she laughed, but Leopold was out by then.

***

It was the noise of landing, not the jolt, that awakened Leopold. His dreams of Edna, and her veal dinner with pear pie for dessert, vanished with the creaking and cooling and steaming of the thrusters.

"Leave the Dice!" Kate commanded, as the uniforms piled out.

The blonde stood at the threshold and peered into the light, then turned to Kate. "It's just Helena to greet us," she said to Kate. "Please remember what we discussed." Then she darted through the opening. That left Kate and Leopold alone inside the craft.

Leopold tried to flex his frame and, to his surprise and relief, succeeded. His left knee, his right elbow and hand, his toes. The link between his brain and musculature was starting to work again.

"Hera's mistake," Kate said slowly and evenly, "was tactics. She responded to small provocations with aggressive confrontation. It shortened the game, but increased the fukkin stakes."

"I thought it was leverage," Leopold said weakly.

"It was. More leverage and she would have prevailed. But she could have won the verdammten thing with the leverage she had. If she'd used it in smaller gaijin doses. Do you understand why I'm telling you this, Dice?"

"No," Leopold responded.

"Helena is out there by herself. Which means she's already talked to Zu and the gaijin Council. She'll have a proposal for me. Her leverage is she won't let me and my girls back into Titus unless I verdammten well agree to it."

"Is that more leverage than you have?"

"Yes, even though I have you. Our ship can't go anywhere else. We had just enough fuel to go and return. But once we're inside, well, then the situation changes."

"So what are you going to do?"

"Bargain for terms," she said, her voice now a whisper. "But here's the deal, Dice. In the end you control what happens to you. It'll be your choice, and there's only one fukkin choice that guarantees your safety."

"Yes?"

"Choose to be my thrall."

"You mean, wear white, cover my head, follow you around, and…and…"

"Yes, and be my sex slave. Go on, say it."

"Yes, that," Leopold said, nearly gagging.

Kate's voice turned into a husky growl. "There are worse fates, Dice. I saw you looking at me. But you have to pledge yourself to me. Take an oath. Like my other thralls. I will be your master. I will fukkin own you."

Leopold gulped. *What would Edna think?* He was not prepared to make any decisions, let alone one as consequential as this.

"What would you do with me?" Leopold asked.

"I'll be the first to get pregnant on Titus in a very long time. And I'll control who else has access to you. That will give me unprecedented gaijin status. And leverage. In exchange I'll treat you well the rest of your life. You have my word. Even after your beans stop working."

She leaned over and whispered seductively in his ear. "And you'll get to eat chicken once a week!"

Then Kate stood up in all her magnificence. "And remember this, Dice. No one can protect you on Titus except me. Not Helena. Not Zu and Little Zu. No one."

Leopold lay there, trembling. Would Kate keep her word? Would she really protect him the rest of his life? He fingered his necklace, remembering Duncan Hillyer's words. On Titus, everything without an approved use is discarded.

The primary rule.

To which there are no exceptions.

***

Chin high, Kate strode through the opening like a conquering warlord. She barked orders, then several uniforms clambered back on board to offload Leopold. The wheels of his cage clattered on the metal landing deck, then they rolled him to Kate's side. Her soldiers stood at attention in rows.

The cargo bay was tight quarters, and Leopold's eyes widened when he saw the Titan craft from the outside. A piece of junk! He was amazed it could fly at all, much less in space. It looked like it couldn't dust a cornfield.

Kate stood face to face with the thinnest woman Leopold had ever seen. Helena! He thought she might vanish if she turned sideways. Her pure gold blouse and pants billowed against the acrid steam still shooting from their ship. The only thing whiter than her skin was her hair.

She took two quick steps over to Leopold's cage, then put her hands behind her back as she bent over. Like she wanted to see but was scared to touch.

Frowning, she examined him from head to toes but did not remove the blanket.

"So," Helena said, in her bored, aristocratic voice. "This is he."

"Large as fukkin life," Kate responded.

"While you were out adventuring," Helena said. "Council met informally."

"Council can't meet without Guardians," Kate said.

"Hence the word *informally*," Helena rejoined. She returned to where she'd stood before, face to face with Kate.

"Shall we cut to the chase?" Helena said, softly but with an edge.

Kate shrugged. "Might as well. You always do."

"Council will not permit your re-entry until acceptable ground rules are in place."

"I could kill you here and now," Kate growled.

"Indeed," Helena said, "but then you'd never gain entrance."

"They'd let us in eventually," Kate said.

"Or not," Helena said. "Zu would preside over Council in my absence. With Little Zu beside her."

"So what ground rules do you and the two Zu's have in mind?" Kate asked, baring her teeth in an insincere grin.

"The gentleman belongs to all of us," Helena said.

"I found him," Kate said. "Finder's keepers."

"The public right is supreme," Helena said.

"Under Code, he can choose to be my thrall," Kate said.

"And has he done so?" Helena asked, raising both

eyebrows, risking a thin smile.

"Discussions are on-fukkin-going," Kate said, eyes dancing.

"Until they are concluded in your favor, he is part of our body," Helena said, her face a mask again. "The public body. The *Titan* body. He is a unique resource. There must be rules and procedures governing access to him."

"If you're referring to his verdammten gaijin seed, he might have something to say about that."

"He shall be consulted, of course."

"But in the end Council decides?"

"As always."

"And until then?"

"My personal security can serve as an escort," Helena said.

"I offer mine as well," Kate said. The two women sized each other up.

Helena sighed. "And if Zu were here, she'd offer Little Zu."

"So, it's an Honor Guard for the Dice," Kate said. "We each choose one."

"Until Council decides," Helena said.

"And the Dice will need a medtech around the clock. He's not out of the gaijin woods yet. We have the 'E,' and we've brought one from the trawler. A Seph."

"How thoughtful!" Helena exclaimed with faux enthusiasm. "But I'm sure Zu has one of her own to offer."

"I'm sure she does, but I insist on the Seph. A neutral gaijin party. I don't want the Dice waking up some morning with his beans in one of Zu's aquariums."

Helena took a deep breath, then nodded decisively. She offered her hand. "Agreed then."

Kate took it and shook. "Agreed."

Helena peered at Leopold again. "He damned well better work," she said.

"A-fukkin-men to that," Kate said.

***

They stashed Leopold in a small cubicle near the cargo bay. He spied a broken-toothed comb inside the door. And a piece of twine around the handle to help the door stay shut.

Someone used to call this home. Someone who'd been hastily evicted for Leopold's benefit.

And Edna joined him. They hung her portrait over his cage. He gazed at it during his lengthening periods of lucidity.

Outside the cubicle was a railing and below that the Atrium. It was the only open space in the entire space station. Leopold leaned over the edge of his cage to take a look. A few primitive tables and chairs amid containers of plants and vegetation. No people.

The Seph, continually checking on Leopold, came and went as she pleased. The Honor Guard made themselves comfortable in the corridor. From the Guardians, Kate chose the petite soldier with the kohl-rimmed eyes, whom they called Baby. Under thirty, she was the youngest person on Titus. From the Techs, little Zu, black as a sealed airlock, was taller than Kate and at least fifty kilos heavier. Helena chose a quiet intense woman with bird-darting eyes called Murry. Apart from muttering into her wristcom at periodic intervals, she didn't say a word.

By the end of that first day, Leopold's condition stabilized and he gained more control of his movements. He tried sitting up, but collapsed from the vertigo. The Seph pronounced devitrification complete, then disconnected the tubes except for his IV.

That evening, when everyone but Leopold was asleep, a wall panel in the cubicle silently slid open, and Helena walked through, as elegant as an icicle. She tied the twine tightly around the door handle. A necklace glittered from her neck.

"We need to talk," she said.

"Yes," Leopold replied.

"I don't know where you come from or what your life experiences have been," she said quietly. "Perhaps in time I can learn your story. But for now I need you to understand Titus. How we operate. And why."

Leopold said nothing.

"We live on the edge of a razor," Helena continued. "Our world ends each night, and the next morning we're all surprised to still be here. Every day is touch-and-go whether we have enough air to breathe, water to drink, food to eat. It's been that way for so many years I've lost count. Our society is fragile as an ancient eggshell. We survive only because the bureaucracy—the Crats, they call us—exercise total control. We embody and implement the public right. Without us, there is no Titus. Regimentation is survival. It may sound harsh, but there is no other way."

"I thought there was a Council," Leopold said.

Helena's back stiffened. "A convenient fiction to give the Techs and Guardians a sense of participation. But make no mistake. Nothing happens unless the Crats want it to happen. Unless *I* want it to happen."

Leopold thought about Duncan Hillyer. And that disgusting mouthpiece he wore. "What about the Silent?"

Helena tossed her head in irritation. "We can't everyone be rulers. For all of us to live, some must serve. It is how effective societies work. Too much participation is anarchy. And anarchy means we all die."

"So where do I fit in?"

"You don't, unless you sublimate yourself to the public right. We shall draft rules and establish procedures to ensure that any expansion of Titus occurs in an orderly and supportable manner without upsetting the status quo."

"Expansion?"

Helena glanced at the door to make sure it was still shut tight. "Pregnancies," she hissed sourly. "You know, babies." She nearly spit out the word.

"I think Kate has other ideas," Leopold said.

"She always does," Helena replied. "Trust me, I'll find ways to mollify her. But you must not choose to be her thrall. The consequences for all concerned would be devastating." The way she said *all concerned* let

Leopold know she was talking about him. Threatening him.

Leopold noticed Helena was trembling.

"It would upset the balance of power we have worked so hard to establish since, well, since . . ."

"Since Hera," Leopold finished.

"Yes. So you understand the stakes. If everyone has a voice, no one is heard."

Leopold nodded.

Helena looked at the portrait on the wall. It was barely visible in the gloom. "I am told this was your wife," she said. "What was her name?"

"Edna," Leopold offered.

"Edna," Helena repeated out loud, then grabbed Leopold's arm. Breathlessly, she leaned over. "We are busy revising the rules to govern access to your, how shall I put it, your functionality. Let us finish this process while you get stronger. Kate will push. Zu may as well. You must resist. Time will out in the end."

Sounds came from the corridor. Someone turning over in their sleep? Or maybe the Honor Guard hearing voices? Not taking chances, Helena darted into the dark opening in the wall.

"Think of Edna," she said, then silently closed the panel behind her.

***

Next morning the Seph decided Leopold should get up and move. He couldn't walk yet, so they procured a chair with wheels. When Leopold saw the L-OID dumped into a corner, he knew where they'd gotten the chair. It smelled of motor oil.

The Seph found Leopold a gown and helped him out of his cage. He literally fell onto the chair. Leopold couldn't have weighed much more than 50 kilos, but still the weight was too much for his legs. The Honor Guard took turns pushing him down the corridors, lifting him through hatches, and hauling him up and down the ladder-like stairs.

The procession moved slowly as Leopold absorbed the sights and sounds and smells of Titus. Befitting a low-orbiting space station, it was mostly corridors and cubicles. Leopold caught his reflection against polished doorframes and realized he looked like Mahatma Ghandi. All skin and bones, and bald.

The people scattered and hid when they saw him coming. But then he'd see their heads pop out from around corners, under desks, and behind chairs. And from dark corners. Even the Silent quietly ventured out, mouthstraps tightly in place. Leopold heard a buzz, an undercurrent of murmur. Word had spread. They all knew who he was, and what he represented. They all wanted at least a peek.

And a touch.

As they rumbled by, the wheels of Leopold's chair clattering angrily, hands would reach out, some tentatively, some aggressively, seemingly from nowhere. At first Leopold huddled tightly. But then he learned how to offer a bit of his gown, which hung on him like drapery. A sleeve here, a hem there. And how people grabbed it! Like it was a lifeline. Like they were sick and one touch would heal them.

Gradually, Leopold began enjoying the attention. He developed new gestures and facial expressions. As they maneuvered past openings, he would extend his arm to make it easier for someone to reach out for the fabric. And he learned how to gently jerk it from their grasp after they'd had what in Leopold's judgment was a sufficient touch.

Sometimes he saw eyes in the distance, and he smiled and waved. A few waved in return.

And Titus surprised him. At first he thought it dirty. Then he realized it was just old.

Dilapidated. It wasn't designed to operate for so many years. The station reminded Leopold of a shack in Appalachia. You could repair it and sweep it out each day, but it was still a shack.

Parts of the station were no longer lit, although starlight entered through uncovered hatches. This is where the Silent lived. Guardians with nightsticks and wearing flashlights on their heads patrolled at periodic intervals. Trouble was not tolerated. The Honor Guard did not let Leopold enter the unlit areas. *Too difficult to see*, they lied, eyes to the floor. Leopold frowned and sniffed. It smelled like bleach. Or chloroform.

Then they pushed through swinging doors into an area stuffed with machines, monitors and screens. Little Zu smiled for the first time, and Leopold realized this was where the Techs lived. A hand-lettered sign hung crookedly from the ceiling: *Tech-No-Land.*

They pulled up in front of a tiny cubicle, and an animated discussion broke out among the Honor

Guard, with fierce whispers and strong gestures. Little Zu towered over the other two. Baby, her eyes shining like sapphires, rested her gun hand on a hip holster. That's when Leopold realized she was carrying the Grav-gun. Kate had loaned it to her. The third guard, Murry, stood back and, worried, spoke fast into her wristcom.

Then the door swung open and a tiny black woman stepped out, chin high. She had fine aquiline features and raven black hair down to her waist in back. She motioned with both hands like she was conducting an orchestra.

Little Zu drew herself up to her full height and pursed her lips. "Zu says she will speak to the Dice here in the corridor." She glared at Baby and Murry. "You can stay to listen if you wish."

Baby and Murry exchanged nervous glances, then shrugged and leaned against the wall.

As long as they could listen and report, it was all right.

Zu moved her hands, and Little Zu interpreted. It wasn't signing, exactly. It was more the way ballet dancers moved their arms and hands. As in, this gesture means dance, this one, magic, and this other one, stay away. But somehow Little Zu knew in great detail what Zu wanted to say.

"We are the nerve and brain center of Titus," Little Zu said, her eyes fixed on Zu's weaving and waving hands. "If our equipment fails, Titus dies. If our monitor-and-control algorithms have even a hiccup, Titus dies. If even one day goes by where we do not do our job perfectly, Titus dies."

Leopold was mesmerized by Zu's motions.

"The Crats and the Guardians have a high opinion of their own value," Little Zu said, "but neither can say that."

"What about me?" Leopold asked.

"Zu feels strongly that you belong here. It is the best solution for Titus. For the body. It permits growth without disorder."

"I don't know what that means," Leopold said. "Belong here, how?"

"We would surgically remove your testes, house them safely in our equipment, and produce and distribute your seed in a controlled manner to ensure the survival of the human species."

Leopold involuntarily clenched his thighs together. "What about the rest of me?" Leopold asked.

"Zu says we would protect you forever to honor your sacrifice."

Leopold glanced at Baby's Grav-gun, nestling against her hip. Narrowing her eyes at Leopold, Baby pawed at it.

Kate will hate me, and Helena will be furious, and I will have no leverage. And forever is a very long time.

Zu raised her eyebrows, as if she knew what Leopold was thinking.

"Please tell Zu I'll take it under advisement," Leopold said to Little Zu. He was pleased with the turn of phrase. He'd heard it on TV, but this was the first time he'd used it. He wasn't entirely sure what it meant. Just that he didn't want to make a decision right then and there. He wanted to keep his options open.

Baby smiled, and Murry whispered with relief into her wristcom. Zu sighed and Little Zu shrugged.

As the makeshift procession left the cubicle, Leopold thought he heard a rustling sound.

He turned, but Zu hadn't moved a muscle. She stared at him, no expression on her face. "Tra-la-la," she said.

***

Leopold awoke the next morning feeling alive and refreshed. The cryo was peeling off now in thick layers. Leopold was becoming himself again. He stood without buckling. With the aid of a rusty bent stanchion, he could walk. The Seph found him clothes, and he dressed carefully.

This day he wanted to make a good impression.

As the Honor Guard assembled itself, Leopold leaned over the railing to survey the Atrium one level down. He enjoyed the green. The life. He inhaled what he imagined was its fragrance. It was the only thing on Titus that reminded him of Earth.

Against the Atrium's far wall, something hung that wasn't there the day before. A limp blue robe. Then Leopold saw the two motionless feet underneath, and he knew.

He rushed to the stairway and would have tumbled down headfirst if Baby hadn't caught up and grabbed his elbow. Then Murry took Leopold's other arm, and the two women helped him to the bottom of the stairs.

Using his stanchion as a cane, he shuffled, spindly-legged, to the blue cloak, then roughly pulled it down.

There hung a naked Duncan Hillyer, his eyes unblinking and his mouthstrap shoved far down his throat. His arms were tied together so he could hold a sign. Written in red, it said: LOOSE LIPS SINK SHIPS.

Leopold realized immediately the sign was for him. That slogan. It dated from World War II. No one else on Titus would know what it meant. He wondered how long they'd searched databases to find it. Somehow they must have discovered that Hillyer had talked to him.

This was a warning, a threat even. Was it the Techs? Hillyer worked for them, and they certainly had database access. But Kate was capable, and Helena was cunning. It could have been any of them.

His Honor Guard stared quizzically at the sign. "What does it mean?" Murry asked.

Leopold pursed his lips. "It means Hillyer spoke when he wasn't supposed to."

"He's not supposed to fukkin speak at all," Baby said. Little Zu nodded in agreement.

"Yes," Leopold said, grinding his teeth.

The Seph averted her eyes.

"Let's walk," Leopold said.

Gradually Leopold's anger and fear subsided, and he grew stronger as they walked the corridors of Titus.

This time Leopold listened hard to the murmurs. When someone reached out, Leopold leaned in to hear, his own swaying necklace providing a rough translation. *You are the one*, they seemed to say. *The one we have been waiting for.* Were they really saying that? Or was it merely what Leopold wanted to hear?

You are the hope of our world.

Energized, Leopold spent as much time on his knees as standing—looking for the Titans, seeking out the physical contact. He glad-handed like he was running for Congress. No, like he was already in Congress and running for reelection.

His gestures from the day before became even more pronounced. Smiling broadly at his reflection in the corridor siding, Leopold looked like a gargoyle. He offered his hand and the hem of his garment to anyone who didn't shrink back.

And he began speaking to them, even though he knew they wouldn't understand. But they would hear the tenor of his voice. They would sense the courage in his words even if they did not know their meaning.

At first, he offered platitudes, such as *Be strong!* or *Persevere!*

But then he personalized his commentary. *Yes, I have come—I have heard your summons—Yes, I am the hope you seek.*

Yes, I am the one you have been waiting for.

Leopold's Honor Guard became nervous. Baby kept reaching for her holster. Murry talked even faster into her wristcom. Little Zu licked and re licked her lips.

And then Leopold walked into the minefield.

Speak, he said. *Speak your mind and you can move mountains.*

"You need to be more gaijin careful!" Baby said, concern giving way to anger. "Some people are forbidden to speak."

"Says who?" Leopold said, remembering Hillyer.

"The public right," Little Zu said.

Leopold sucked in his breath. "The public right is wrong," he hissed. Everyone stopped in their tracks.

"These are my people," Leopold said. "They have a voice. They are entitled to be heard."

And then he repeated himself for good measure. "The public right is wrong."

At that moment, they were in Tech-No-Land. Down the corridor he saw a tiny black woman with glorious flowing hair watching him. It was Zu. She had heard everything he said. She stared at him without emotion. Almost pityingly. This time she made no gestures with her hands and arms.

"Tra la la," Leopold said to her.

***

Bright white lights flashed quickly, then repeated in a pattern.

"We need to get you back," Baby said, eyes upward, taking Leopold's arm.

"My place is here," Leopold said, pouting. "With my flock."

"Your place is back in your cubicle," Little Zu said. "If you know what's good for you."

"They're trying to shut me up," Leopold said.

"I don't know who 'they' might be," Baby said with

annoyance, inclining into her earpiece, "but the Sephs just shot a verdammten recon drone so close it's nearly up our gaijin asses. Two more on the way. The white lights mean we're on battle alert."

Helena met them at the cubicle. She looked like a stormcloud. "Have you lost your wits entirely?" she said to Leopold.

"You have eyes and yet you cannot see," Leopold said.

Helena shook her head aggressively. "You are a little boy playing with matches. You have no idea the harm you could cause."

"The public right is wrong."

Helena slapped him hard. "Never say that again. To me, or anyone else here on Titus."

Leopold rubbed his jaw. "So the Sephs have come knocking."

"Yes, they want you back. I've been in nearly constant communication with Hwee-boon since Kate boarded their trawler. They just upped the stakes. We need to think clearly, and for that we need calm."

"She's probably mad about Lorelei," Leopold said.

"She doesn't care about Lorelei," Helena shot back. "Why do you think they dumped Lorelei on that trawler in the first place? Hwee-boon hated her. It was a miserable assignment."

Murry ran breathlessly up to Helena. "We have a riot in the second corridor down under. The Guardians are on their way. Kate is loaded for bear."

Helena paused for a second, then made up her mind. "Go!" she said. "Go, go, go."

Murry followed Baby and Little Zu as they ran to the scene of the conflict. Suddenly forgotten, Leopold followed, stanchion in hand, as quickly as he could manage.

It was the Silent. They were sitting cross-legged against the cold metal siding in the corridor leading to their unlit living space. They had removed their mouthstraps and, eyes closed, were chanting.

The public right is wrong! The public right is wrong!

One of the Guardians, the older blonde Leopold had seen on the trawler, shouted at the Silent. She led a team of Guardians, who bent down to strike selected chanters. She cajoled, wheedled, then threatened. Titus was under attack from the Sephs, she said, and everyone must maintain discipline. Still, the chant continued.

Leopold smiled. In only a day he had made a difference!

Then Kate showed up, Helena at her side, both scowling. The blonde looked to Kate, who nodded, once.

Then the blonde shouted orders Leopold couldn't understand, and the Guardians attacked the Silent with their nightsticks. More Guardians joined in, and the blood flowed. The chant gave way quickly to cries and wails and moans. The Guardians dragged the rioters down the corridor to their dark living space. The sound of truncheons beating flesh and bone continued for some minutes. Leopold felt sick. The floor was smeared red.

Leopold limped back to his cubicle, led by the tap-

tap-tapping of his cane. His strength was gone, and he hurt all over. He lay on his mattress and sighed. Sometimes cryo seemed like death. Other times—this time!—it didn't seem so bad.

The Honor Guard was gone. Kate and Helena, too. And Zu. Everyone and everything, it seemed, was gone.

The Seph nurse quietly let herself in, closed the door, then tied it shut. She began massaging Leopold to relax his muscles. His breathing slowed. His tensions ebbed. His boiling thoughts simmered. Then she worked her way down his abdomen, and up his thighs. He felt sensations he hadn't felt in more than forty years. As he began to respond, he raised his head.

"What are you doing?" he asked.

"Shh," the nurse whispered, finger to her lips. Then she dropped her clothes and climbed on top of him. It happened in an instant, and then he realized how much he'd wanted it. With every fiber of his being. More than anything in the world.

Even more than Edna. He briefly thought of her portrait, there on the wall. "I don't even know your name," he said to the nurse.

"Shh," she whispered.

***

Leopold awoke to a new sound. A constant low-grade rustling. Like persistent winds over a desolate Iowa cornfield. He lay there, remembering the night before. The Seph nurse was gone. He peered up at Edna's portrait. For the first time, he didn't know what to say.

He heaved himself over the mattress and stood without help for the first time. He wasn't ready to run sprints just yet, but he was erect and mobile. He flexed his knees. He even did jumping jacks. His body protested, but it complied.

Outside, the Honor Guard was gone except for Baby. She leaned over the railing to peer down into the Atrium. Leopold joined her, and his jaw dropped. The greenery was gone. So was Hillyer's body. And the space was filled to overflowing with people. Titans milled about, some shuffling their feet. Others crouched, flexing to stay limber. It was all eerily silent. No one said a word.

They had come in all shapes and sizes. Some even wore white, signifying they were some Guardian's thrall. Others wore the mouthstrap. He recognized several from his perambulations around Titus. Crats and Techs were mixed in with the Silent. But there were no Guardians, except for a few thralls.

"What are they doing?" Leopold asked.

"They're fukkin lined up," Baby said, not taking her eyes off the crowd.

"They're in a line?"

"Fukkin A," Baby said. "See, it starts over there, then snakes there, and up and around there, and then down that gaijin corridor." As she pointed with her finger, Leopold finally saw it. Like when you stare at a page of dots and suddenly your eyes see a dinosaur.

"What are they lined up for?"

Baby smiled like she thought Leopold was joking.

"You really don't know?" she said.

"Should I?"

"They're lined up for you. The Crats posted it yesterday. Sign-up starts in thirty minutes for volunteers to receive your gaijin seed."

Leopold was dumbstruck. "Half of Titus must be down there."

"More if you count those down the verdammten hallway," Baby said, gesturing.

"They're here for me!" he said, as if talking to himself.

"The rest would be here too, except they have fukkin jobs. Titus doesn't run itself."

"There are no Guardians down there," Leopold said.

Baby shrugged. "Kate said no."

"Little Zu and Murry?"

"They're out there. Somewhere. Maybe down the corridor."

Leopold smiled like he'd won a lottery. "They all want me!"

"They want security," Baby said. "You get pregnant, have a baby, you got it made. Or that's what everyone thinks. With our tech, any female can get pregnant."

But Leopold wasn't listening. "Halloo!" he called from the railing, waving.

Everyone looked up, some pointing. A murmur arose from those not wearing a mouthstrap.

An enormous beaming smile enveloped Leopold's face, and he began marching in place, his feet moving up and down to music only he could hear. If he'd been handed a saxophone or a trumpet, he could have been in a marching band.

In that moment, Leopold realized why they had killed Hillyer. It wasn't a warning or a threat. It was a sign of weakness. They were desperately scared of him. None of them could draw a crowd like this. Leopold had power.

He had leverage.

"Quite a fukkin crowd," a familiar voice said. It was Kate.

"Come to admit defeat?" Leopold said.

"No, Dice. Come to tell you my offer from before is still open, but the window's closing fast. One way or another, decide now."

"Now I think maybe you're the one who should wear white," Leopold said, smirking. He could not take his eyes off the crowd below.

"Watch yourself, Dice. Wars are for warriors. Politics, for politicians. And you're neither fukkin one."

"You think I'll make Hera's mistake. Bad tactics."

"Your mistake isn't tactics, Dice. It's strategy. Big fukkin difference."

Leopold waved his hand dismissively. "Tactics? Strategy? Call it what you want. In the end, it's all about leverage."

Then he laid his hands out over the railing towards the people below. "And that's what I call leverage."

"Boom!" Kate said, a strange smile on her face. "That's the sound of my verdammten window closing. Baby and I will leave you here. You know, to commune with your gaijin people."

"I am preparing a list of my requirements," Leopold said grandly. "Please assemble Helena and Zu at your earliest convenience so I can inform you all."

"Whatever you say, Dice," Kate said with practiced amiability, as if she didn't care. Then she motioned to Baby, and the two walked off, Kate whispering furiously in Baby's ear. Baby looked at Leopold like she might never see him again.

But Leopold's attention had already returned to the throng. His feet began marching in place again. He smiled, nodded his head, and waved.

***

It was the pilot who came to get Leopold. The one with the black butch hair who'd shaken his genitalia back on the transport.

"They're waiting for you in the cargo bay," she said.

"They?" Leopold asked.

"Kate, of course. And Helena and Zu."

Leopold nodded, then gestured. "Excellent. Please show the way."

He touched the woman on her shoulder. "May I ask what you're called?"

She seemed startled and confused. "You mean, what's my name?" she said at last.

"Yes, your name."

"Evie."

"Evie," Leopold pronounced out loud.

The three women stood quietly as the pilot showed

Leopold in. He approached them briskly while the pilot quickly let herself out.

"So how do you wish to proceed?" Leopold asked.

"We have something for you," Helena said smoothly. Smiling, she showed him a burnished silver object in her hand. Then she pressed a button with her thumb and a blade snapped out. Before Leopold could react, she slid it easily between two ribs on his left side.

At the same time, Kate produced a wicked curved shiv and jammed it into his right ribcage.

"Zu?" Helena said, raising her eyebrows.

Zu walked behind, and Leopold felt the icy shock of a third blade entering his back.

For a long moment, they all stood there. Leopold, his mouth open and eyes wide, trying to comprehend the searing pain. The three women stood still, hands firmly clasping their blade handles, no one moving, no one speaking.

Then, as if on cue, the women pulled out the blades simultaneously, and Leopold collapsed to the cold metal floor like a sack of potatoes. Blood spurted in all directions.

"I still think the Grav-gun would have been easier," Kate said.

"We all needed to participate," Helena responded. Then she bent over Leopold's body, keeping her distance to avoid staining her gold gown.

"How could you do this?" Leopold croaked. "I am the only path. How will the species survive?"

"We decided it was more important," Helena said, "to maintain our structure of authority. As you know, there is a fragile balance of competing interests here on Titus. A narrative, if you will. Preserving the fabric of that narrative was and is our priority. Unfortunately, you did not fit into it."

"Then the human race dies with me," Leopold gasped.

"I don't know about that," Helena said. "The three of us will survive. As will Titus. And the Sephs. As to what happens after I am dead and gone, well, how much should I care? What matters is the public right, here and now."

Leopold rolled onto his back, moments from lasting unconsciousness. "What will you tell my people?"

"We'll think of something," Helena said, turning to Kate. "A latent cryo infection, perhaps."

"A slip and fukkin fall," Kate offered.

"Yes, something sudden," Helena added. "And unexpected."

Leopold tried to speak but could not. A final word escaped. It might have been *Edna*, but no one could be sure.

"You needn't worry about your wife," Helena said as Leopold sucked for air. "We'll keep her portrait safe."

"Edna's one of us now," Kate said.

Helena stepped back as the expanding circle of blood approached her feet.

Without emotion, Kate watched Leopold struggle. "It was risky," she said to Helena, "posting the gaijin sign-up notice yesterday. We could have given the Dice more fukkin time. Another day at least."

"We needed to know," Helena said emphatically. "Before the situation worsened beyond our capacity to regain control."

"So what have you told Hwee-boon?" Kate asked.

"I told the Sephs we've decided to give the gentleman back," Helena said. "And so we shall. The airlock over there should do the trick. Hwee-boon can chase after the carcass all she wants."

"What about the Seph nurse?" Kate asked.

"Hwee-boon hasn't mentioned her, so I assume she's ours. If we want."

"Well, we eliminated the 'E,' so we're down a verdammten medtech. Any problem to keeping the Seph?"

"I see no harm," Helena said. "Zu, what do you say? She'll be one of yours." Zu wiped her blade on her pants and shrugged.

"Then it's settled," Helena said. "We keep the Seph and go back to the way things were."

Kate nudged Leopold with her foot, but he was dead.

"Tra la la," Zu said

SALVAGE MISSION, PART 4

"Quinn, we've spent years salvaging derelict ships and stations, but we have never found anything like this before," Pope said. She was unable to keep the awe from her voice.

"Does the manifest help in any way?" Quinn asked.

"Our usual channels for selling salvage range from second-hand space ship dealers to parts resellers." Pope was at a loss. "I don't know where to begin."

"Let's have another story in the meantime," Carter said. The eagerness slipped into his voice.

A Meadow in the Mountains: Le Mas de Saint-Paul, by Vincent Van Gogh, 1889. Oil on canvas.

Havero Colony Transport, Catalog #: 115

4. PARIS IN THE RAIN

S. C. Megale

"Oh, John." Her head pressed into the sleeve of my arm. Her voice a whisper like wind in the sand. "What's on that mountain?"

I stood at the open window and watched the sky. It draped around the single peak on the horizon like a silver cloak.

"I don't know, my love." My hand reached across my chest to hold the side of her head. "But I will take you."

I kissed her. Flecks of my orange beard stuck to the black of her hair. Then I moved away.

I shook the box of oats in the kitchen. They blurred as one color into my bowl. Janice stayed by the window gazing at her mountain and leaned on the cottage wall. Her body curved like an S in her purple-black dress. The spoon stroked through the oats without a sound, and my russet eyes glanced up at her as I ate.

I tightened the coat around me when the bowl was empty. The brim hat hung at the foyer and I grabbed it at the same time I grabbed the sickle. On silk hinges I opened the door with one hand, and then turned and gazed back at my wife.

She didn't sense my stare. I left.

My boots sank into the stone pathway as I walked to the fields. Brushes of golden wheat seemed to sway only when they were in my periphery. I wondered what I would hear if they moved and rushed the way my wife does. I believe they would sound like her. The still mountain would sound like me.

I lifted the sickle. I grasped the wheat. And then I swung.

It was like dragging a blade through water. Around me the colors saturated as night gave way to day. Stars faded to white. Everything I cut and did not catch floated to the sky like embers.

Sweat rolled down me and dripped flesh onto my shirt. The outlines of my fingers stuck together. I plodded up the hill back home, carrying a bundle of wheat.

Janice sat at the bench next to the windowsill daisies. Her hands were in her lap, and somehow she always managed not to smudge them together. Her head was bent to the roof. I followed her gaze.

What was a thatched roof yesterday was tin today. Bright blue. Janice and I locked eyes but did not speak.

In bed that night, we lay. The roof was louder now, each droplet of new color tinging onto it. Janice's eyes were not closed. I held her in my arms.

And that is when we heard the echo. A hiccup. A mournful skipping in the distance, like human misery.

"John." Her fingers curled at my chest.

"Rest, little one."

"Will they touch the mountain?"

When the spirits sob, always we wake to some-thing changed.

"They would never."

Its mighty shadow made periwinkle all that touched the world the next morning. The mountain remained as dark and large as ever.

Still the wheat would not sway.

I closed my eyes and swung.

Only until the remnants floated to the sky did I notice the little specks of rose enhancing the wheat. I looked up at them, the bundle in my arms.

It was wheat no more.

I trudged home.

"But we cannot eat wildflowers," said Janice.

I set the bundle down on the bench and pressed my palms into it. I hung over it, eyes still closed, and breathed, fighting the turpentine of my tears.

"They are just flowers now," she said.

"But they are beautiful," said I.

I turned away.

That night, the spirits did not cry.

I hacked my sickle at everything, desperate for an edible reap. The oats were low. Janice was thinner at the window gazing at her mountain.

When I was far enough into the fields, I cried out to the distance. I attacked the ground with my blade and my anger.

Color chipped away. So much that I found white, clothy ground beneath. My chest heaved. My inhales were squeaks. I gazed at the odd soil and lowered to a crouch. Then I ran my hand along it. My fingertips left a stain.

Janice swept the last spoonful of oats towards her mouth. She stopped. And she held the spoon out to me.

I stood. Leaned over the table. My hands touched either side of her soft jaw.

"You will go hungry," she said.

"Do not think of that."

"How can I not?" Tears filled her eyes.

I dropped my forehead onto hers and plummeted my voice to a rasp. "Think what is on that mountain."

We rose before the morning that next day. Something felt empty in my stomach, but I kept my head down to the chill and led the mule by the rein. It mowed through the long grass with me, tent and water on its back, and my wife holding it steady upon the saddle.

We neared that mountain.

Miles wound through mosaics of copper and purple

hues. Bronze leaves fell into lapis water. Our cottage shrunk to a dot in the distance, and it felt like that mountain was all we could see. It stretched the sky.

On its face, I saw no grooves. Only steel colors that borrowed from the clouds. The peak swirled together white and grey and canary yellow.

"Let us rest here." I extended my arms to Janice. She shifted into me and I carried her to her feet. Her body trembled against me. Joy shook her speechless as she clutched her black cloak and absorbed the majesty of the mountain before us. I absorbed only her reaction. "We will sleep at its base and climb it tomorrow." Somehow, I would find a way.

Under the tent, we rubbed the oils of each other together. We were hungry. But we were happy.

Then, sometime in the middle of night, the sobs reverberated. I woke with a start. Minutes later woke Janice, and she tore at our tent. I stumbled after her.

But it was too late.

The mountain was gone. Janice screamed and fell to her knees. I fell with her, on all fours, and clawed for her as she tried to charge for the empty space that used to be the mountain.

"John!" she wailed. "John…"

I held her, and she wept into me. "John…"

I shook my head and watched as new colors flooded and folded into the void of the mountain before my eyes.

"I will bring it back to you," I said. And I rocked her as I watched the colors mix like auroras. "If it takes centuries, I will make you your mountain."

But it seemed that we rocked there forever.

Years passed. The landscape slowly changed. More buildings were added, and food inside. But no other people.

Janice closed the window for good. She stared instead at the dust bunnies in the corner of the cottage. But she held a daisy in her hand. I picked a new one for her each day.

Then one night, the echoes of mourning spiked to shouts and everything quaked. I was thrown off the bed and hit my head on the floor. Splatters of permanent shadow lashed everywhere in the room, and were sticky when I touched it.

"Janice," I said. "Janice, where are you?"

A stripe of black covered all but her hand holding the daisy.

"Janice!" I yelled. I fell over the stripe and tried to scratch away, but the hues of her life twisted and muddied the more I tried.

I wretched and hit my fist upon it.

My gold and purple world corrupted and changed into endless night and a maze of streets. Buildings rose like stone pillars and had rows of windows like gap teeth. Smells of pasta and sewage filled the air.

I lay flat at the rain gutter each night. I know they meant to erase me too and missed. My body rolled with grief. The only thing different about my sobs was that they changed nothing.

That mountain. I promised her it. If it took

centuries, I would remove all of this and make it for her.

I'd wait for them to create her again.

The night became colder, and lines of silver dotted the sky. Everything started to shine with light.

I rose to sit at the curb.

A few blocks away, a clunky sound accompanied the hiss of water.

Then I saw a glint.

On a current surging for the rain gutter, my sickle floated to me. It bumped into my boot.

I grasped it. Stood.

Strength came over me.

I closed my eyes and swung.

***

Five hundred years later.

Richter rattled his flashlight. Thick batteries clanged around. "Come on." He hit it with the butt of his wrist.

"Is it dead?" said Wren. Her seven-year-old voice was tiny. She tried to take it from him with little hands.

"Nah, I got it." He hit it once more, and the flashlight flickered to life. It shot a beam over metal tile and a thick, EMPLOYEES ONLY door.

Wren frowned, as if sad the light worked after all. "But I'm sleepy," she said. She hugged a stuffed elephant. "Can we go home now?"

"Soon, Wren, I just want to see it before Mom and

Dad have to give it over to the Curator."

"But who cares?" said Wren. "I can paint things. I'm a good artist."

Richter swooped Wren up into one arm and grunted. "You are a good artist, Wren."

"I have lots of colored pens," said Wren.

"You do."

"I know when things are missing."

"Uh huh." Richter chewed and popped black gum.

"So let's just go home and I'll draw for you!" said Wren.

"Would you stop whining? It's a Kasglow, Wren! The last oil painting on earth. It's worth, like, 1.6 billion."

He glanced over his shoulder and flashed his employee ID tag at the lock. It beeped and clicked open.

"Well. Is it pretty?" Wren yawned.

"I don't know." Richter's voice was hushed with maniacal wonder. "I've only ever read about it. I've wanted to just…be *near it.* My whole life. Even just once."

"Was it still worth 1.6 billion after the artist killed himself?" said Wren.

Richter halted and craned his head to look at her. Her fingers were in her mouth.

"You're not supposed to know about stuff like that," said Richter.

"Why did he do that?" said Wren, innocent.

Richter sighed and kept walking. "It's hard to blame

him, Wren. The guy spent his life painting over *one* canvas when it wouldn't sell. I'd cry every time I had to do that too."

"Why did he paint over them?" said Wren.

"They were expensive in the 1800s."

"What's the one that finally sold called?"

"I don't know, something stupid," said Richter. "*Rain in Paris*?"

They approached the door with the wheel lock at last. Wren gazed at the security camera.

With a groan, Richter hauled open the 6-inch-thick door. He nodded towards it with his head and whispered. "Come on; pretend we're cave divers." Wren ducked her head with him.

The room was empty. Save for one easel, covered in red tarp.

Richter set Wren down and took a deep breath. He exhaled through his mouth. "Ready?"

"Uh huh…" said Wren.

"Count," said Richter.

Wren tilted her head and paused, as if considering whether or not to indulge him.

"Okay…Three," she said.

He grabbed the tarp.

"Two." Pause. "One."

Richter pulled. The tarp billowed down to the ground.

Silence. Richter and Wren stared. Finally, after what seemed like a full minute, they stepped forward to look closer.

There was no Paris. Nor rain. The Kasglow signature was still there in the corner, but everything, everything, was white canvas except for one giant mountain in the center. Paint chips were on the floor.

Atop the mountain, in almost refrigerator-art proportions, but professionally painted, stood a man with a brim hat and an orange beard. He held a daisy in his hand. Somehow, even from his tiny features, he looked sad.

"What…what is this?" said Richter. "I don't understand."

"This is *Paris in the Rain*?" said Wren.

Richter crouched at the signature. "It's…it's Kasglow. It has to be. There's no other oil painting left."

A beat. "It's annieclimantic," said Wren.

"Anticlimactic," Richter corrected. He shook his head, not rising. He must have been too engrossed to hear the click of Wren's pen. But he shot up at a scratching sound.

Wren was in front of the canvas.

"What are you doing?!" he said, tugging her away.

Too late. Wren had doodled a woman next to the bearded man.

"Wren!" He turned her to him and she stared up at Richter innocently. "You just sketched on a Kasglow!"

Wren glanced back at the painting. "He looked sad."

They turned back to the painting together once more.

And froze.

There stood the man atop the mountain. Next to him was the woman; somehow the daisy now in her hand.

SALVAGE MISSION, PART 5

"Quinn..." Carter's voice fell off.

"What is it, Carter? Spit it out." Quinn looked up.

"This next one…" Carter held it up so he could see it better. It didn't have an ornate frame like some of the others. Just the canvas. "It's…it's a Monet."

Quinn had heard of this artist. "Wasn't he like the founder of the French Impressionist movement?"

"Yes. In the 1880s," Pope answered over the radio. "That painting is over 700 years old."

"Shall I read the story that goes with it?" Lex 1.1 asked.

"Yes," Quinn replied.

Palm Trees at Bordighera, by Claude Monet, 1884. Oil on canvas.

Havero Colony Transport, Catalog #: 61

5. TROMPE L'OEIL

Erica Rue

Every morning, they're laughing at me, those damn birds. As soon as the sun tints the horizon, the cacophony begins. The green scaly ones chuckle in short bursts—hehehe hehehe. The long-beaks draw out their throaty guffaws—haw haw haw. The feather heads simply click at me with pity, like they know I'm going to die here. I ditched my armor weeks ago, but not as soon as I should have. I kept clinging to it like hope, sweating out all of my fears into its thick protective layers, only to find myself drenched in them.

My stomach rumbles. Time for breakfast. The Dians could have killed me already, but I think they'd rather let me starve. We had enough intel to know what we could eat, and they have some sort of a giant squirrel that tastes pretty good, when I can catch it. At least the Earth First Coalition provided adequate survival training before dumping us on this rock, and I'm grateful for it, but that's about where my gratitude ends. I'm just another son that will never come home.

Time for the morning routine. I turn on my radio, not because I think I'll hear a call for evac, but because I think there must be others forsaken like me. The days are getting shorter, and colder, and soon the jungle will stop providing. I just want to find another human, if it means I won't die alone.

I eat a few raw roots I dug yesterday. They taste like spicy carrots and I barely notice the dirt anymore. It's almost like seasoning. As I break down my solitary tent, I hear the radio crackle. The first time it did that, I got excited. I rushed over and sat with it at my ear for an hour before giving up. Not this time. Weeks of random static is enough to crush hope, but not habit.

When I first hear the voice, I think it's my imagination. I can't tell it's real until I figure out that I don't imagine voices in such poor quality. The voice is male, distant, and accented, though I can't place the origin.

"Anyone else out there?"

I don't even think before responding. "Specialist Rodney Baker, here."

"Thank God." The voice on the other side sounds relieved. "Private Elijah Clark."

"What's your location, Clark?" I say. Another human being, at last. God, it is good to hear a voice outside my head for once.

"Compass broke. I'm trying to get to the extraction point."

"Hate to break it to you, but they're not coming. They're long gone."

"No, I picked it up yesterday, they're coming. One last ship."

My heart pounds in my chest. Could it be true?

"What'd they say?" As much as I hate those lying Earth First Coalition bastards, I'm surprised to find myself eager to see their hideous logo on a shuttle.

"In three days, at dawn. Extraction point Gamma."

"Gamma? Fantastic. I'm just under three days from there. Where are you? Let's figure this out."

After a few minutes of listening to his description of his surroundings, the sun, and using my own location, we determine that he's a little closer to Gamma than I am, but we'll both make it in time. I'd like to meet up, since we're so close, but we're separated by the Backbone.

The Backbone is a natural rock formation that acts as a wall, right smack in between us. It won't descend back into the ground, what we call the Drop, until we are almost on the extraction site, so there's no way I can reach him. I tell him to head straight for it anyway, and I head toward my side. We don't have to see each other to feel companionship, and it's an excellent guidepost.

"Once you hit the Bone, follow it toward the setting sun. We'll meet at the Drop," I say. The boy sounds green. Even without his instruments, he should be able to find his way. They trained us for this. It's almost like they planned to leave us here. When he reaches the end, he'll wait for me, and we'll use my compass to make it the rest of the way to Gamma.

We agree to check in twice a day, morning and night, unless something of note happens. And with that agreement, I turn off my radio and follow the Bone. When the others were hustling back to bases for last call, I was lying in a ditch on deep surveillance, all comms off. Someone was supposed to come for me in case of evac, but they were either dead or a raging coward. My relief never came.

But I am a good soldier. Obedient. Patient. So I stayed in that ditch for longer than I care to admit. By the time I figured what was going on there were no vehicles to collect me. In fact, there was no one at all. I chide myself again for all the times I worried about them, how I thought things must be going terribly to stop them from reaching me.

The day's walk is uneventful. I see no enemy Dian soldiers, and I encounter no hostile animals. No squirrel dinners, either. After I set up camp, I turn on my radio and start cleaning off my spicy carrots as I wait for Clark.

He crackles in, sounding distant, right after I take a big mouthful.

"Still there, Baker?" What is that accent? Maybe when I see him, I'll be able to place it.

"Affirmative. Run into any tangles today?"

"Negative. Sooth sailing."

"Good," I say.

There is silence over the radio for a moment before

Clark speaks.

"So, Baker, how did you get…overlooked?"

I tell him, but I leave out the details of how long I waited.

"That's a tough break."

"What about you?" I ask. Kid probably got lost.

"My squad was pinned down, and they didn't send air support. Some died, but most ran off. Might be out here somewhere."

"Pinned down and you're still standing? Those Dians are poor shots."

"Yes, sir," he replies. "Have you ever gotten a good look at one of them?"

I realize he's changed the subject. He sounds uncomfortable. Best not to press him. "Only images from training, and those were grainy and terrible. You remember. The only ones I saw were in full armor, but I hear they're beautiful in person. Like something out of a fairy tale."

"Makes you wonder what we were doing here in the first place," he says. I laugh to myself. This kid is greener than summer leaves. "Don't you think it's weird they sent us here when we were so outgunned?" Clark asks.

"We didn't come here to win the war. We came here for a latch and snatch, grabbing as much tech as possible before escaping alive."

"What do you mean?"

"We're here to line the pockets of a suit we'll never wear."

"You think they made money from this trip? But

the travel was so expensive."

"Government subsidies. The promise of new tech worth a fortune and a half back home. Take your pick. They didn't get everything they wanted, sure, but they wouldn't have left without something."

Clark is silent for some time. I'm no college type, but I understand what makes people tick. And men like the suits back home? Always looking for their next break. A few of the tech moguls ponied up cash for a stake in whatever gets brought back.

"Look, Clark, the Earth First Coalition leaders are snakes. They are the reason we're stuck here on Dian." The pay was enough to make the slogans seem appealing. One poster, the one that I remember best, featured a tall tree with feathery bluish leaves, sprouting planet-shaped fruit, with the phrase CARPE DIAN in thick block letters at the top. I could have made a poster like that. I had the artistic talent, but sketches and paintings wouldn't pay the bills.

Carpe Dian. It was a play on words simple enough to make men like me feel smart. Back then I didn't know what the pull of invisible strings felt like. They tried to sell it as a pre-colonization sweep, but we all knew it was a raid. That's what the weapons and survival training had been for. We came, we saw, we failed, and now I'm decaying in this heavy heat while they fly away, tails between their legs.

"So you don't think they'll come back? The war is over?"

"They got what they came for. I honestly can't believe there's still an evac shuttle. It must have gotten lost, too, and just now received its new orders: GTFO."

"GTFO?"

This kid must live under a rock back home. "Get the eff out," I say, "Haul ass."

After an awkward silence and an uncomfortable sign off, I am alone again. I have nightmares that night, for the first time in almost a week. I think it's because I finally have something to lose again, even though my new companion is nothing more than a voice, a stranger on the wrong side of the Bone.

The next morning our check-in is brief. We've got a lot of ground to cover. The day inches by and when the time comes for our evening chat, I'm exhausted. Clark's in a strange mood tonight.

"Did you ever kill one of them?" he asked.

I pause. Unpleasant memories bubble up to the surface, but I push them aside.

"I don't know. I've blown up a lot of their birds." They sent a lot of drones out into the forest after our retreat, and we'd taken down quite a few.

"I heard that they pilot their birds with a neural interface, and when you take one down, the agony for them is unbearable. Lasts for days."

A pang rips through my stomach. Hunger? No? Poisonous food? No, the roots were bland and safe. Guilt? The Dians were the enemy. In my head, I cycle through the hollow lies the officers told us. Threats had been made, life-saving technology had been withheld, treaties had been rebuked. What I had seen as slights by the Dians, I now understood as logical responses to

Earth's unreasonable inquiries.

"I didn't know." I don't want to think about the harm I've done. I just want to survive a few more days, go home, and forget any of this ever happened. I tear my mind away from those thoughts and our conversation long enough to hear a sound, like a metal file rasping against a rough surface. It sends goose bumps rippling over my arms. I reach for my sidearm and say one word over the radio.

"*Kylix*."

I turn off the radio and check my pistol. I'm on my last three rounds. Armor piercing. The *kylix* knows where I am, and if I'm going to face it, I want to be outside where I can maneuver, not stuck in a tent.

I can't see the *kylix*, and I can't hear it anymore, but I know it is there. A *kylix* is like a cross between a snake and a wolf, and its scales are hard as steel. I try to catch the glint of moonlight off its shining scales, but only darkness greets me.

Then, a flash from my left. I turn and fire two quick shots. A whine and a thud tell me that I've hit my mark. Another silvery spark gleams on my right, but I see it too late. A second *kylix*. My last round misses. The *kylix* is already on top of me, slashing my chest and legs with its claws in its desire to knock me down. It's unfortunate I'm out of ammo, because from my position, pinned under the beast, I can access its vulnerable underbelly. I shriek in pain as the *kylix* sinks its teeth into my shoulder. I can't taste good. All lean muscle and tendons. With my left arm mangled and my right arm pinned, I stand no chance against this beast.

I can't reach my boot knife, but as I stretch for it anyway, I can feel my pant leg wet with blood.

This is the end. My shoulder is warm and numb. The *kylix* has released it, freeing up its jaws for my throat, but it hesitates. That's when I hear it, the low hum that I know all too well. The *kylix* hears it, too, and backs away, rushing off into the shadows. This fear we share in common. The pilot drone must be close if I can hear it. I haven't heard one for weeks, but maybe they are still looking for us.

I press my right hand onto my shoulder and get up. The *kylix* is gone, but I'm not safe yet. The pilot drone is manned by a real Dian, and once he spots my tent, he'll set it on fire and report my location if he can't find me. They'll follow my blood trail and kill me.

As I crouch in the dense undergrowth, I rip off a scrap of uniform to staunch the blood flow. When the humming reaches its peak, I stay absolutely still, knowing that my tent will be easily discovered.

Except the humming fades, and no weapons are fired. Strange. Almost as strange as its presence out here. What could the pilot drones be looking for now except stragglers?

The coast seems clear, so I try to get up, but I'm too dizzy. The corners of my vision flash white, and I lie back down. The adrenaline is wearing off. I need to get back to my crappy tent and use what little first aid I have before it's too late. I begin to crawl, and the short distance stretches out hopelessly in front of me, but I find new resolve. If I keep moving, I may not die here all alone.

I make it to my pack and grab a few mirabands—miracle bandages. No clue what's in them, but they can stop the bleeding and disinfect the area. They were designed to stitch a man together for a few hours while rescue came. No idea how they'll hold up over the next couple of days, or if they'll even work on these wounds.

I grab my water bottle. There's no time to sterilize the water, so I really hope these things do the trick. My hand shakes as I lift the water bottle and rinse off as much blood as I can from my shoulder. I can see it out of the corner of my eye, but I don't look too closely before slapping on two large mirabands. The simultaneous pain and relief sends another jolt of adrenaline through my system, allowing me to sit up.

I am a bloody mess. The front of my uniform is torn and blood stained, but that cut seems minor. My left leg, however, aches where the *kylix* dug in with its back claws to get leverage. I can see the long, deep scratch in the moonlight, caked with dirt from my crawl.

"Shit." I grab my last two mirabands and cover up the deepest part of the wound, leaving the shallower part exposed.

After that, I drag myself back into my sad little tent and try not to close my eyes, because I know that once I close them, I may never open them again.

***

I'm not sure where I am at first, but it's dark and everything hurts. That's when I remember the *kylix*. I'm starving. How long have I been out?

I lift myself up, slowly, and look around for the radio. I turn it on, and when I speak, I hardly recognize my voice.

"Clark? You there?" I cough in an attempt to clear my throat, but it just sends a bolt of pain down from my wounded shoulder into my chest. The scratches there are shallow, but they certainly feel abundant.

"Shit, Baker, I thought you were dead."

"The night is young. Don't count me out yet." I open up one of my last ration tins. It actually tastes good.

"It's been a whole day. Evac's gonna be here morning after tomorrow. I'm still on schedule, though. I'll have them wait for you."

Bless this dumb kid. "Don't waste your breath. They won't wait."

"Maybe they can come get you where you are."

"Yeah, maybe," I say, though I don't believe it for a second. There's a reason they choose an evac site instead of picking up men from the jungle. Hell, we're not even supposed to be in the jungle. This is where they told us to run if everything went to shit.

There's a long pause. Maybe Clark has figured it out. I'm dead. There's no way to get me, no time for me to get to Gamma. His next words surprise me.

"The river," he says. "You can't be far from it."

He's right. I've tried to keep close, because hey, it's water. Not too close, though. Between the hungry animals, who also like water, and the openness of the area, I try to make my trips brief.

"What about the river?" I ask, but I see where his

mind is headed.

"It'll be a lot faster than hiking."

He's right again. Sure, I'll probably get shot by a drone for my trouble, out in the open, but it's the only chance I have.

"It's worth a try, I guess. And Clark," I say, "thanks." I try to suppress the tears of hope and gratitude welling in my eyes. For all my casual talk of being dead already, there's something inside me that won't let me quit. There's a part of me that desperately wants to survive and the logical pessimist inside my brain is finally willing to listen.

The next few hours hurt like hell, but the mirabands did their job and stopped the bleeding. I pack up camp and leave behind anything I don't need, including my now-useless sidearm. I feel naked without it. It takes me twice as long as it should to reach the river, but I tell myself it's the darkness slowing me down. I'm jumpy after my encounter with the *kylix*, and my hand frequently twitches to where my gun used to be. The pack digs into my shoulder, but after a while the pain fades into pressure. My leg only gets worse as I continue and just before it gives out, the sound of running water hits my ears like air conditioning on a hot day.

The river itself isn't that large, but the way the tree line stops and makes way for the river sand before the water even starts makes it appear bigger than it really is. The darkness is lit by a meager sliver of moon, and the light is just enough to work by. I collapse onto the sand and give my leg as much of a break as I can while

I fashion the tent and a bamboo-like tree into a raft. There are enough suitable fallen pieces to make the work go quickly in the moonlight, and I can even do some of the work sitting down.

By the time the sky starts to lighten, I've got something I'm pretty sure will float and my leg hurts just a bit less. There is even enough time to make a little paddle out of a stick and my breakfast tin. I've used a bit of the waterproof tent canvas to make a little bag, which I tie around my neck. I fill it with my radio, my last ration, and my compass. Just in case.

***

It's only been light for an hour, but it's already hot. After another hour, my shoulders are pink. But the river is moving. It's not taking me quite parallel to the Bone. First it will swing out, taking the long way, but it's still faster than dragging myself across land. I don't even know if the river will get me there fast enough, and I've got to keep an eye on the Bone. I can still see it peaking above the trees, even as the river pulls me away from it.

I turn on my radio.

"Clark, you're missing out on the river cruise of your life. We'll come back sometime, I'll show you the sights."

"You're in a good mood. Guess you haven't run into any of those eels."

"What eels?"

"The ones that turn your mind inside out."

"You must have gotten a different briefing."

"Nah, a guy on my patrol decided to rinse off the jungle stink and something bit him. He couldn't see straight for days. Couldn't even remember to eat and drink water."

"What happened to him?"

"Just try and stay on the raft," Clark says.

I'm not sure how I manage it, but I fall asleep, only to wake up a few hours later with the worst chapped lips you can imagine. I check for the Bone and it's still easily visible over the tops of the trees, closer than it was. I'm on my way back in. As soon as it drops out of sight, I'll have to find a place to exit the river. I feel like I'm moving slower now than when I first started. Out of the corner of my eye, something breaks the surface of the water, and I see its slimy tail disappear into the dark water.

It was bound to happen. This part of the river is deeper. We don't have a lot of intel on what's in the rivers. Our advance probes prioritized what was vital to the mission. Layouts of the cities, facilities with minimal security, how to survive if we had to retreat into the jungle. They didn't anticipate the need for river rafting. I hear another splash behind me, but by the time I turn, the culprit is gone. My shoulders stay tense, but I don't see any more appearances. Probably just fish catching bugs, and here I am getting myself worked up about it.

A few of the trees covered in pink blossoms stand out among the rest, and for moment I imagine that I'm back on the Madre de Dios. Except I am alone on this river. There are no miners tearing up the river bottom and filling the water with mercury in desperation for gold. Everything back home serves an economic purpose. *Even my life.* This place is different. Here, I am the only intruder on the river.

I see the Bone sinking lower, and soon it will be below the tree tops. I can also see the occasional rock popping up out of the water. The water is moving fast enough now that I don't want to take too long to get to the river bank.

I hear the rapids before I see them. Fast, shallow water filled with rocks, and my improvised paddle isn't getting the job done. I think I'm close enough to swim, but I remember the creature I saw earlier, breaking the water's surface, and convince myself I can make it by paddling.

I'm close to the bank now, but something nudges the raft. I see that slimy tail splash just feet away. The creature knows that soon the shore or rapids will take me out of its reach.

The raft lurches and I jab in vain with my paddle. The creature knocks the raft again. On the verge of losing my balance, I grip the raft with both hands. The paddle plunks softly into the water and I stay on, gripping the raft's edge with my weak left arm.

With a mighty splash, I'm in the water before I can react. Almost immediately, I feel excruciating pain tear through my calf on my bad leg. It's biting me, pulling me down. I tear at it with my hands before I think to grab my boot knife. I stab it, and manage to slice into my own leg as well, before pulling it back out. I let out a gasp of bubbles before I swim to the surface and gulp in air. Its tail also breaks the surface. It's thrashing in pain, or maybe anger, but eventually that stops. I tuck my knife away and do my best to float in my wet clothes.

My raft is already too far down river for me to salvage, along with my pack, about to hit the rapids. I need to reach the shore, but my progress is too slow. I feel the water getting choppy and soon, I'm not swimming. I'm being swept away.

The first rock I hit is mostly underwater, so the pain is unexpected. I try to grab onto rocks and fight the current, but all I get for my trouble are cut-up hands and exhausted arms. After getting washed away for the second time, I realize that the only way out is through. From this point on, I do my best to keep my head above water and away from rocks. Losing consciousness will be a death sentence.

I alternate between choking and crashing, and test the limits of how long I can hold my breath before finally the ride is over. The river is calm, like nothing happened, and I frog kick to the bank. I am alive.

I am alive. My limbs are bruised, my ribs must be cracked, and my spine…I whirl around, looking for a glimpse of the Backbone peaking over or through the trees, but I can't tell. I can't be that far past it, can I?

I pull my radio out, but the water proofing wasn't meant for such a long submersion. I try Clark, but all I get is a little burst of static. I rest a little longer on the river bank, drying out as best I can, grateful for the heat for the first time.

"The plan's the same," I say to myself, "Get to the Drop. Get to Gamma. Clark will be there."

***

I'm soaked and limping, but dammit, I'm almost there. A wet compass is still a compass, and using the sun and what I remember about the river's path from the maps they showed us, I've chosen a direction. I can see a silhouette, even though there's almost no moon tonight. The darkness reminds me of the river, and I shiver, wondering what it's hiding now.

"Clark," I say. But once I get closer, I realize it's just a tree. My mind must be slipping. The trees keep going fuzzy, or shining with a strange colored halo of dark pinks and blues. My calf, where I got bitten, stings with every step, and I think the damn eel poisoned me. Or maybe my body is failing for a million other reasons.

I'm at the Drop. The Bone is to my back, but I don't see Clark anywhere. He should have been here already. Maybe he moved on ahead. I try my radio one more time with no luck, before heading to Gamma, but I leave it on. It's already dark, and the clock is ticking. I'm not sure if my broken body will get me there in time.

It's been barely twenty minutes when my radio crackles and I hear his voice. He's distant.

"Baker, the *kylix*, it got me."

"What's your position?" I say, heart pounding in my chest.

"My side, right along the Bone. Close to the Drop,"

he says. I might make it to Gamma. I might make it to Clark. I cannot do both. I close my eyes and know what I have to do. I won't leave Clark to die alone. We'll call evac. We'll tell them to wait. It's amazing how I can believe the lies I know I'm telling myself. The human mind is incomprehensible.

Suddenly I am running, or coming as close to it as I can. He is back by the Bone, close to the Drop. An old hymn is playing on a loop inside my head, keeping my pace for me, and it's like I can hear the organ music in the rustling leaves. The hallucinations are getting worse. I get snatches of his words and his moans, but there's no time to process them. Soon, I can hear his groans without the radio. He's there on the ground in front of me. I kneel down to touch him, and he flinches under my fingertips. It's really him.

"I can't," he says.

"You're gonna make it."

I dig in his pack for his mirabands. Just two left. I slap them on his leg, or what's left of it, and he cries out. He won't even be limping anytime soon.

"We're getting out of here, Clark," I say, unable to see the pain on his face for the darkness. Somehow, I sling him across my shoulder. He is impossibly light, or maybe it's just the adrenaline. I don't know when the sun will come up exactly, but I know there's not much time.

***

My grandma always used to say, "Mind over matter." But she would always chuckle afterwards, and clink her cane against her metal prosthesis. The war had taken her leg, and now a different war will take her grandson. I will never get to tell her she was wrong.

Gamma is close, but I'm completely spent. Clark is still out, and getting heavier every passing minute. The sky is getting lighter, and the tree roots and branches block my progress. My heavy boot doesn't quite clear the latest tree root and I fall, unable to catch myself. Clark goes down with me and my vision blurs again. I've gotten used to the strange colors of my hallucinations by now, but the pulsing still sends me reeling. I roll on my back, panting, and the canopy leaves above throb in that angry rhythm. I roll over just in time to get sick on the ground, mostly, rather than myself. Dawn is almost here.

I check on Clark, and in the faint light, he almost looks like one of them, face so pale it looks white, braids still hidden under his helmet. He deserves to go home.

I can't carry him, so I drag him, careful to avoid my vomit. I can't focus my eyes on my compass, so I just keep going. It's either the right direction or it's not, but I need to keep moving regardless.

I see it. The upside-down L that means I'm here. This is Gamma. I drag us both into the clearing and look up at the sky. Did we miss them? Is it too pink, or not pink enough? Is it even pink, or am I imagining that, too. Why is it spinning? Why is it humming?

It's the ship. It's here, but why is it humming like that? Our ships don't hum…

It's a trap. The Dians are here to kill us after all. I

collapse next to Clark.

"It's all right, Clark. It's nice to have a brother by my side here at the end." I feel him move and I turn to look; he's removed his helmet. His dreadlocks are spread out, but they're as pale as his face. He's kneeling over me.

"You're going to be okay, Baker, evac is here."

The hallucinations have completely taken my mind, because Clark looks just like a Dian.

***

I think I'm awake. The air is stale and smells of antiseptic, which is how I know I'm not in the jungle anymore. The Dians have me now. I'm in a science lab, or something. I sit up, but I feel dizzy. A Dian comes in, and gently pushes me back down onto the bed.

"Relax, Baker, we are healing you. Give your body more time." I recognize that voice. It's Clark. He lied to me. Why? What do they want with me?

I hop out of bed, feeling only a dull ache in my leg. I won't be a test subject. I won't be an experiment. I try to speak, but my words slur. Then my thoughts. The bed rises to meet me and I lose awareness of my surroundings.

***

I'm not scared anymore, now that the eel venom is out of my system. The world is no longer dancing in vibrant colors, though there's not much to see from my hospital bed. No window. I'm awaiting my trial or whatever the Dians do to men like me.

My first visitor aside from Clark and my doctors is an older Dian. His face doesn't give it away, but his demeanor and dress impress upon me his age and status. After a word with the doctors, we're walking in a bright garden, side by side. I'm walking, pain free, though it's only been a couple of days. His face is humanoid, but white and pudgy. His eyes are dark, and his chin-length hair reminds me of snakes, thick white strands that can move all on their own. In fact, I don't think it's really hair.

"Is Clark okay?" I ask. "Or, he was never hurt, was he?"

"No, he wasn't. He thought you would come for him, and he was right. You saved Clark, even though it meant risking your own evacuation. Why?"

"He saved me."

"How?"

"The river. Keeping me sane. Giving me a goal. Take your pick."

"But your only chance to go home, to survive, was going to leave without you."

I shrug. I can't put it into words. Plus, how do I claim to have any honor when my species just started a war to steal technology? How do I tell them that I hate myself, when they just saved me?

"There's one more thing. Why did you lie to Clark?"

I feel my face grow hot. "What do you mean?"

"When he asked if you had ever killed a Dian, why did you lie? Others we observed bragged about their kills."

He knew. They knew. All this time, they knew, and they hadn't shot me with a drone and been done with it all.

I'm sobbing. After everything from the last few days, I can't hold it in any longer. I was supposed to defend the entrance to the facility. A hospital, they said, full of miracles for back home. Once the team was inside, we felt the explosion, the ground tremble beneath us, and we knew it was over. We attempted rescue, but fire blocked everything except the way out. That's where they were waiting. Two dozen Dians, holding us at gun point.

I don't say any of that. Once I regain some composure, I simply say, "My commanding officer gave the order to fire."

"But you are still responsible for your actions."

On Earth, I am innocent. Just following orders. That doesn't mean that I don't feel the weight of what I've done. The Dians kept missing. They were herding us away, but we didn't hold back. I didn't hold back. I don't know how many I killed, but I did it knowing that something was wrong.

"You're right. I am. Why didn't you kill me? I'm not special."

"No, you aren't, but does it matter? Your people left you, and we wanted to understand what humans were like. We can find a place for you. You can make amends."

"What do you mean?"

"Stay with us here, and we will find your talents and put them to use. You can atone."

I know what to say, but not how to say, so I just look up at him and choke out the words, "Thank you."

"Will you stay?"

"Yes." I am ready to accept whatever punishment they have planned.

I think I'll be doing manual labor, hauling crates of something heavy, bathed in the stench of hard work, but he really means it. They find my talent, the way I can add value. I've always loved drawing. I doodled my way through school, but now I paint. I sketch. I shade. I bring their world to life with a palette of rainbow hues, even when color can't do it justice.

Earth got what they came for, and from what the Dians tell me, they got more than they deserved. The Dians let them take the technology. The caches they raided, the ones that were enough to send them home? Planted. Full of defective weapons, but the medical tech, the tech they would have traded to us anyway, was all there.

Many paintings later, the Dian I knew as Clark sits with me as I paint yet another landscape. He looks around the studio, and asks, "How many more will it take?"

I keep working on the detail of a red *murwa* flower that grows up the trellises of the gardens here in the city. "For what?"

"For forgiveness."

My fingers hesitate mid-stroke before pulling the brush through unevenly. I will have to paint over this mistake later. I put the brush down and give my friend my full attention. "Why don't you tell me?"

The thick white tendrils on his head flare out for a moment, a sign of Dian frustration. "You have made your amends with us. It is time you forgave yourself." Clark grasps my shoulder in farewell and then he is gone.

I look at the mutilated *murwa* flower. The damage isn't so bad. I could probably just fix it, but I paint over it anyway. On Earth, x-rays can reveal the secrets of old paintings, attempts that have been abandoned and painted over. I wonder how they would feel, seeing the layers exposed, their secrets revealed.

I put down my current work, and move to stand before one of my first paintings here, a *halsan* tree with its blue feathery blossoms, the one from those recruitment ads. Its branches are full of the long-beaks and feather heads I got to know during my solitude in the jungle. I've trapped a piece of my darkness underneath their cackling beaks. I don't know the answer to Clark's question, how many more, so I do the only thing that I can. I keep painting.

SALVAGE MISSION, PART 6

"Quinn. Carter. Are there any other markings on the body besides CURATOR marked on the helmet?" Pope asked.

"Yes. The breast patch says K. WALTON," Quinn replied. "The emergency vac suit is in bad shape. It lost integrity long ago. The moisture is completely gone. And the body totally desiccated. Skeletonized."

"We will need a DNA sample," Pope said. "Can you send it back with the drone?"

"Will a hair sample do?" Quinn detached the helmet and handed it to Carter. The sample was easy to collect. The drone headed out as soon as it had it. Quinn replaced the helmet as the next story began without delay.

The Bear Calls Renard to Appear Before the Council of Animals, by Hendrick van Alcmar, 1650 – 1675. Engraving.

Havero Colony Transport, Catalog #: 199

6. THE ARCTANTHROPIST

Jeffrey C. Jacobs

"A perfect, waxing gibbous!" First Shift Officer Ursula Arktos looked up from her keyboard to gaze upon the nearly circular, black spot on the ceiling of the blanched-white room. Dense, black curls framed her round face as her lips curved into a smile. Within the Spartan walls of the Rest and Relaxation chamber, she really liked how the graphic stood out.

Fourth S.O. Siddhartha Sing scoffed. She was glad the Senior Officer's breakfast aligned with her supper, and vice versa. He'd been in command since before she'd reawaken, having been the eleventh revived. No-one alive had ever met the original crew. "What are you up to now, young lady?"

She pointed to the spot. "Look, Sid, isn't it beautiful? Just like back on Earth!"

He brushed his hand through his holographic, Sudoku Cube, causing it to disappear. "Why'd you put a spot on the roof?" The ancient lines of his face were etched into a scowl.

"It's supposed to be the moon. It's a new subroutine for my night display."

Sid pursed his lips. "It's black?"

She rolled her eyes. "Well, of course it's black. If it was moon color you wouldn't be able to see it. I'll add the texture when I upload it to the Olive Orchard display."

He shook his bald head. "Young lady, how long has it been since they woke you?"

"Two years." She rubbed her hands together, still staring at the ceiling. She reminisced about the time before she was frozen, all those countless light years away. She could still picture the cottage she once called home, in the shadow of the Acropolis monument, as it was in 2115.

"Has it only been that long? One loses a sense of time in the monotony of interstellar travel. I could have sworn Helen passed ages ago." He sighed.

Having been the seventeenth revived, with still over a century to their destination, she knew many of the remaining 83 would still be in cryogenic storage when they arrived at Kepler 186f to manage the embryo gestation cycle. Yet, for those who never made it, death was always hard when you were only had six people to interact with, and with each death there was one less person who would make it to their destination. She remembered how morose Sid had been when she'd replaced Helen. "Are you alright?"

He cleared his throat. "Nothing time can't mend. Just like being homesick. You grow out of it."

It grated on her, his stoicism. She couldn't be so callous. "What's wrong with trying to create a little bit of Earth out here?" Ursula crossed her arms and tilted her head.

A chime rung out before Sid could respond. "The time is 11:55." The ship's computer voice was chipper and feminine. "Sid, prepare for work." Every four hours began a new shift like clockwork. As the Shift One Officer, Ursula began at midnight. But now was her designated sleep cycle.

Sid stood and straightened his white shirt and trousers. His extruded seat and table melted back into the Smart Material of the ship's floor. "Well, that's my cue. Best you get to bed, Ursula. See you when I get off duty." The door slid closed behind him as he exited.

The light in the room dimmed.

Ursula saved her work and dismissed the black orb from the roof. After a few more tweaks at the keyboard, she uploaded the routine to her quarters and closed her display.

***

As she left the now featureless R&R, the light in the main hallway dimmed before her, bathing the normally brightly lit corridor in a muted gray. She made her way through the rotating, donut-shaped vessel. She couldn't see beyond fifty or so meters of the corridor ahead as the floor curved upward along the circumference of the ship's habitat. Each section dimmed as she entered, preserving the twilight ambiance in preparation of her sleep cycle. Behind her, the passage restored normal lighting.

En route to the habitat sector, the light dimmed as usual, but then lit back up slightly. She heard someone approaching from the opposite direction.

Second S.O. Gwyneth Garrett entered the corridor. She was a few centimeters shorter, and five years older than Ursula, with pixie-length, tawny hair. Gwen brightened when she spotted Ursula. "Hi! Hi! Thanks for your help during the first half of my shift. The Sleeper Count always gives me the creeps." She giggled.

"No problem." She liked visits to the Sleepers Sector. She found the twilight walks excitingly mysterious.

Gwen halted in front of Ursula. "Off to bed?"

Ursula crossing her arms. "Yeah."

Gwen blushed and cleared her throat. "Well, um, if you need any company, I'll be in the R&R room with supper. Call me?" She raised a finger and spun it in front of her.

Ursula frowned. She wished Gwen could take a hint but understood how frustrating it was when your whole world consisted of only five other people.

Gwen walked down the hall, crestfallen. The light dimmed again when she receded.

Ursula sighed. It wasn't that she didn't like Gwen—she was a rather attractive woman, after all—but she just preferred guys. She reached her quarters and the door slid open.

The computer chimed as she entered. "Welcome Ursula, please sleep well."

The spacious room contained a sleeping palette and a mirror above an empty basin built into the wall. The walls were otherwise blank except for her one and only, most prized possession from Earth, a family heirloom. The worn parchment contained just a sketch, but its value was incalculable, coming from the master himself, Leonardo da Vinci. She found the rough strokes gave the bear study an almost supernatural glow. She always liked bears.

She went to the mirror and raised her fist adjacent to her open mouth, moving it back and forth. A bubble formed on the wall, expanding into an arm holding a tooth brush. It brushed her teeth, and she spit into the basin. A spigot popped from the wall and water poured down the bowl, flowing down a drain which opened up at its bottom. When the surface was clean, the wall returned to normal.

"Computer, please integrate and display Orchard One with Moon using lunar texture." She removed her white uniform with its Space Science Core logo, placing it on a peg which projected from the wall as she approached, and put on the nightgown laying on her bed.

After a few moments, the ship replied. "Orchard One integrated. Activate?"

She crawled into bed. "Activate."

The plain walls faded to reveal rows and rows of

Olive trees in every direction. From one of the trees, her sketch seemed to hang as if pegged. The floor took on the look and texture of clumped dirt, and above the canopy scudded low clouds. Behind one, the white of her moon shown through.

"Computer, set alarm for 19:30."

She shut her eyes as a soft breeze ruffled her covers, and she listened to the sounds of a babbling brook, created not far behind her head.

***

It's chasing me. In the night, I'm running, but it keeps following me. The leaves brush against my skin, but I keep moving.

Forward.

I can sense it following me. It knows where I am. I can't keep running. I need to fight back.

A cool breeze ruffles my hair.

To the left, there is a box. It's beeping. "Stop beeping!" It doesn't stop.

I approach the box and study it.

I swipe it with my hand. My hand hurts. I swipe harder. I swipe again. Spaghetti comes out of the box.

I eat the spaghetti. It's chewy, with stiff noodles.

It tastes like hard candy. It's no longer following me.

Someone's coming. I flee, returning to my cave.

The sun is coming up.

***

The alarm crescendoed. Ursula awoke with a start. The sky was blue and the sun was peaking over the horizon to her right, through rows of Olive trees.

"Computer, close Orchard One."

"Please specify location."

Ursula blinked. "What? Right here. In my room." *Stupid computer.*

"Unable to identify who initiated request. Requested action unclear."

A bird nested in a tree next to her bed and began singing.

She raised her voice. "Computer! Dismiss Orchard One from Shift One Sleeping Quarters!"

The olive trees and blue sky faded. They were replaced with the default white background, with the Da Vinci bear the only thing to break the monotony.

Ursula thrust off her covers. Her nightgown was coming apart at the seams. She wondered how it could have become so damaged in just one day. It hadn't seen this much distress in the years she'd had it. *Rough night.* She made a mental note to have the computer generate a new one when it was feeling more cooperative.

She made a lifting gesture to the wall, where a bin opened. She undressed and threw her sleepwear in the created hamper. The space closed and disappeared. She brushed her teeth.

She stepped to the far corner of the room, and then twisted her hand clockwise. A curtain extended from the wall, and water began to flow from the ceiling, collecting in a drain which opened between her feet.

After a few minutes, she swiped her palm in front of her. The water stopped and a jet of hot air replaced it. It dried her just enough to keep her from sweating.

Then the curtain melted back into the wall.

She walked over to the wall adjacent to where she created the hamper, and pulled her hand toward her belly. A drawer manifested from the wall, and from it she retrieved fresh underwear. She grabbed her uniform from its supporting peg, the hanger fading into the wall. She dressed quickly.

Outside, she was nearly bowled over by Fifth S.O. Kawsu Mutombo's tall, muscular frame. He was svelte, the perfect specimen of a man and not much older than her.

"Sorry, Ursula! The computer controller's been damaged!" He was already half-way down the hall as he yelled.

Her shift didn't start for at least another four hours, but she wasn't in the mood to see Ilyusha before he began his sleep cycle or Stéphie before she began her shift, so she chased after Kawsu. She could have breakfast later.

***

She followed Kawsu into the computer room. He stood next to Sid, who sat cross-legged beside a mangled mainframe amid the rows and rows of signal lights.

Kawsu crossed his arms. "Any change?"

"No." Sid rubbed his chin. "The entire computer subsystem has been shredded. It can't self-repair."

Kawsu ran his hand along his scalp. "Well, we're still on course. At least there's that. Do we have a backup we can restore from?"

Sid frowned. "No, the backups were taken out forty-five years ago during a gamma ray burst."

Ursula counted out the rows of lights. "Isn't that the CPU for the Internal Sensor Array?"

Sid turned to face her. "Oh, Ursula, good morning." He bowed his head and smiled, then turned back to the machine. "Yeah, it's the Orientation and Identification subsystem. It's why we've been having trouble getting the computer to recognize us."

A chime rung out. "The time is 19:55. Unknown Shift Six, prepare for work. Unknown Shift Six, where are you?"

Sid pointed upward. "See."

Kawsu patted Sid on the shoulder. "Sid, you've put in a full day, why don't you get some rest and have some supper?"

Sid stood and dusted his knees. "Fair enough. Ursula, care to join me?" He extended his hand and beckoned.

She shook her head. "I want to see this malfunction for myself. I'll be by later."

Sid winked at her as he left. "Well, just promise you'll wish me goodnight, young lady."

"Hey, Sid, before you go, um…" Kawsu cleared his throat and his dark skin looked a shade redder. "Please let Stéphie know we're in here." Kawsu quickly knelt and took Sid's place by the damaged computer, hiding his face in the damage.

Ursula bristled when Kawsu mentioned Stéphie. She walked to Kawsu and stood over him protectively, her head barely above his glistening, smoothly shaved scalp. She admired his physique. He was rugged, strong, and yet clever. Her mind wandered.

"Ursula." He was looking up at her.

She blushed and turned to the destruction. "Er, what could have caused it?"

Huge scratches cut through the smart-materials of the wall and wires spilled out. The surface flickered as nano-machines tried in vain to mend the gash.

Kawsu grasped one of the loose wires. "No idea. Mice?" He raised his eyebrows and formed a moue.

"Mice?" Sixth S.O. Stéphanie Wagner called out from the doorway. "Surely it's better with the voice recognition and hand gestures, n'est pas?" She was tall and middle-aged, though quite athletic. Her long, blond hair trailed behind her as she approached.

Kawsu twisted to face her and waved. "Oh, hey Stéphie. Sorry you have to begin your shift like this."

Ursula nodded, though didn't take her eyes off the havoc. She wished Kawsu gave her as much attention. "Evening Stéphie."

Stéphie stood next to Ursula. "Zut, alors! Oh, you think this could be caused by the rodents?" She shook her head. "No, there are no rodents 317 light-years from Earth. I've never seen this."

Kawsu stared up at Stéphie, wide-eyed. "I'm sure you've seen a lot in your twenty years aboard."

Stéphie chuckled. "Please do not make me feel so old."

Kawsu patted a spot beside him. "Oh, you don't look a day over thirty, Stéphie. Perhaps it was one of the rams come down from the gardens?" He shrugged. "Now, do you think you can help me? I don't have any idea how to fix this pile of spaghetti."

Ursula's stomach rumbled.

"Oh, ma petite, why aren't you eating?" Stéphie nudged Ursula. "Come on, I can handle this. It's not my first kernel rebuild. I'll see you at midnight." She knelt and pulled up a terminal.

Kawsu leaned in close to see Stéphie's screen.

Ursula cleared her throat. "Right. See you then." She caressed Kawsu's beefy bicep. "And feel free to visit me when you get off duty."

He waved a hand behind him. "Sure."

***

On her way back to the R&R area for breakfast, Ursula heard a shouting down the corridor.

"Derrmo! Computer, Dim lights!"

The chipper voice responded. "Unable to identify command location. Please specify."

"Eto pizdets! Why is it always me?" Third S.O. Ilya Brezhnev was naturally bald, with a monk's pate, about twenty kilo overweight, and ten years her senior. He stomped toward her, oblivious to her presence. He looked to be voicelessly muttering again, but Ursula had never recognized what he was saying and had assumed it was just a nervous tick.

"Good evening, Ilyusha!" Ursula winced. "It's awful that the lights aren't working."

Ilyusha stopped his storming and straightened his stance, looking directly at her. He smiled nervously.

"Oh, Ursula! I didn't notice you! How are you? About to get breakfast?"

Ursula smiled politely. "Yeah, and get in some research, then exercise."

Ilyusha fidgeted. "You know, I could stay up a little later, if you want to hang out." He studied his shoes. "But I don't suppose you'd be interested in that." He looked back up at her, wide eyed.

She sighed. "Go to bed, Ilyusha."

He shrugged and his smile faltered but recovered quickly. "Well, I could get up early and we could hang out during your shift. I mean, I guess you'll be pretty busy but I would be happy to help you."

She rubbed her temple. She wished she could tell him to stop asking her out all the time, but she knew hurting his feelings could jeopardize the interpersonal dynamic, and he was just so sensitive. "Stéphie and I should have it covered."

He bit his lip. "What about I find you after breakfast? I mean, I know you probably just want to eat in quiet, but…"

"Go to bed, Ilyusha."

He slumped and skulked past her. "Goodnight, Ursula."

***

When Ursula got to the R&R, Sid was sitting alone, on a white chair, in front of a white table. On the table rested a bowl and pieces of naan. He grabbed another piece of bread and dunked it into the bowl. He pulled it out covered in red curry.

"Hey, Sid." She found a space, in an open corner of the room and squatted when she felt the rising section of floor beneath her posterior. She then put out both her hands, palms down, and lifted both. A block formed in front of her, making a table.

She raised her hand, curled it around an imaginary glass and put it to her lips.

The table grew a white cup, then it detached. After she grabbed the cup, the middle of the table sunk into a basin, a drain forming out the bottom. A water spout protruded from the edge.

Ursula filled the cup, then the sink popped back into a flat table. She took a sip of water, then she pointed back at the empty surface. Ursula was in a hurry so chose something light with minimal preparation. "Greek breakfast three." She remembered the location issues the computer was having. "In the R&R room, leftmost table."

After a few moments, the middle of the table sank, and then rose again with a plate of black olives, feta cheese, and dill, drizzled in olive oil.

"Not hungry today, young lady?" He grabbed another piece of naan.

She popped an olive. It had a nice texture for something grown in a multi-level, two-hundred-hectare greenhouse. Yet, it just couldn't match the freshly plucked ones fed by a natural sun. But she was on an adventure. Farther out than any human being had ever ventured. It was exhilarating. "I'm good." She grabbed some cheese, impressed that the nano-machines could construct it without any milk cattle or rennet.

They ate in silence. When she'd finished, she tapped the table twice, and the middle of the table with the empty plate sank down again, returning flat.

She circled her fingers and put them around her eyes, as if wearing goggles.

At the back of the table, a board started forming. Eventually, it made a screen.

"Show American History, 2000 to 2050."

Sid cut a glance at her. He had finished his meal and was already on a new game of Cubic Sudoku. "Oh, surely you're not going to watch that!? It's so depressing!"

"You have to eat your broccoli before you get dessert." The video began playing.

When it was finished, she looked back at Sid. He was still playing games. "Don't you ever study?"

Sid nearly fell back, then looked at her, wide-eyed. "What?"

"I mean, we have four hours for breakfast, entertainment, and fitness before work, four hours for dinner, entertainment, and more fitness afterward. You could be doing anything now. The computer library is massive. The gym is first rate. All you ever do is play that game." She folded her arms.

He chuckled. "Ursula, I've seen every video in the library at least twice in my fifty years since awakening. And I'm too tired to work out after patrolling the lower levels. Right now, I need a real challenge. These Sudoku puzzles help sharpen my mind. And at my age, it's all I can do to keep from becoming dull."

"You're far from dull!" She laughed. "But Sudoku? I just don't find it all that difficult."

"Well, I guess not for a doctor of maths like you, but not everyone is so blessed my dear."

She winced. She resented it when she was reduced to just Ursula the Arctan, the maths nerd. But this was Sid. He reminded her of her father. "The world needs engineers too, Sid. But, enjoy your puzzles. I'm just glad to have your company. You are a great mentor."

He was likely the next one to pass away. She was glad her assignment let her spend more time with him than anyone.

He smiled politely, then returned to his game.

Not quite ready for her morning workout, she selected a documentary on the extinct Grizzly Bear. She had seen that one before but figured Sid was right, she should relax. And it was one of her favorites. The bears were so adorable. She wished she could have a pet one on the ship, like Byron. She chuckled to herself.

When the video finished she downed the rest of her water, got up and stretched. Her table and chair melted into the floor. "Well, I'm off to get some exercise in. See you later."

"Be well, young lady."

She left the R&R.

***

Ursula proceeded down the corridor about a half kilometer until she arrived at the quarter-hectare gym sector. On the left was the workout equipment. She decided to head right, for the pool. She opened one of the changing bays and tried to pull a drawer from the wall.

"Error: unknown user access to garments."

She rolled her eyes. "Computer, Shift One swim clothes."

A drawer opened and she found the one-piece swimsuit inside. She removed all her clothes and placed them in the now empty drawer, which then sealed in the wall. She put on the swimming costume and then stood in the corner and initiated a shower.

She exited the changing room and entered the pool area. The Olympic-sized pool still amazed her. She stood at the head of the pool, with the far end curved upward to eye level. The water followed the same contour of the ship as a whole, neither spilling nor sloshing.

She did laps, first crawl, then breast, and then a back stroke, swimming lap after lap and losing track of time.

The computer chimed. "The time is 22:00. Time to check the Sleepers."

She knew Kawsu would probably handle the rounds this time as Stéphie was the computer expert.

She got out of the pool. She considered going to the Sleepers to see if she could meet Kawsu. *Too bad he's not here.* She imagined him taking a swim in the pool in a tight thong.

She could surprise him. If he was doing the Sleepers check, she could meet him there and accompany him. It'd be a chance for them to get to know each other better.

She returned to the changing room, showered and retrieved her clothes.

***

The Sleepers Sector sat divided, fifty sleepers on the left, fifty to the right, in rows two deep by twenty-five units long, spanning a hundred meters, with entrances at either end. Ursula couldn't see the far side from where she was due to the ship's curvature. She cracked the door on her right and peeked in. Row upon row of cryogenic boxes lined the walls. Green lights stretched into the dark, with weak illumination above each cubicle to allow for observation. The cold made her shiver.

"Kawsu? Are you in here?"

The place was silent. Kawsu was probably in the other one. She shut the door.

Suddenly, the lights went out.

Stéphie's voice came over the speaker. "Desolé! I accidentally disconnected the light circuits. Won't be a moment."

"Computer, torch. Shift One, Sleepers Sector."

She felt along the wall, next to the left entrance, until she found a drawer. She picked up the flashlight and aimed it at the door.

As she approached, it swung open, knocking her to the ground and flinging the light from her hand. As she passed out, she thought she saw Kawsu.

***

My stomach growls. I'm hungry. I crave salmon.

I can smell the flesh through the door. I enter.

It's dark. It's brisk. I am in the middle of a stream. There is ice to the left of me, ice to the right. I see through the ice, I see meat. I try to break the ice to access the submerged delicacy.

I swipe and I swipe. Finally, I am able to stick my hand in and noodle for the fish. I taste the cold flesh. It soothes my palette.

I've had my fill. I scratch my belly.

I think I hear someone. I leave the cold region, and step into the warmer air. I wish to rest, to digest my meal. I nod off.

***

Stéphie's voice greeted the restored illumination. "The lights, they are fixed. Again, my apologies."

Ursula found herself on the floor. She flexed her jaw. It smarted. She massaged it and found flakes of dried blood. Nothing felt broken. The door must have knocked her out.

As she stood, she noticed the flashlight lying next to her, pointed upward. She tapped the wall and returned it to the drawer provided.

The computer chimed. "The time is 23:55. Unknown Shift One, prepare for work. Unknown Shift One, where are you?"

Perhaps she could find Kawsu with Stéphie. *Did he see her, sprawled on the floor?* Her jaw still felt tender. She pulled herself upright and headed to the Computer Sector to begin her shift.

***

Stéphie still sat by the terminal in front of the flickering gash. She didn't hear Ursula's arrival.

Cautiously, Ursula entered. "Hello, Stéphie. Make any progress on the repair?"

Stéphie spun in her chair. "Oh, bonjour Ursula! My goodness, this is très compliqué. I am so sorry for all the problems." She hid her face in her palms and shook her head.

Ursula frowned. "Were you able to figure out the cause?"

"Oh, my! No. It's senseless. I can't imagine it was a computer malfunction. It looks as if the wall, he is ripped open. I can only guess one of us did it. But then who?" She stared at Ursula, wide-eyed.

Ursula shrugged. The thought of sabotage made her shiver. She thought she knew everyone. She thought she could trust everyone. *Could one of them be a saboteur?*

Stéphie stroked her chin. "Where were you at about 17:30, yesterday?"

Ursula stepped back. "I was sleeping."

She tossed up her hands. "Je ne sais pas. It could be anyone, I guess, but if you were fast asleep, I suppose that is your alibi. If only the computer, she was working, we could make sure." She shook her head.

Ursula moved to stand over her. "Need any help?"

"No, thank you. I should be able to manage. I hope. Maybe you should just check on the rest of the ship."

"Okay, then. Just try not to shut off the lights again." Ursula started to chuckle, but her jaw throbbed. "Aou." She rubbed her chin.

"Oh, are you alright?" Stéphie rose to examine

Ursula's chin. "Oh, là, là! How did you get that?"

Ursula stepped back. "I guess I walked into a door when you disconnected the lights."

Stéphie put her hand to her mouth. "Ursula, it looks like someone hit you!"

Ursula turned to leave. "I don't want to talk about it."

***

Ursula went in search of Kawsu. She remember seeing him when she passed out. She felt bad for interfering in the 22:00 Sleeper Count, and she wanted to apologize for getting in his way. She hoped he'd not seen her incapacitated like that. Ursula wandered back to the R&R room.

Gwen was seated, finishing off some sausage and eggs. She heard Ursula enter and immediately waved. "Hi! Hi!" Morsels of food fled her lips as she spoke.

Ursula nodded. "Hello, Gwen."

Kawsu had his back to her, facing the wall. She could see a half-eaten plate of couscous and mock-goat with bread on his table, next to a dish with artificially smoked salmon.

She went over to him. "Kawsu, how's your meal?"

He didn't respond.

"He doesn't like to talk while eating." A piece of meat stuck out of Gwen's teeth.

Ursula tapped Kawsu on the shoulder. "Say, Kawsu, what's your plan after supper?"

Kawsu swallowed his food and dropped the piece of bread he was holding into the plate. He turned to face her. "I'm gonna watch some videos about the mission goal. Kepler-186f sounds very interesting."

She had seen that video file, but as she was destined never to gaze upon a planetary surface again, she'd avoided it. Not when they still had 131 years to go. It wasn't worth it. "Why would you want to watch that when we could hang out?" She tapped him in the chest playfully to punctuate the last sentence. "I could spot you at the gym."

"I like to be informed, even if it won't be me." He returned to his food.

Gwen wolfed down the last of her breakfast. "We could hang out!" She waived her hand wildly.

Ursula turned to go. "I'll see you at 04:00, Gwen."

As she left the room, she turned back to look at Kawsu. *Why was he ignoring her?* Her jaw still ached.

***

Kawsu had some nerve brushing her off like that. He'd been pretty friendly to her before. It didn't make any sense. Unless… No, it couldn't be him. He was too much of a gentleman for any shenanigans.

She started her patrol shift, wandering past the crew quarters. The lights over rooms three and four were red. Hopefully, Ilyusha and Sid were sleeping well. Of the three defrosted men, Sid was far too old, and Ilyusha, well, he was bald. And Kawsu was so handsome and close to her age. She hoped Kawsu was just having a bad day. She put her hand to her cheek. It still smarted.

But then anyone who'd just vandalized their primary

computer would naturally be in a bad mood. She regretted the thought. But it made sense. It was, after all, Kawsu who'd found the sabotage.

Her pain flared. "Aou!" *Where was Kawsu during the Sleeper Count? Could Stéphie be right? Could Kawsu have assaulted her? Was that why she passed out?*

Maybe he hit her with the door as she was trying to get a flashlight. It could have been an accident.

She didn't know what to think. She continued to wander the halls of the residential sector, then decided to get some exercise. She headed to the lifts and descended to the cramped, basement level. She liked walking these corridors as they were about fifty meters longer than the crew level and had about three percent more gravity.

She watched the ballast tanks as she surveyed lower level nine. Everything seemed in order here. *But if it wasn't Kawsu, then who?*

She walked the next few levels, passing through layers of the aquarium. One of the octopuses followed her with one eye as she passed from platform to platform. *Oh, Mr. Eight-Legs, what should I do?*

Maybe it had something to do with the sleepers? Could one of them have awakened early? She resolved to do a berth by berth, thorough survey during the next Sleeper Count.

She considered going to the gym to see if Kawsu may need someone to help him workout, but decided it wasn't worth the risk, just in case.

Somewhere near the top level of the ocean habitat, the computer chimed. "The time is 03:55. Unknown Shift Two, prepare for work. Unknown Shift Two, where are you?"

Since Stéphie was about to go off duty, she decided to check out her progress. Maybe she could figure out how to make the repair. She headed up to the main level.

ᛉᛉᛉ

Gwen had replaced Stéphie at the terminal. She turned and waved her hand above her head as Ursula entered. "Hi! Hi! Pull up a chair!" She pointed next to her.

"Hello, Gwen." Ursula sighed and summoned a chair and terminal.

"Look, the computer keeps trying to reset but the base kernel is corrupted. Half of the read-only memory's damaged." Gwen pointed to a magnified image on her screen of one of the embedded circuit boards built into the wall.

"Okay, but how do we fix it?" Ursula crossed her arms.

Gwen swiped across the screen. Computer code flashed up. "Stéphie was working on rewriting it. But she was stuck with some of the math functions used by the Fourier transforms."

Ursula rolled her eyes. "Which ones?"

"Well, let's see. There's Inverse Tangent."

Her old nemesis, the Arctan function, her university epitaph. "You've got to be kidding me?"

"What?" Gwen regarded her with puppy-dog eyes.

"You know, I'm a lot more than just the maths nerd."

Gwen grabbed her in a massive hug. Ursula didn't return it.

"You're more than that to me, Ursula."

Ursula chaffed as Gwen stroked the bridge of her nose. "Gwen, please."

Gwen put on a fake pout then grinned. "Okay! Okay! So, what do we do?"

"Well, the ATAN function is actually pretty simple, if slow. Basically, it's just a repeated sequence, just the value, x, minus x cubed over three, plus x to the fifth over five…"

Gwen lightly shoved her. "Okay! Okay! I got it! Math was never my specialty. I studied horticulture."

Ursula sighed. "Look, Gwen, I can handle implementing the trigonometric algorithms and optimizations. Why don't you go check out the upper-level gardens and I'll work on this."

Gwen locked her fingers together and shook them at her. "But I want to hang out with you? Please? Pretty please?"

Ursula rubbed her scalp, her curly bangs tickling her fingers. "I already checked the lower levels, and your specialty is plants."

Gwen pouted again. "Okay." She started to rise, but halted before her chair could dissolve. "But do you want me to do the Sleeper Count with you?"

"I'll be fine, Gwen. Go make sure the olive trees are still bearing fruit. I want to have a tapenade for supper. And make sure none of the sheep or chickens are missing. Kawsu thinks one of the animals may have damaged the computer."

Gwen nodded, then, regarding her one last time, walked toward the exit. Just before she left, she turned back to Ursula and waved vigorously. "Bye, bye! Bye, bye, Ursula! See you later!"

Ursula worked for hours, trying to implement the various algorithms, testing them and making them faster. She was able to implement a number of them in terms of others, but getting them fast enough for the computer to work in real-time was the challenge.

Before she could finish, the computer chimed. "The time is 06:00. Time to check the Sleepers."

She sighed. The firmware rebuild would have to wait.

***

Outside the Sleeper Sector, she pulled on a wall beside the closer set of doors. "Computer, Shift One parka, Upper Sleeper Sector."

A shallow closet opened and she put on the coat within. She decided to enter the top, right bank. The Berths were numbered in pairs, with Berths Ninety-Seven and Ninety-Eight by the door, followed by Berths Ninety-Three and Ninety-Four, with Berths Ninety-Five and Ninety-Six in the adjacent chamber.

Normally, she just casually strolled down the rows of bodies, verifying the lights were all showing a positive status. But she decided given the mystery of the damage to the computer, she'd better check each one manually. She hoped Kawsu had done so too, but she wanted to be sure.

She proceeded down the pairs of cryogenic pods, checking each for damage. She rubbed each glass, making sure the body was sound. She paused at Berth Seventeen, dark and empty. She'd spent 162 years asleep here. She stared into the glass case. Life had been so simple when she was still asleep. She knew being assigned with such a low number, she'd never see Kepler 186f. She envied those she'd just passed, with green lights still illuminated.

The last three rows were empty since they had already been awakened. The lights for each one, like hers, had been extinguished. So far, no one was missing. None of them could be wandering around the ship, damaging equipment.

Next to her pod, a green light indicated the next body to be revived. She rubbed the glass for Berth Eighteen and froze. She knew that face! She went to the name plate and brushed off the frost. Chang Yuping. "Ping! No!" *Had he been here the whole time? What was he doing here? Was he stalking her? Typical Ping, that's why we broke up.* She thought she'd moved past that. And now, here he was, back again. *Please let Sid outlive me. I don't want anyone replaced by you!* She knew that was next to impossible. She'd have to deal with him at some point. She was just thankful Sid seemed to be in good health for a man in his eighties.

She gently thudded her fist against the glass. "Damn you Ping!" She shivered, not entirely from the cold.

She was thankful she hadn't recognized anyone in the previous forty berths. She rushed through the remaining three rows of vacant pods, then crossed the hall to check the other fifty. She passed six more empty pods, then, with trepidation, she moved on to Berth Nineteen.

Ahead, rows of green lights illuminated the path. She continued her verifications. She didn't recognize anyone else.

As she approached Berth Forty-Nine, she blinked. As the last row of lights came into view, she saw one of the them was actually red. *Could it be an escaped Sleeper?* She shivered. She would deal with that last, she had to make sure no-one else was missing. She resumed her checks.

Scanning Berth Ninety-Five, she noticed something sticky on the floor. The red light was in the next row. She quickly verified Ninety-Five, Ninety-Six, and One Hundred then turned to face Berth Ninety-Nine.

Congealed blood dripped from the berth. The mangled remains had been viciously slaughtered. It was just like the computer, only with intestines and flesh instead of wires and paneling. *Were those bite marks?* She clutched her churning stomach. Fortunately, she'd not eaten since 20:10. She bent over and dry heaved.

After some time, she wiped her mouth as she gingerly stepped around the gore. Next to the red light, she brushed off the tag. *Rest in peace, Rebecca Johnson.* She said an Orthodox prayer for her.

Thankfully, eighty-two crew members were present and still in good condition, more than enough to complete the mission, but she wondered now if there wouldn't be more attacks. *Would the killer stop at the Sleepers? And why didn't Kawsu notice?*

"Computer, at what time did Sleeper Berth Ninety-

Nine go offline?"

The voice came back. "Sleeper Ninety-Nine went offline at 22:27."

That was during Kawsu's shift. Could Kawsu have done this!? Did he hide it from Stéphie? How could he keep this a secret? Someone was dead!

Protocol would normally be to sound an alarm, but that might alert the killer. She didn't want to risk that. If it wasn't the a rogue Sleeper who was responsible, it had to be one of the crew.

She needed to tell her shift mate Gwen, but first she had to see Stéphie. *She'd know what to do.*

***

She found Ilyusha alone, watching geology videos in the R&R room.

"Where's Stéphie!"

Ilyusha spun around. He gawked at her, wide-eyed. "Oh, Ursula. It's you! How are you? I don't suppose you'd like some company during your shift? I can watch this video later." He fumbled behind him with a close screen gesture.

She glared at him. "I don't have time for this Officer Brezhnev! Just tell me where Stéphie is and go back to your worthless rock stories. Your shift starts in just over a half-hour. You can do your patrols then." She'd had enough with his flirtations. "I have no desire to spend time with you, ever! Just tell me where Stéphie is."

"I… I… I don't know." He was shaking. His eyes looked glassy, though she couldn't see tears.

She took a deep breath and went over to him, laying her hand on his shoulder. “Ilyusha, I’m sorry. That was rude. Of course I enjoy your company, just not, um, romantically. But, please, do you have any idea where Stéphie could be? The 22:00 Sleeper Count was inadequate. One of the Sleepers is dead.”

Ilyusha stiffened. “What? Someone’s dead? Bozhe moi! How?” He wiped his nose and locked his focus on her.

“That’s what I want to find out. I think Kawsu did the count but he’s sleeping. Stéphie might know something.”

“I’m coming with you.” He stood.

She was tempted to say yes. “Listen, Ilyusha, we need to let Gwen know. Can you find her? She’s checking the upper levels. I don’t want to send out a broadcast message in case the murderer hears. Then meet me at Berth Ninety-Nine.”

Ilyusha nodded. “Right! But call me at the slightest bit of danger, I mean, if you don’t have anyone else, promise?”

“I promise.”

***

“Stéphie!” There was still no answer. She was now in the pleasure sector. She saw a green indicator over one of the bays. She thrust open the door.

Stéphie was on a chaise-lounge, half-naked. The room was unusually warm, with simulated wood panels and a fireplace at her feet.

"Pierre embraced her, caressing her supple flesh…" The computerized voice had adopted a deep baritone.

"Merde!" Stéphie's hands darted from her body, then she pulled a cover over her to gain some modesty. "Computer, stop His Master's Wood! Shift Six, pleasure room!" She turned to Ursula, beet red over all her still exposed flesh. "Ursula! Please. Do you not respect the 'me' time in Greece? You know I'm not la gouine! Not that I have a problem with that, if it's your thing, but I think Gwen…"

Ursula put up her hand. "Listen, Stéphie, I don't care what you do in your free time. What I want to know is, did Kawsu do the 22:00 Sleeper Count?"

Stéphie pulled her covers tighter. "Er, I think so. He wanted to stay with me, but I insisted he do it so I could keep working on the computer." She turned onto her side to face her. "What's the point, anyway? You go in, see eighty-three lights, and go about your business. What's the big deal?"

Ursula sighed deeply. "One of the Sleepers is dead."

She sat upright, letting the sheet drop from her breasts. "Dead. Non! C'est impossible!" She put her hand over her mouth.

Ursula turned away. "Stéphie, just put your clothes on and meet me outside."

"This is no time to be prudish! Someone's dead! Besides, the human body is nothing to be ashamed of."

With her back to her, Ursula raised a hand. "It makes me uncomfortable."

"Fine."

In the corridor, she waited a few minutes before Stéphie came out in uniform.

"Okay, I'm dressed. Now please explain. Where is the body of the dead Sleeper?" She regarded Ursula with wide eyes.

"Berth Ninety-Nine."

Stéphie wrapped her arms around Ursula. "I'm scared."

Three hugs in one day, this was getting to be a habit. She returned the embrace. "It'll be alright, Stéphie."

"The time is 07:55. Unknown Shift Three, prepare for work. Unknown Shift Three, where are you?"

***

Stéphie followed Ursula back to the Sleepers, where she found Gwen, Ilyusha, and Sid in parkas, examining Berth Ninety-Nine.

Sid was the first to see them, and immediately went up to greet them. "Is this the only berth you found attacked?"

Ursula nodded.

"Oh no! Oh no! What can we do?" Gwen started shaking.

Ilyusha gently placed his hand on her arm. "Get a grip Gwen. We stand united. We can't all die."

"Where's Kawsu." Stéphie nudged Ilyusha to get a better look at the body.

"Kawsu? Do you think he did it?" Sid raised an eyebrow.

Gwen turned to Ursula. "None of the animals are missing."

"He's certainly strong enough." Ursula crossed her arms. "And he was scheduled to do the Sleeper Count when the murder happened."

Ilyusha stepped forward. "It's all pointless. We have no plan. What can we do?"

Gwen raised a finger. "We should avoid him." She pointed at the four of them, each in turn. "Each and every one."

Sid cocked his head. "Just go about our business as usual, as if he wasn't here?"

Ursula forced a smile. "Right now, all the evidence is circumstantial. But I agree, we should try to avoid him for the time being. Until we have more proof."

Stéphie yawned. "Oh, I'm sorry. It's been a long day, and I never even got to finish my private time. Not that I need it now. The mood, she is long gone." She waved her hand in front of her in a sailing motion.

Sid put his arm around Stéphie. "Get to bed. We'll handle it from here."

"Yes, yes, but lock your door!" Gwen made a locking gesture with her hand.

Stéphie regarded Ursula. "Bien sûr! I've already learned my lesson about unwanted guests." With a further yawn, she left.

Now it was Ursula's turn to blush.

Sid cleared his throat. "As for you Ilyusha and Gwen, best you get to patrolling since it's your time on duty. And try to keep together."

"Bye bye, bye bye!" Gwen's eyes lingered on Ursula as she left.

Ilyusha stopped in the doorway. "What about the computer? Are we to be lambs to the slaughter?"

Ursula shook her head. "I've just had the shift from

hell. Surely it can wait until tomorrow?"

Ilyusha nodded and began to turn, then stopped. "But that means we can't track Kawsu?"

Ursula's lips curved into a half-grin. "He can't track us either."

Ilyusha nodded again and finally left.

Sid stroked the back of his neck. "Well, I'm in no mood for breakfast. We might as well tidy up."

They summoned mops and a pail from the computer and did their best to clean the mess.

Sid cleared his throat. "Computer, compost Sleeper Berth Ninety-Nine."

"This command requires secure access. Please confirm identity and access code."

"Shift One, code One Eight Six Foxtrot."

"Initiating disposing of Sleeper Berth Ninety-Nine."

Ursula turned to Sid. "So that's it?"

Sid frowned. "For now."

***

They made their way to the R&R and sat close.

Sid pulled up another Cubic Sudoku. He stared at the screen, but didn't make any moves.

She chose some Sherlock Holmes videos to watch. She wanted to see how the master would solve the case definitively.

After a while she yawned. She was having trouble keeping her eyes opened. The adrenaline rush which had propelled her through most of the morning was finally wearing off.

"The time is 11:55. Unknown Shift Four, prepare for work. Unknown Shift Four, where are you?"

Sid rose slowly. "I'm going to find Ilyusha."

"Be safe, my friend." She hugged Sid, then went to bed.

She locked the door. The simulated moon was full.

***

The air is fresh. I want to run. But a stone is blocking my cave entrance. I will the stone away. I exit into the sun.

I stroll along the path. The path is empty. I want a challenge. I want to swim in the lake and be free.

I find the lake, curved up in front of me. Only I'm not alone. Swimming in the lake, in a tight thong clinging to his chocolate body, there he is, Kawsu.

He's so handsome. Such a perfect specimen of a man. I want him. I need him.

He doesn't see me watching. He's focused on his laps.

He's no murderer. Not this trim athlete. I start to feel warm inside. My hair stands on end.

He's swimming toward me. I want to snatch him from the water and hug him, feel his strong arms around me.

Here he comes. He looks up. He sees me. He screams.

"Bear!!!!!!"

He's so smooth and slick. Nothing hirsute nor bearlike about him. Why must he protest?

He turns to swim away.

Don't be afraid Kawsu. I'll protect you. I jump in the water and paddle toward him. He's fast, but I'm stronger and faster. I grab him!

He struggles below me. He's playing hard to get.

His bubbles tickle my belly.

I cling to him, pressing him against my flesh, feeling him against my breasts. His muscles pulse.

He's struggling. Why is he struggling? Can't he tell how good we are for one another? Like Sid and Helen?

There aren't any more bubbles.

Finally, his struggling stops.

All his movements stop. His body is limp. He's lifeless.

I release him and swim back to shore. He floats in the water.

I'm alone. He hangs there, motionless. He never loved me. If only he took the time to get to know the real me. Goodbye, Kawsu.

I skulk back to my cave.

***

"Computer, dismiss Orchard One from Shift One Sleeping quarters." Ursula thrust open her eyes. She was restless and sweating. She wore just her underwear, having forgotten to order a new nightshirt in all the events of that morning. When she lifted the covers, she found them soaked through. Despite her perspiration, the amount of damp gave her pause.

She had the computer assemble some dry sheets, got cleaned up, and put on a fresh pair of underwear, then suited up.

She found Stéphie in the R&R room, eating breakfast.

"Hey, Stéphie, you run into Kawsu?"

Stéphie waved. "Oh, good evening, Ursula! No, I've not seen him, thank goodness."

Ursula scanned the room. "Where's Ilyusha?"

"Oh, he stopped by for a quick supper then left. He said he was going to do an extra shift to cover for Kawsu and keep Sid company."

Ursula nodded, pulled up a chair and ordered breakfast, a little hardier than yesterday. "Remind me to thank Ilyusha and apologize for being so short with him earlier."

"Zut, alors. After this morning, I think everyone has a right to be a bad mood."

Ursula watched a short video on Polar Bears while her food was being made.

Stéphie craned her neck. "Oh, Ours Blanc! I love those!"

Ursula froze at hearing her name. "What did you say about me?"

Stéphie chuckled. "Non, pas Ursula, Ours Blanc, the French words for polar bear. Did you not know this?"

Ursula shook her head. "That's weird. No, I didn't."

Stéphie put her hand to her mouth and made a popping sound. "And now you know."

Ursula scratched her chin, then pointed up. "In Greek, it's arkoúda."

The food came and Ursula ate fast. She wanted to complete the computer repair before she got in a few laps at the pool. As she was finishing her meal, the computer chimed.

"The time is 19:55. Unknown Shift Six, prepare for

work. Unknown Shift Six, where are you?"

That question was getting annoying.

Stéphie got up. "I'm going to find Ilyusha so he can get his rest. Will you be okay?"

Ursula shoveled down her last bite and stood. "I'll go with you, at least as far as the Computer Room."

***

Ursula bid Stéphie good luck and entered the Computer Room, locking the door behind her.

She spent about an hour finishing up the last suite of trigonometric and other missing functions, then told the machine to reboot.

The lights flickered and the machine chimed.

"Software Version 4.2 loaded. Good evening, Shift One Officer Ursula."

Ursula smiled broadly. She retrieved the surface texture plan from storage and coaxed the nano-machines to make the final repair to the wall based on that template. They started pulling the tongues of material together immediately. It would probably take thirty minutes for the breach to completely heal.

Ursula rose and stretched. Not bad for a day and a half's work between her and Stéphie. It was time for her daily swim. Today, she deserved it!

Hopefully, Kawsu won't be there.

***

Ursula cautiously made her way to the Gym Sector, but didn't see anyone.

In the changing room, she quickly suited up and opened the door to the pool.

It was the smell that greeted her first. She bristled. There was Kawsu. Dead.

She grasped the door frame.

"Computer, summon Sid and Stéphie!"

The body floated near the center of the pool, bloated. The chest looked bruised, as if crushed by a blunt force.

Stéphie arrived with Sid. "Chouette! You got the computer working!"

Ursula pointed to the pool.

Stéphie fell back, against the wall. "Mon Dieu! What should we…?"

Sid put his hand on Stéphie shoulder. "Steady on."

"But we're in danger, n'est pas?" Stéphie shook.

Sid bowed down to get a closer look. "He must have committed suicide."

"Do you think?" Stéphie hugged herself.

Sid tilted his head from side to side. "Makes sense. Felt guilty for killing the Sleepers, so he ends up killing himself."

Stéphie shook her head. "By drowning."

Ursula stared off toward the far end of the pool. "I had a dream about him last night, you know. About Kawsu."

"You did? Was it scary?" Sid turned to her.

"Not exactly." Ursula blinked.

Stéphie looked up. "Computer, clean the pool and compost any organic material found."

As the pool started draining, Ursula followed Sid and Stéphie into the hall. "So, what do we do? I've never been through an active crewman loss before."

"We activate Berth Eighteen." Sid folded his arms.

"Ping."

"Qui?"

"Chang Yuping, an old friend. My ex-boyfriend. Of all the times to call him up."

"Oh, that's romantic, he followed you up her and scheduled his awakening after yours!" Sid beamed.

Stéphie nudged Sid. "She said ex."

"Oh. Sorry Ursula." Sid cleared his throat. "Anyway, awakenings require the full, remaining crew and are timed to occur eight hours before that person's shift is to begin. For Shift Five, that would be at 08:00, tomorrow, right before you go to bed Stéphie, and just as I'm scheduled to wake."

"Oui."

Sid stroked Stéphie's arm. "I'll try to rise early so you won't have to stay up too late."

Stéphie grasped Sid's hand. "Merci."

The computer interrupted. "The time is 22:00. Time to check the Sleepers."

Ursula groaned.

Stéphie patted Ursula's shoulder. "Don't worry, Ursula, we'll take care of it."

Sid nodded. "Listen, I ate while you were fixing the computer. Why don't you go back to the R&R and wait for your shift to begin. I'll finish out this shift."

She hugged Sid. It had to be Kawsu who committed the murders. She had to keep telling herself that. *So why didn't she feel safe?*

***

Her shift was uneventful. She tacitly patrolled with Stéphie, and then Gwen, focusing on the upper, greenhouse levels. The alarm she'd set for 07:45 sounded and she and Gwen silently headed over to the Sleepers Sector.

They met Ilyusha, Sid, and Stéphie there, all in winter coats.

She and Gwen summoned their own, then they all went into the lower, left compartment, heading toward Ping.

Sid whispered to her. "Now, you start us out. Tell the computer you wish to revive Berth Eighteen, your shift number and the command code."

Ursula nodded. "Computer, revive Berth Eighteen, authorization Shift One, command code One Eight Six Foxtrot."

"Accepted."

They each in turn repeated the awaken request in order of shift.

Finally, Stéphie spoke. "Computer, revive Berth Eighteen, authorization Shift Six, command code One Eight Six Foxtrot."

The light next to Ping's Berth moved from green to yellow. Ursula could hear the sound of pumps running.

"Activating Berth Eighteen. Crew will be informed when revival is complete."

"That's it." Sid stretched.

Stéphie yawned. "Well, if it's all right with everyone, je suis crevé."

"The time is 07:55 Ilyusha, prepare for work."

"I guess that's all the fun." Ilyusha nudged Gwen.

They left together.

Only Sid remained. He let out a deep breath. "Thank goodness that's all over. Let's go get something to eat, young lady."

***

Ursula sat close to Sid as they ate breakfast, though she avoided looking at him.

If Kawsu didn't kill the Sleepers, if he didn't damage the wall, if he didn't kill himself, as it didn't seem he could have, then who? Who was covering up?

"Everything okay, young lady?" Sid was staring at her.

She shook her head. "I'm fine, Sid. Just thinking. Are we sure it was Kawsu?"

Sid sighed. "Only Kawsu was strong enough to break into the computer or smash that cryogenic pod. It must have been him. He was the one who discovered the damage. He was the one who was doing the count when Berth Ninety-Nine was killed. It must have been him." He reached over and hugged her. "It'll be alright, Ursula, you'll see. Sometimes, we just get a bad apple. It's why they overstock the Sleepers. In theory, you only need about thirty-six Sleepers for a colony mission like this, with maybe twenty more to get the incubation chambers humming. We have nearly double that capacity. The whole project is built with redundancy to keep us from failing."

"I guess." Ursula sighed and released Sid. She pulled up some Poirot videos. Perhaps Agatha Christie could put her mind at ease.

In the middle of Murder in the Mews, the computer chimed. "New Fifth Shift Officer Yuping Chang will awake in five minutes. Prepare indoctrination."

Sid rose and headed to the door. He turned back to Ursula. "You coming?"

"Nope." She remembered her indoctrination. They were going to welcome Ping and take him to a simulation chamber to bring him up to date, only to send him out a few hours later. It had been disorienting for her, but nothing Ping couldn't manage.

Sid left and she continued to watch her video. Just as Poirot was sneaking a peak into some cupboard under the stairs, Sid returned, followed by Ping.

"Ursula! You're okay! I was worried about you!" Ping was a little taller than her, with straight, black hair and a round face. He rushed over to her.

She sighed then stood, allowing him to hug her. While they embraced, she glared at Sid in the doorway.

Sid mouthed an apology, then came to tap Ping on his shoulder. "We should be getting you to your training now."

Ping pushed back from her. "Sorry! It's just so good to see you again, Ursula."

Much as it pained her, it was good to have a familiar face around, someone who knew her back on Earth. Someone who clearly wasn't involved in the incidents of the last few days.

Sid put his arm around Ping and started to lead him out.

Ping halted. "Listen, ah, Siddhartha…"

"Please, call me Sid, young man."

"Okay, Sid, do you think Ursula could be the one to give me the tour?" He looked pleadingly at her.

"Oh, I don't think…" Sid loosened his grip.

Ursula waived her hand. "It's fine, Sid." She turned to Ping. "Let me show you around."

Sid threw up his hands, then pulled up a chair and started another Sudoku session.

***

"So what's it been like?" Ping trailed behind her like a puppy dog on her heels.

"Mostly uneventful, except for the events which caused us to defrost you." She tried to keep a safe distance without seeming unfriendly.

"Kawsu, right? That's awful. But are they sure he was the one who attacked the Sleepers?"

Ursula paused. "What makes you think that?" She thought maybe she was paranoid for not wanting to accept the simple explanation, biased from being directly involved. But Ping wasn't there. He had a detachment, and yet he clearly could see things just didn't add up.

"Well, Ursula, are you sure it wasn't…" He fidgeted. "Wasn't you?"

Her nails bit into her as she clenched her fists. "What the heck are you talking about? I was asleep during the attacks!"

Ping sighed. "Well, I guess you couldn't have. After all, it's not like there are any full moons in interstellar space."

She stepped back. "What do moons have to do with anything? This is lunacy!"

"Ursula, you're a werebear. We've talked about this before." His eyes pleaded with her.

"Werebear? Are you fucking insane? You're supposed to be a Scientist!" She turned away to continue their walk. "There's no such thing as werebears."

"Fèihuà! You *are* a werebear, an arctanthropist. You and your entire family. Don't you know Arktos is Ancient Greek for Bear?"

"You're nuts, you know that Ping? This, *this* is why we broke up." She stormed away.

Ping ran to catch her. "Fàng gǒupì! Ursula, we broke up because you're a werebear, and you're still in denial about it!"

"Oh, and I suppose the moon I coded up for my room is the reason for all the disasters? Because it's little me, turning me into a big, scary bear?" She turned and raised her hands above her head and growled at him. "Look at me, the huge grizzly, come to eat you." She bent over with uncontrollable laughter.

"You're not serious? You didn't actually simulate a moon in your room, did you?"

"So?" She put her weight on her left foot and crossed her arms. He had some nerve asking her about her private bedtime configuration. She decided she'd had enough, the sooner they got to the training sector, the sooner she could be rid of him. She turned with a flourish and continued down the hall.

He followed. "How long have you had it?"

"A couple days." *Where was he going with this?*

"And when did the troubles begin?"

"Yesterday. So?"

"Zhēn de! You don't see the connection?!" He put his hands to his head.

"It's a coincidence. You and your conspiracy theories." She stopped. "We're here."

She opened the door to the Training Sector, and started up the program, then left him.

***

Sid was pacing the R&R room when she found him. "Oh, Ursula! Good, you're here! Which theme should we use for the welcome party?"

She remembered how delighted she'd been to walk into the R&R the first time, totally dark, and have Ilyusha, Sid, Stéphie, and even Kawsu, yell 'Surprise.' Gwen, of course, had been sleeping.

"You know, he was always fond of Nuclear Music, you know, what did they call it? Deeko?" That was one thing she always liked about Ping, his eclectic taste in everything.

Sid knitted his brow. "You mean Disco?"

"Yeah, that's it, you know with the sparkle sphere?" She cupped her hands around an imaginary globe.

"One disco ball, coming up!" Sid looked skyward. "Computer, activate Discotheque 1979."

A bowl descended from the ceiling and shaped itself into a disco ball. The lights dimmed just enough so she could see the reflections but not quite dark.

Ursula started to gyrate, pointing her right finger in the air. She tried to sing. “Oh, oh, oh, oh, keeping a life, keeping a life.”

Sid chuckled. “Something like that.” He pulled up a terminal in the wall. “Here, let me choose the play list. Why don’t you order snacks?”

She opened a terminal on the far side and browsed the registered food items which could fit on a canape. After a few minutes, she had four items.

“Let’s get this party started, you all!” Stéphie entered in a sexy dress.

Ursula and Sid both stared at her.

Stéphie shrugged. “Couldn’t sleep. Plus, I want to meet the new guy.”

Sid clapped his hands together. “Welcome aboard! Why don’t you help Ursula select dishes for everyone? Find something Alsatian for folks to snack on.”

Stéphie joined Ursula at her terminal.

They had about ninety minutes, assuming Ping aced the training program, as Ursula knew he would. He may not be grounded in reality, but one thing was for sure, Ping was quite clever. It’s what’d first drawn her to him.

Ursula nudged Stéphie and whispered. “Are you sure we’re safe now? Do you think we should cancel the welcoming party?”

Stéphie put her hands on Ursula’s cheeks. “I trust Sid. If he says we’re safe, we’re safe. Don’t worry.”

Stéphie and Ursula chose a number of dishes from a variety of regions. Eventually, they had about eighteen selected.

"I just checked his progress. He's almost done!" Sid closed his wall monitor.

"Computer, summon Gwen and Ilyusha." Stéphie rubbed her hands together.

A few minutes later, Gwen entered, greeting them twice, followed by Ilyusha.

"Places, everyone." Sid gathered them all in the middle of the room. "Computer, turn off the lights."

It was totally dark. With no light to reflect off of it, even the disco ball was invisible. They waited.

Suddenly, the door opened. In the crack of light, the disco ball glowed. Just like a sparkling moon.

***

Fresh meat is everywhere, and I'm hungry.

SALVAGE MISSION, PART 7

"Quinn, I just confirmed with that DNA sample that the curator is Kate Walton," Pope said.

"I am surprised that it came back so fast," Quinn answered.

"Quinn that is, was, *THE* Kate Walton. The one who wrote *The Colony of Days*. The last Poet Laureate of Earth. She disappeared just before the Exodus War."

"Even I read *The Colony of Days*," Quinn said. "It was required reading in school."

"That was the first book to make me cry," Carter added absently.

"Kate loved to write," the AI inserted. "Shall I continue?"

"Please do." The answer came from Pope this time.

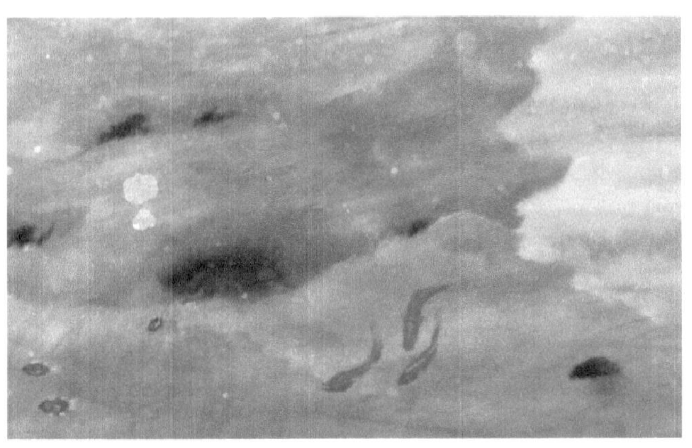

Lurking, by Peter Dube Jr., 2018. Acrylics on canvas.

Havero Colony Transport, Catalog #: 273

7. THE LITTLE COTTAGE

Peter Dube Jr.

Edward Whitmore stared at the gate to the little white cottage and remembered the stale voice of the attorney: "As the closest living relative of your brother, Jacob, and as your having been in the military at the time rules you out as a suspect, you are to inherit his estate and all his belongings." How strange. Edward was to live here, after Jacob had…died here.

Inheriting this amount of wealth meant the military was no longer an option. When he reported to his superiors he was congratulated and immediately sent to out-processing. So, with no other options prepared, Edward opened the gate.

He looked around the overgrown lawn and wild garden. Jacob had been a reclusive painter who had always let his art dealers manage the sale of his works. The few pieces Edward had seen were insane abstracts Jacob had managed during one or another of his fitful migraines.

Little Jacob never did make sense, Edward thought as he approached the door. He reached tentatively for the handle. He took a deep breath, taking in the smell of fresh air, pine, and lilacs. Would the inside still be a mess like in the police photos? There had barely been enough for Mrs. Cruz, the woman who delivered his groceries each week, to recognize him.

"Shame there'd been no one closer to the man living nearby. Poor Mrs. Cruz nearly fainted at the sight," the lead detective had said. "Most gruesome thing I'd seen in all my years."

"Thanks." Edward had glared at the man. Edward had seen some pretty awful things in his life, but nothing quite compared to the horror of what must have happened to Jacob.

Edward opened the door. A whiff of oil from paintings, and the clean smell of linen hit his nose before he realized he needed to open his eyes. The house appeared white and pristine. To the right, in a gilded gold frame, was a gorgeous deep ocean scene. Edward was entranced, staring at all the seaweed that seemed to undulate slowly.

A miraculous trick of the light. Edward smiled.

That was when he saw the eyes. They were staring at him from a dark cave in the coral: silver and completely inhuman. A shiver ran down his spine.

It is only a painting, Edward thought, and laughed

anxiously.

He leaned in to get a closer look. Tentacles. Octopus or squid? He was no marine biologist. But wait... There was something near the mouth of the cave. Something shining. A bracelet? What did it say?

Jacob A. Whitmore.

Edward jumped back. He had gotten Jacob that bracelet, after Jacob had admired his dog tags. Why would that happen to be in a painting right next to his murder scene? Goosebumps crawled across Edward's skin. He decided it was best to venture onward.

The rest of the house was filled with similar ocean paintings, but the deeper he got into the house, the darker and stranger the paintings got. The worst paintings were those in the master bedroom. They were of an underwater temple—only, the temple belonged to nothing human. It was covered in paintings up the wall and on the ceiling. On one side was a giant statue in an alcove that looked more like a sarcophagus. And where the other statues had eyes of stone, this one had eyes of the night sky. It seemed to be watching. Waiting. Edward had to leave the room.

He decided that the first thing he would do is sell the paintings. He had seen people set up and take down an exhibit before and did not think it would be that hard. He was wrong. When he tried to take down a painting, he found that he couldn't remove it; it was as if it, and the other paintings, had been mounted directly onto the wall.

It took hours to find tools in the cottage. He found his brother's journal, but he did not want to pry into the life of a madman, at least not before he attempted the task at hand. It took a lot of work, but he managed to pry the golden frame off the first painting near the front door. That is when he found that the painting was painted *directly onto the wall* and was a part of the house itself.

Frustrated, Edward went back to the study to read his brother's journal.

> If you are reading this, then I am dead. My life's work has now become yours. My house is not what it seems. My so-called paintings are not what they seem; they are…

He was so distracted that he did not notice the dripping sound from the hallway.

> …gates to another dimension. Gates which I have sealed. The things that exist there are beautiful, terrible, and trying to get in. In my research I have found a way to stop them. I only sell the gates I have permanently sealed. Those I cannot permanently seal become part of this house. You are to protect them at all costs to make sure nothing from the other side escapes. They change, adapt. They watch you and wait for any opportunity…

Sloosh. Edward jumped out of his chair. There was

water seeping in through the crack beneath the floor. He dropped the journal on the table and grabbed the chair, ready to throw it at whatever may be on the other side of the door. He tentatively approached. He slowly turned the handle. He swung the door open and raised the chair to strike.

There was Jacob. He was sopping wet. He slowly looked up and stared at Edward with cold, silver eyes.

SALVAGE MISSION, PART 8

"The Havero Colony Transport was a colony ship off the books," Pope said from the bridge. "It was privately funded. They filed fake flight plans like so many ships those days to avoid attacks. When it disappeared, everyone figured it was lost in the war."

"So much lost," Carter said in just a whisper.

"Would you like to hear the last story?" Lex 1.1 asked. "It is the longest of them all."

"Thank you, Lex," Quinn replied. "Yes."

The Dancers, by Edgar Degas, 1900. Pastel and charcoal on paper.

Havero Colony Transport, Catalog #: 226

8. CLASH BY NIGHT

David Keener

DAY ONE

01. Planning

Behind Coalition Lines, 14:54
Amazon River, 320 km east of Manaus

Emily Dunkirk pushed open the door of Kushner's cabin and a waft of cool air hit her in the face, a welcome relief from the oppressive tropical humidity outside. She was the last to arrive at the meeting, thanks to the deliberately late notice from Ester Tomkin, Kushner's assistant. The other team members had already dragged the room's wicker furniture into a rough circle. A holo projector resting on a coffee table in the center displayed a slowly rotating, three-dimensional satellite view of the city of Manaus, looking somewhat the worse for wear thanks to regular bombing by the Chinese.

Heads turned to acknowledge Emily as she entered. Ignoring Ester's ill-concealed smirk, she took a seat next to Captain Ahoub, a tall, fit Egyptian in his late thirties. He was the commander of *Khufu*, the thirty-meter-long riverboat they were traveling on.

Steven Kushner was standing in what Emily, after past experience with the mission commander, assumed was a carefully practiced pose. With his designer outdoor gear and trademark salt and pepper hair without a single strand out of a place, he looked like a high-powered CEO on a safari. She looked over at Tomkin and noticed that she was holding a microcam focused on him.

Emily shook her head.

Unbelievable. Was it too much to ask for a leader who was focused on the job and not public relations?

What they were doing was dangerous. No matter what risks they mitigated with their planning, they were going into a war zone.

Fang Li, the leader of Ghost Team, sat on a couch, impassive as always, delicately holding a cup of tea in his scarred hands. Ghost Team was the five-person mercenary team hired to assist with the mission. They had a history of working with the Monumentalists, including one previous recovery mission with Kushner. Ophelia Foxx, Ghost Team's Electronics Warfare Specialist (EWS), sat next to Fang; she was in charge of anything electronic, from comms to the drone swarm that provided surveillance and security for their activities.

With a pointed glance at Emily, Kushner said, "Now that we're all here, I can tell you that the mission is go." He nodded gravely, facing directly at Ester's hand-held camera. "We're going in. It's up to us to rescue the One World United Art Exhibition, which went missing here in Brazil during its worldwide tour thirty-two years ago. More than two hundred priceless works of art, thought lost forever, but now they've surfaced." He paused, lifting his chin minutely to look more resolute. "We *will* rescue these works of art. We will not let these precious artifacts of our global culture disappear again. We are the Monumentalists."

Despite herself, Emily felt goosebumps on her arms. Kushner might be an insufferable idiot, but he really was an excellent orator.

Even if he wasn't really a *believer.*

An immense amount of artwork had gone missing during the Time of Troubles that had descended on the world in the latter part of the twenty-first century. Global warming had generated a toxic mix of war, famine, man-made plagues, terrorism and population migrations. The situation had been ripe for looting on a scale not seen since World War II, when the Germans, Russians and many others looted every museum and art collection they could. Their organization, the Monumentalist Foundation, was dedicated to recovering lost and stolen artwork. It was a spiritual successor to the Monuments Men, formed during WWII to find, preserve, and return artwork stolen during that smaller-scale conflict.

Emily had gotten involved with the Monumentalists in college, helping to recondition recovered paintings that hadn't been stored properly by their looters. An art historian and soon-to-be museum curator after this mission, she believed wholeheartedly in the organization's mandate. Kushner, on the other hand, seemed far more interested in glory, not to mention the completion bonus for a successful recovery. She wouldn't be surprised if he had a ghostwritten memoir, or maybe a biographical documentary, in the works.

The mission commander paused long enough so that his opening statement could easily be edited into a dynamic soundbite. "Ophelia will provide a detailed briefing." He gestured in her direction, then stooped to pour himself a cup of tea.

Ophelia stood up, a slim Nigerian with close-cropped hair and non-military gold hoops dangling from her ears. "This is Manaus," she said. "More than 1400 klicks up the Amazon River from the coast. Actually just a short distance up the Rio Negro, which feeds into the Amazon. Currently one of the strongpoints still held by the Batistas, though not for long if the Chinese have anything to say about it." Emily knew that resource-hungry China had made stabilizing Brazil a priority and were backing the faction that, largely thanks to their extensive help, appearing to be winning the decades-long civil war.

Ophelia grinned. "The Batistas are losing. Badly." The city projection darkened into a nighttime view. As details faded, a tracery of glowing lines appeared and outlined the buildings. Explosions rippled across the city. "Near nightly bombing by the Chinese, mostly focused on the downtown area, military targets and infrastructure."

Fang said, "We figure they're going to make a big push in about ten days, once they've softened up the opposition enough."

"How sure are you?" Emily asked.

Fang gave her a considering glance. "They could move sooner, maybe in five days, if they're willing to risk a phased roll-out. But they're typically more conservative than that."

Emily nodded. Fang had formerly been Chinese Army Special Ops, so they'd have to trust his insights into Chinese military activities. She still wondered how he'd ended up as a mercenary.

"Folks," Kushner said gravely, "this gives us a ten-day window to get in, get the paintings and get out before the big push starts."

"Five days," Emily corrected. "We need to be conservative, here." Kushner shot her an irritated glance. He hated being upstaged.

"Right," Ophelia responded. "Over here on the southeast side of the city, the *favela*." The map zoomed in on that area, then several windows appeared around the edge showing photos of watery channels lined by rickety-looking shacks, sometimes even stacked on top of each other. "Think of it as a poverty-stricken Venice, made of wood and scraps. Our target is a low-rent warehouse complex on the edge of the *favela*." The image obligingly focused in on the complex. "Six warehouses, surrounded by razorwire. South side has a dock extending into a private lagoon that's set off by more fencing that extends underwater. Looks like eight to ten guards at any given time.

"The word from the Fuzzy Pandas is the paintings were delivered this morning, to the warehouse closest to the dock." At that, smiles broke out around the room. Knowing that the cache was heading toward Manaus, they'd already made arrangements to infiltrate the city by boat. Not the *Khufu*, but a smaller, nondescript local vessel. "Our hackers confirm that this is just temporary, before they get transshipped to the buyer, so the paintings won't be here for long."

Emily leaned back. "Do we know who the buyer is?" She ignored Kushner's glare.

"Negative," Ophelia said. "We know the seller, a General Marcos Diego, but security on negotiations has been too tight to ID the buyer. We only know *where*, because the Fuzzy Pandas cracked the subsidiary comms." She spread out her hands and smiled radiantly. "Batista online security rots."

Kushner walked over and stood next to Ophelia. "Before we discuss taking the complex," Kushner said, "I think we'll need more refreshment." He gestured at the teapot sitting next to the holo projector. "Emily, go get us some more tea, please."

She raised her eyebrows. "Seriously? Isn't that what you have an assistant for?"

Kushner struck a command pose, then said in his mellifluous command voice, "Now, Miss Dunkirk."

While Tomkin tried to hide her triumphant smile, and the others looked away in, perhaps, sympathetic embarrassment for her predicament, Emily stood up, fuming. She grabbed the tray the teapot was on and left the room.

She returned a short time later with a new tray, sweating from her foray into the stiflingly hot outdoors. By then, they were discussing the extraction, i.e. - what had to happen in order to get away with the loot. She poured out a cup of tea, and added two lumps of sugar, just the way Kushner liked it.

Kushner said, "The getaway boat drops the cargo container with the paintings in the water here." He pointed to a spot downriver from Manaus. Emily took advantage of the pause and handed him his teacup. He nodded with mock graciousness and took a sip. "Then Ghost Team's APC hooks up to the container and travels underwater to rendezvous with the *Khufu*."

Emily had seen images of the cargo container, which was almost half as long as the trailer of an eighteen-wheeler truck. It would be on the boat they'd be using to infiltrate the city. She had no doubt that the APC could get to Manaus underwater, although how quickly was a good question. But dragging the cargo container back downriver some seventy klicks seemed problematic to her.

"Do we have an alternate egress?" she asked, sitting

down next to Captain Ahoub.

Fang said, "Upriver, fifty klicks and then overland. We have a route mapped out." OK, so one alternate egress. And if the enemy twigged to their underwater capability, then both alternatives were compromised.

Kushner frowned at her. "We've taken all the variables into account."

Emily tried not to goggle at him. Anybody who thought they'd identified "all the variables" in a lightning heist of two billion credits of priceless artwork from behind enemy lines right before a big military push was, well, an idiot.

The mission leader continued on as if she hadn't deigned to interrupt him. "We'll make at least one more stop this afternoon, then time things so we pass Bang Hai in the morning." Emily saw Captain Ahoub straighten up and pay closer attention as Kushner covered details that affected his riverboat.

Ostensibly, *Khufu* was carrying a humanitarian mission chartered by the United Nations—the doctors and medical staff made up the bulk of the boat's passengers. "Bang Hai" was the nickname the Western media had applied to the Chinese forward military base after reporters had revealed the base's extensive use of Brazilians as "comfort women" for the troops.

Kushner straightened up. "We can do this, folks. We have the expertise, we have the plan and we will bring the world's cultural heritage home." He held a resolute pose for a moment, playing to Ester's camera.

As the meeting broke up, Ahoub flashed her a wide grin and patted her hand, before he left. Tomkin sauntered out without collecting the tea service, having apparently decided that Kushner had made it her responsibility.

"Emily," Kushner said, "stay after for a minute."

Once the cabin door closed behind Fang and Ophelia, the mission leader cleared his throat. "I expect loyalty from my troops, not insubordinate and uninformed questions."

Emily straightened up and considered him for a long moment. How big a fight did she want to have with him? Was it worth it? Would it change anything?

She gritted her teeth and said, "Understood."

He nodded and gifted her with a smile that didn't reach his eyes. "I'm glad you see it my way." He patted her on the shoulder and watched as she collected the cups, saucers and teapots on a tray.

Outside, still seething, she heaved the tray into the river.

02. Playing Catch-Up

Behind Coalition Lines, 16:15
Amazon River, 307 km east of Manaus

Emily caught up with Captain Anton Ahoub in his usual place. Whenever he wasn't on the bridge or in his cabin, he was always at the bow. The *Khufu* was a working riverboat, not a tourist craft, and she had to pick her way over ropes and around machinery to get to where he stood leaning over the railing.

Without looking at her, he said, "Kushner doesn't like you."

She snorted. "You think?"

He turned toward her. "If I may ask, Em, how did you end up working for him?"

"Think of me as the gift he didn't want. He wasn't given a choice." She leaned on the railing next to him. At his raised eyebrows, she added, "He's done four recoveries for the Monumentalists. The first three were successful, I mean, like really successful. Textbook precision operations. People thought he walked on water."

"And the fourth?"

"The Clementine Recovery, named after a billionaire art collector who hid his collection during the Time of Troubles. And then died without revealing its hiding place." She shook her head. "Mostly junk, he didn't have much in the way of taste. But twenty-six of the paintings, oh my. World-class. Totally.

"After the Fuzzy Pandas dived on the collection's location, Kushner spent a week planning the perfect heist. By the time they went in, somebody else, probably the Russians, had found out about it, too. Kushner's team got in first, actually got their hands on the core paintings. But as soon as the competition showed up, he made just about every wrong decision he could. Even Ghost Team couldn't salvage the situation for him. The only saving grace was they extracted without any major casualties, mostly 'cause Ghost Team is savage dangerous."

"So Kushner's not flexible?"

"No," Emily responded. "He plans like a banshee, really, really works hard at it. But as far as I can tell, they're 'green-light' plans. They only work if everything goes right." She grimaced. "If he didn't miss any variables."

"That's not good," Ahoub said. "Brazil, well, she demands flexibility." He patted her hand. "And you?"

She chuckled mirthlessly. "You could drop me in a pond, and I'd start organizing things."

"I believe you," Ahoub said in a bemused tone. "He certainly didn't like all your questions, though."

"Well, the faction of the Monumentalists that doesn't think he walks on water," Emily said, "they jammed me on his team to help with the planning and execution. But he's basically freezing me out. Which is why I need you to fill me on what I missed during my tea run."

Behind Coalition Lines, 20:04
Amazon River, 275 km east of Manaus

Kushner reclined on the couch in his cabin and moved his hands in intricate patterns. The details of his planning were scattered across his virtual sensorium, obscuring his view of the room around him. Based on the latest satellite updates Ophelia had provided to him, he was fine-tuning the route and timing for their nighttime approach to the warehouse complex where the paintings were waiting for transshipment. Floating in with the tide—the Amazon was a tidal river, even this far inland—and gone well before dawn.

The way he figured it, success was all in the planning. With a carefully crafted plan, all you needed was competent grunts to carry it out. That was really the essence of military planning. They'd be in and out like ghosts, with nobody the wiser. Long gone before anybody even knew anything had happened.

Finesse.

This was how you planned a mission.

Tighter even than his plan for the Clementine recovery. He felt a surge of anger. It hadn't been his fault the Clementine thing had gone wrong. Circumstances beyond his, or anybody's, control. Even the best generals lost a battle every now and again. At least he'd gotten everybody out safely.

But this mission, this was going to go smooth. By the numbers.

He started as someone knocked on the door, then he swept the plan details aside. "Come in."

Ester stepped into the room and closed the door behind her. Approaching, she said, "Our little Emily is going to be a problem, isn't she?"

Kushner grinned sourly. "Undoubtedly."

"I have some ideas on how to deal with her." She tilted her head. "Maybe sideline her somehow, let Miller run her part of the mission."

DAY TWO

03. Bypass

Behind Coalition Lines, 10:11
Amazon River, 251 km east of Manaus

Emily gazed through the bridge window at the river, marveling at how many guises the river could take on. The morning sun slanted down, exposing a riot of colors from the vegetation that lined the shore. *Khufu* cut through a light, shallow mist, generated by the cooler water meeting the warming air. She caught a glimpse, then, of just how the mighty river could entrance and ensnare men like Ahoub, draw them in and make them content to make their living on the vast and ever-changing waterway.

It was like a painting that changed every day, sometimes even multiple times in a single day.

Emily turned toward Ahoub and found him watching her closely.

He smiled. "She's a fascinating river, isn't she?"

"Yes, I've never seen anything like it." Right now the river was beautiful like a dream, but only an hour previously they'd been passing dead towns, bombed out ruins where countless people had lost their lives, all swiftly disappearing under the encroaching jungle.

Ahoub pointed at the wide, curved display panel in front of him, which showed about a dozen video feeds from drones and observation points on the riverboat. "Alas, here comes trouble." In one of the views, Ester Tomkin was laboriously climbing the narrow stairs up to the bridge.

Emily groaned. Trust Kushner's assistant to ruin a perfectly good morning.

The door slammed open. "There you are," Ester said accusingly, as if Emily had been hiding from her.

"Indeed," Emily said drily, "here I am."

"Steven has a task for you," she said, somewhat breathlessly after the exertion of climbing the stairs in the tropical heat. She was still trying to score points against her, Emily decided. Ester was the only person who ever called Kushner by his first name. "We're going to be passing the Chinese base soon and they'll be watching us. Steven wants you and a couple other women on deck as a distraction." She held out a flat white box perhaps fifteen centimeters long and half that in width.

Glumly, Emily took the box. As Ahoub looked on with curiosity, she opened the box, revealing a pink, polka dot bikini inside. A very skimpy bikini that she would never have purchased for herself. The type that the Brazilians she'd met on the coast had referred to as *fio dental*, or dental floss.

She glowered at Ester who was trying reasonably hard to look like she wasn't pleased with herself for humiliating Emily again. Then she looked sidelong at Ahoub, who was smiling because, well, he was male. Enough said. She punched Ahoub in the upper arm with one knuckle extended, which had to have hurt just a bit but only made Ahoub smile more widely.

War Zone (Coalition-Dominated), 11:22
Amazon River, 238 km east of Manaus

Emily Dunkirk hated sunbathing with a passion.

She was a doer, somebody who accomplished things, not a debutante who lounged around like some sunscreen-covered model with a sediment tan looking to be ogled. She was the type of person who went to the beach and actually went swimming. She hated even more that she'd been ordered to lie out on the forward deck of the *Khufu*, along with the three prettiest females of the ship's medical staff.

In Kushner's estimation, despite their United Nations credentials and their cover as a humanitarian medical relief effort, a bit of a distraction couldn't hurt as they traveled up the Amazon River past Bang Hai.

A deep rumble in the sky distracted her. Shading her eyes with her hand, she looked up and saw a sleek-looking jet fly overhead, then turn upriver. Her implant helpfully superimposed "Chengdu J-46 Fighter Bomber" on her vision, thanks to a geo/military data upgrade provided for the mission by Ghost Team. At successive intervals of about a minute, seven more fighter-bombers followed. Probably heading to

Manaus to drop more bombs on the rubble. Hopefully the bombing wouldn't destroy the warehouse that was the target of *Khufu's* secret mission.

As the bombers rumbled into the distance, the riverboat cruised slowly by the extensive base that occupied the southern bank of the river.

After another thirty minutes, she'd had all she could take.

"I'm done." Emily stood and slipped into her sandals.

The other women, two nurses and a young doctor from Global Doctors, looked up at her and giggled. The doctor, Gwyn Chambers, a long-limbed blond from Australia, said, "You've got to learn to relax, Em."

"I'll relax later." By which she meant, after the mission was done. All they'd just done was pass the first hurdle.

Of course, the others didn't know about the mission. They weren't stupid. They knew something clandestine was going on, but they really were here for the relief effort. As long as they could administer aid to people in need, they honestly didn't care about world politics or hidden purposes. It heartened her sometimes to think that people like her scantily-clad companions, as well as the other members of the relief effort, existed. People willing to go to extreme lengths for low or non-existent pay just to help other people that they'd never met.

As far as she'd been able to discern, the prevailing opinion on board was that the hidden objective of the relief effort was American-spawned espionage. This, despite the fact that no single nationality dominated the mission participants that had padded the relief effort's roster. Nobody had gotten a whiff that it was all an elaborate cover for a heist.

She picked up her towel, wound it around herself and walked back to her quarters. While she quickly changed into cargo shorts and a sleeveless flowery top, a message popped up in her sensorium from Miller, her foreman among the mission's art contingent.

> Ester just sounded me out re: could I handle the art stuff if you're not available
>
> They're planning something
>
> Watch your back

She smiled grimly, then left her cabin and made her way down to the aft hold. She put her hand on a scan plate next to the door. There was a hum and a green glow as her hand was scanned, then the door clicked as the lock released. She pulled the door partly open, then slipped into the compartment beyond, a cavernous space that ran approximately a third of the length of the riverboat.

Ceiling-mounted white lights shown down on *Paladin*, a sleek, high-tech military APC belonging to Ghost Team. The front of it looked like a tank, complete with a dangerous-looking main gun. The back was elongated, with room to transport a small military unit.

Emily stopped in her tracks and started laughing.

Instead of its usual drab, military coloring, the APC was bright pink with white polka dots. Just like the bikini Emily had been wearing only a short time before. The APC had highly advanced digital camouflage capabilities; somebody had clearly programmed it to emulate her bikini.

Travis McCloud popped out of the hatch on top of the APC, grinning from ear to ear. He was a large, broad-shouldered military vet from the Republic of Texas, with long, shoulder-length, sandy hair. "Howdy, darling. Loved the outfit."

She stopped next to *Paladin* and peered up at him. The lights above turned his hair into a halo around his head, which was easily the closest he'd ever come to being an angel. "Don't count on ever seeing it again."

He laughed and disappeared back into the vehicle as she began clambering up the ladder. A moment later she descended from the hatch into the APC's dim interior. Most of the light came from the bank of screens in front of Ophelia Foxx, Ghost Team's EWS, some of which were showing exterior scenes of the *Khufu* and others showing freeze-frame shots of Emily in her bikini.

"I'm going to kill Kushner," Emily said, glancing pointedly at the screens. "You're not ever going to let me forget this, are you?"

"Nope," Travis said, chuckling. He was sitting in the co-pilot seat, leaning back strategically in a way that emphasized his sculpted chest and impressive musculature. He'd been pursuing her in a steady, good-natured way for most of their journey. She knew for a fact that he'd already bedded at least two of her fellow swimsuit models. Since the other mercenaries weren't around, she assumed they were probably racked out in their bunks.

"When this is over," Ophelia added, "you're goin' viral, girl. I'm going to put these on the net."

Emily shook her head sadly, playing along. "Just what I always wanted to be…a museum curator and a notorious net model. Yay."

Travis pursed his lips. "And your parents never thought you'd amount to anything."

Emily gestured at one of the screens; it was showing a picture of her as she stood up, but the other three women were also visible. "Are men really that easily distracted?"

Ophelia and Travis looked at each other, then, almost in unison, nodded and said, "Yes."

Emily sighed and rubbed her forehead. "We're doomed," she said, pretending to ignore them as they laughed at her. "On the other hand, what are the Chinese up to?"

Ophelia said, "Well, they've got three flybabies following us, just to make sure we don't do anything nefarious too close to their base. They're too busy with other stuff to watch us for long, though."

"Um, flybabies?"

Ophelia gave her a look like she hadn't done her homework. "Little, disposable, solar-powered, micro-drones about a half-centimeter in diameter that float on a tiny air jet." She flashed a grin full of perfect white teeth. "I figure they'll drop the detailed monitoring by tomorrow. I'll surreptitiously deploy some of our own eyeball drones in about an hour...I didn't dare have them out anywhere near the base. Right now, all we've got up is the crappy UN swarm they're expecting us to have."

"Plus," Travis said, "nobody's going to be stupid enough to attack us within close view of the Chinese."

Emily nodded. She was sure the Chinese coalition would simply love the public relations windfall of rescuing a United Nations humanitarian mission, but suspected it would be considerably more difficult to find someone stupid enough to attack them this close to their core assets.

"What about egress? I thought that part of the plan looked weak." They both stared at her with blank expressions. "Look," she said, mildly exasperated, "I'm not going to go running back to Kushner."

Ophelia and Travis exchanged a look, then Travis said, "Best is obviously a quick in-and-out with nobody the wiser. Otherwise, all scenarios are dealing with a limited set of options. You can get the cargo container out by boat, get it out by dragging it behind the APC or hide it somewhere for later retrieval. That's pretty much it. The biggest problem with a contested pursuit is disengaging from enemy forces for long enough to make any of those options viable."

Ophelia added, "Kushner may be satisfied with his two alternatives, but if the shit hits the fan, the situation is going to be much more fluid than that."

"Yeah, that's what I thought."

Travis grinned at her. "Hey, you're smarter than I look."

04. Unplanned Deviation

War Zone (Coalition-Dominated), 15:36
Layola, 192 km east of Manaus

Emily leaned on the railing next to Doctor Gwyn Chambers as the riverboat eased slowly toward Layola's decrepit excuse for a dock, their third stop of the day since passing Bang Hai. Their impending arrival had already been noticed, as well as the giant red cross emblazoned on the sides of their vessel that announced its humanitarian mission. Children thronged toward the dock, waving and yelling. Drums sounded a staccato rhythm.

According to her implant, Layola had once had a population of some twenty thousand. That must have been a long time ago, because most of the town had long since been reclaimed by jungle. All that remained was a ramshackle village that looked like it had been built out of the loose wooden debris of the old one. Towering trees were growing where paved streets had been and colorful orchids covered mounds that had probably once been homes. It looked like one of Monet's impressionistic paintings, but overlaid with a tinge of despair that the master painter had never tried to capture.

"The drums announce that we're welcome visitors," Gwyn said, brushing a blond lock away from her face. "Otherwise, they'd go into hiding." She glanced over at Emily. "Especially with all those children. They're much prized by some of the war bands running rampant in Amazonia."

"Amazonia?"

"This whole region," Captain Ahoub said from behind them. He took a position at the railing next to Emily. "They've always been culturally distinct from the rest of Brazil. More so, now, after so many years of war."

Emily smiled at him. "How do you stand it?"

Ahoub quirked his lips. "It's a beautiful land, at least when nobody's shooting at you. And I try to spend most of my time well away from the front lines." He rubbed unconsciously at his neatly trimmed goatee. "The trick is to know when the front lines change."

Gwyn asked, "And you can tell this?"

He shrugged. "So far." He pushed away from the railing with a smile and walked away to direct some of his crewmen.

Gwyn craned her head to look at Ahoub as he walked away, then looked back at Emily. "You go, girl," she said.

Emily colored. "I'm not—"

"You should be," she said, chuckling at Emily's embarrassment. "Dr. Gwyn has spoken."

Emily shook her head in bemusement. It wasn't

worth arguing about. She hadn't come on this mission for romance. And she didn't need the distraction, either.

As for the riverboat captain, Emily suspected that Ahoub's success had a lot more to do with his relentless attention to detail than any sort of sixth sense regarding possible danger. She wondered why he'd accepted the mission; he didn't seem like the type of person to deliberately venture into an imminent war zone.

On the plus side, *Khufu* had gotten a few strategic upgrades out of the deal, including upgraded comms to facilitate interfacing with Ghost Team and an obsolete, but still useful, UN-caliber drone swarm. Not even close to what Ghost Team had, but better than most of the other low-margin river runners. Ahoub's ship had already possessed a salvaged Tempest P-12 Defense System (another helpful identification compliments of her implant's military data upload from Ghost Team), so *Khufu* was reasonably well armed.

On the negative side, anywhere between here and Manaus could become the front lines at any time. And any untoward revelations regarding *Khufu's* secret mission could jeopardize their UN-mandated protection as a humanitarian mission.

At least Ahoub was cautious, as she knew well from working with him on the security arrangements for these humanitarian stops. Ahoub had the Tempest gun unit deployed from its internal storage compartment as a visible deterrent whenever they made landfall. Emily was all in favor of visible deterrents. She figured the best way to avoid trouble was to make sure it never started.

In addition, Ahoub had four crewmembers on guard duty carrying Mannlicher smart guns, a popular automatic weapon from South Africa. Travis McCloud and Laney Sanders, two of the three combat operatives from Ghost Team, provided security for the medical tents they'd be setting up on shore. Only the most serious cases, typically those involving serious surgery, would be brought on board.

"Hey, take a look," Gwyn whispered, interrupting Emily's reverie. "Is your Kushner guy actually going ashore?"

She craned her head and spotted Kushner and Ester about five meters away, where the gangway would be deployed once they'd come to a stop.

"I guess so," she said. "Probably wants to get some footage of himself fraternizing with the little people."

They watched as the boat drifted to a halt. Ropes were exchanged with natives on the dock, and tied off. Within a few minutes, *Khufu* was securely docked and the crew was sliding the gangway into place. Kushner marched down the gangway, flanked by the Ghost Team mercs and followed by two more of *Khufu's* security people. Ester filmed the procession from the deck.

Emily said, "Sometimes I hate it when I'm right."

War Zone (Coalition-Dominated), 16:22
Layola, 192 km east of Manaus

Laney Sanders, call sign Ghost Three, stood outside the main medical tent and cursed the weather under her breath. A rainstorm had swept through, dropping rain on her for about thirty minutes and leaving her totally drenched. The only upside seemed to be that the rain had temporarily driven the mosquitoes into hiding. This is what she got for losing the damn coin toss with Trav, Ghost Two, who'd gotten the cushy duty of being on guard within the tent.

He'd also sent her several taunting messages, in his own inimitable Texas style. Her favorite, during the height of the rainfall:

OH, NO, I can't take the
DRUMMING on the roof

The natives didn't seem to be bothered by the weather. They'd patiently stood in line, the lure of real medical attention obviously outweighing any desire for shelter. At least it had been a warm rain.

From the corner of her eye, she spotted Kushner stepping out of one of the rickety buildings, where he'd taken shelter. He was followed a moment later by his lackey, Ester. Laney raised her eyebrows as it became apparent that Ester was filming him. She couldn't recall any secret missions she'd ever been involved with in which the principal felt a need to record his activities. She watched askance as Ester passed him, then, walking backward, recorded a three-quarters view of the mission commander striding confidently through the village.

Finished with her shot, Ester approached Laney. "Kushner wants to get a shot with you next."

Laney fixed her with an icy stare. "No."

Ester's eyes widened in surprise. "What?"

"I said no." She pivoted slightly to face the woman directly, moving her rifle to parade rest and deliberately drawing Ester's attention to the weapon. "Working mercenaries don't want publicity." Behind Ester, Kushner suddenly clutched his right side, then keeled over.

Laney keyed her comm. "Kushner's down, looks medical, but we need a security check and a doctor."

Ester looked around wildly, then screamed when she spotted Kushner lying in a crumpled heap.

"*On it,*" Ophelia said. "*No enemy activity in your area. No heat sources but the line of natives.*"

Ester screamed, "Help him!"

Laney strode over to the mission commander, looked down at his contorted posture. Over comms: "He's still breathing, but he's definitely unconscious."

Doctor Gwyn Chambers burst out of the tent with Travis right behind her, carrying a medical bag.

05. Command & Control

War Zone (Coalition-Dominated), 18:15
Layola, 192 km east of Manaus

Fang leaned back in the APC's padded chair and looked on impassively as Ghost Team discussed what they were calling either the "Command Crisis" or the "Emily Situation," depending on who was speaking.

"Look," Armel said, "she can't be worse than Kushner." He was Ghost Team's APC driver, and also, at twenty-nine, the youngest person on the team. The rest of them inescapably looked liked military veterans, but he simply came across like a thin, black, middle-class teenager, someone who should be playing online twitch games with his friends, not piloting a multi-million-cred piece of military gear.

Laney said, "I like her, but she's a rank amateur. She's going to get somebody killed."

Ophelia rolled her eyes. "You just think she's *muy caliente.*"

"Well, she is," Laney and Trav said at the same time.

Laney added, "Doesn't mean I want to work for her."

"Situation goes south," Trav drawled, exaggerating his Texan accent for effect, "like if Kushner can't do it, is she going to stand and deliver? Or head for the hills?"

"Stand, I think," Fang said. "She's got some backbone."

"Kushner's gone soft." Ophelia put pictures of Kushner and Emily side by side on the main screen. "He's thinking retirement, not mission. Whatever Emily Dunkirk is, she's stubborn. Is she trainable?"

Ghost Team wasn't a democracy, but whenever possible Fang liked to get everybody's input. They were all stakeholders in the outfit, after all. Laying his own interpretation on top of the discussion, Armel was positive about Emily. Ophelia was ambivalent about Emily as mission commander, but had more serious issues with Kushner. Trav and Laney were clearly concerned about her reliability under pressure. As for himself, he thought that Kushner had Emily beat on planning, but Emily had a better grasp of the dynamic nature of an operation.

"I don't see any justification for executing the escape clause," Fang said. "We've had worse clients. Anybody remember Kurdistan?" Everyone but Armel grimaced. That had been before he'd joined their team. Kurdistan had been a nightmare. "Let's just do this by the numbers and get out as fast as we can."

War Zone (Coalition-Dominated), 19:09
Layola, 192 km east of Manaus

"Well, he's alive," Gwyn said, rubbing her forehead and looking tiredly at Emily, Ester and Fang. "We managed to get him stabilized."

"What happened to him?" Emily asked.

"Best I can tell, he picked up a variant of Kielson-Bauer, one of the war viruses from a couple of decades ago. There's pockets of wicked stuff like that throughout Brazil." Gwyn shrugged. "They never got adequate spread on the countermeasures and they haven't had the infrastructure to isolate and eradicate that type of threat in years."

Ester asked, "Is he…is he going to be all right?"

"I can't make guarantees," Gwyn said. "He's not exactly the healthiest specimen of a man his age that I've seen, you know. But we've got quality medical capabilities on board, so, yes, I think he'll pull through. It's going to take a while, though."

Fang asked, "How long until he's recovered?"

Annoyed, Gwyn snapped, "Look, the secret mission you guys got going on that I'm not supposed to know about…yeah, he's not going on it."

"All right," Emily said, relieved that Kushner was going to be all right. As much as she disliked him, she didn't want him to die. She wasn't exactly heartbroken that he'd be sidelined, though. She turned to Fang. "As second in command, I am formally assuming control of the mission." Gwyn looked at her in surprise, apparently unaware of her place in the command structure. Probably not a surprise given how Kushner treated her.

Fang said, “I concur.”

“You can’t,” Ester sputtered. “You’re not qual—”

Fang swiveled and fixed Ester with a glare that silenced her. “The mission command structure exists for a reason. As of right now, Ghost Team answers to Miss Dunkirk.”

Emily glanced at Fang, caught his eyes. “The mission is still go, then.” She looked back at Gwyn. “You didn’t hear any of this. And you won’t speak about it to anybody else.”

Gwyn nodded.

War Zone (Coalition-Dominated), 20:17
Layola, 192 km east of Manaus

Emily closed the door of the *Khufu’s* main room behind her. The coolness was a stark contrast to the muggy heat outside. Miller, a rangy, balding art historian that she’d drafted as the foreman for her team, looked up at her from a couch. A few off-duty crewmen were gathered in a corner watching something on a flexi.

“Any news?” he asked.

“Yes,” she said. “Gather up the *artistes*. Someplace private.” She smiled at the term “artistes,” which had been bestowed in playful jest upon her team by Ghost Team’s own Travis McCloud. Naturally, her folks had seized upon the term with gleeful abandon. It was apt; they were all art historians, museum curators or otherwise associated with the fine arts community.

A few minutes later, Miller had managed to herd all six of her artistes, seven counting herself, into the medical staging room, now unused since the *Khufu* had already ceased medical activities for the day.

Standing in front of them, Emily felt a pang of guilt as her crew looked at her expectantly. "Folks, the mission is definitely still on." There was a smattering of half-hearted applause. "And without Kushner." The applause got noticeably louder, with a few muted cheers mixed in. Kushner was not particularly well-liked. "As of just a little while ago, I officially took over as mission commander."

More applause, as well as a few spirited catcalls.

"About damn time," Miller said. "Kushner couldn't find his arse with—"

"Maybe Ghost Team should be in charge," Sanford interrupted. He was an art historian, tall and gangly and sporting what Emily considered to be a pretentious goatee. "You don't have any tactical experience."

"Oh, shut up," somebody called out. "You're just quoting Tomkin."

Another person added, "Everybody knows you're sleeping with her."

Well, she hadn't known, but now that she did, it felt nice seeing Sanford turn red and shut up. She'd picked him for her team because he was a hard worker, and supremely knowledgeable about art, which generally made up for his incessant complaints. Seeing him quieted by embarrassment was almost like a guilty pleasure.

"Oh, Captain, my Captain," Miller said, eliciting a few chuckles and defusing the situation in his own laconic fashion. "I, for one, think that our odds of success have just gone up."

"Thanks," Emily said. "And thank you to all of you, too, for volunteering. All I can say is, we are not pulling a Clementine, no matter what happens."

She saw nods from most of her team members. They were all here because they believed in the goals of the Monumentalists. As for Sanford, she simply ignored his glare.

DAY THREE

06. Unexpected Hurdle

War Zone (Coalition-Dominated), 16:03
Amazon River, 126 km east of Manaus

Emily stood at the bow near Ahoub's favored viewing position, her face shadowed by a straw hat one of the Layola natives had given her, and watched the sights as the *Khufu* chugged slowly up the Amazon River. She was mesmerized by the famously divided waters downstream from the mighty waterway's juncture with the Rio Negro. Despite the inexorable merging of their flows, the rivers refused to give up their identities, the turgid, sediment-heavy waters of the Rio Negro running alongside the crystal clear Amazon waters for kilometers, a byproduct of differences in temperature, sediment load, density or, perhaps, just sheer anthropomorphic stubbornness.

Except for the occasional Chinese jet passing far overhead, the scene she was observing probably wasn't much changed from 1913, when Theodore Roosevelt, the twenty-sixth president of the now much diminished United States, traveled through Brazil collecting specimens for American Museum of Natural History. She'd reread the former president's account of his travels weeks ago, when the possibility of a mission to Brazil had first been raised.

Of course, the reason it wasn't much changed was heartbreaking. Decades of war and the inexorable encroachment of the ever-present jungle had erased so much. Towns, cities, power lines, roads, farms, and the bones of millions of people, all gone beneath a verdant blanket of green. Between the Time of Troubles and their own civil war, the estimates were that Brazil had lost more than ninety percent of its population.

She'd never thought she'd ever visit Brazil, and especially not the wild, untamed Brazil that Roosevelt had described. After all, the country had been engulfed in civil war for longer than she'd even been alive. She'd also never thought that she'd ever be leading an art recovery for the Monumentalists. Funny how a chance meeting in college, getting involved in art restoration for the organization, had eventually led to this journey up the world's mightiest river.

She hoped she was up to the challenge.

After leaving Layola in the morning, the *Khufu* had spent the day working its way slowly but steadily upriver, making stops whenever Captain Ahoub detected visible evidence of inhabitation, which was, surprisingly, not difficult. In most cases, the natives lined the shore, waving and shouting, and beckoning them in, which was a fairly large clue.

Emily figured it was a testament to two things. Communities still extant at this point in Brazil's interminable civil war most likely had their own lookouts and spotted them approaching. It wasn't as if a big white ship with a giant red cross on either side was inconspicuous. And, as became increasingly evident when talking with patients, despite shocking losses in available tech, there was still a mixed low-tech/high-tech grapevine ensuring that most everyone already knew of the humanitarian mission making its way up the Amazon. As a result, even outlying villages had had time to arrange for their sick and lame to get to a friendly village or, in some cases, just a random section of the shore from which they could flag down the riverboat.

Ghost Team's drone swarm helped in assessing the security aspects of each approach, making sure they weren't pulling into an ambush. While Captain Ahoub's crew provided visibly armed security on deck for each visit, Ghost Team took precautions, as well. Fang had made it clear to her and Ahoub that at least one member of Ghost Team must be in their combat suit at all times during the day, ready for a hard response if it became necessary.

That was only for a real emergency, though. The kind that Ahoub, with all of his experience on the great river, couldn't handle. The others on the *Khufu* knew that Fang and his subordinates were mercenaries, but they didn't know about the heavy gear: *Paladin* and the combat suits for Fang, Travis and Laney. The gear stayed in the hold, until or unless it was needed.

Fang showed up and leaned against the railing next to her with his back to the water. "How's it feel to be the head honcho?"

Emily turned her head to look at the leader of Ghost Team. "You've been talking to Travis too much. You're starting to sound like a Texan."

Fang fixed her with his penetrating gaze. "You didn't answer the question."

"It's scary," Emily admitted.

"Good."

"Good?"

"You're smart enough to be scared." He shifted around so that, like her, he was looking out over the water. She wondered if the river affected him the way it did her. "As long as it doesn't paralyze you, fear is healthy. It makes you plan better and train harder. It makes you focus."

"I think Kushner plans too much, and takes too long doing it."

"And you think you'll be better?"

"Maybe." She smiled slightly. "I'm more adaptable, anyway." She tightened her grip on the railing until her knuckles turned white. "I just want to rescue the artwork, and not get anybody hurt in the process. I don't think Kushner really cares about the art."

Fang raised an eyebrow, which was easily the most expressive she'd seen him being during their brief acquaintance. "The art matters to you that much?"

"Yeah," Emily said. "You want the real reason I'm here?"

Fang nodded.

"You pulled out too early on the Clementine retrieval. Twenty-six priceless, irreplaceable paintings, probably lost to history forever."

Fang stared at her for a moment. "Kushner made the call," he said finally.

Emily shook her head. "It was a bad call." She stood silent for a moment, bemused as she watched a tree branch floating upstream. The Amazon was a tidal river, even here more than a thousand miles from the coast. Twice a day, the current reversed itself in seeming contradiction to the natural order of things. "I want this mission to succeed. The people who funded this mission put me on it, over Kushner's objections, to ensure its success."

Emily leaned on the railing and looked out across the water. "Second-in-command, and he wouldn't listen to a thing I said. We haven't gamed the operation at all. Hell, we don't even have a real backup plan for the extraction."

"Ghost Team does."

"Yay, teamwork. I'm loving all the fine-tuned…" Imitating Travis' Texas drawl, she said, "*…co-ord-i-nation.*" She rolled her eyes. "And I'll give you even odds that the Chinese are already onto this recovery opportunity. The Aggies, sorry, the AAG, their Antiquities and Acquisitions Group, are never far behind the Monumentalists."

"Let's get together to discuss—" Fang stopped in mid-sentence, obviously paying attention to something on Ghost Team's comm net. "Tell the captain there's a Chinese patrol boat up ahead around the bend. They will undoubtedly be coming aboard." Fang moved off at a fast jog.

That wasn't good. They were a UN-protected humanitarian mission, so the Chinese technically couldn't interfere with them without causing a diplomatic incident. On the other hand, if they had the guts to board and inspect *Khufu* anyway, they'd discover Ghost Team, *Paladin* and the *artistes*. End of mission, and a clear diplomatic win for the Chinese.

Ten minutes later, Emily was standing next to Captain Ahoub as a Chinese officer nimbly stepped down from the gunwale of the patrol boat, which was both larger and more heavily armed than their riverboat, to the deck of the *Khufu*, followed by two troopers. Emily wasn't sure what she'd expected, but the officer was a dapper thirty-something who greeted them with a smile and introduced himself as Lieutenant Commander Ye Jing.

Captain Ahoub handed Jing a packet containing the ship's papers and the travel pass issued by the United Nations. "Welcome to the *Khufu*, sir. I'm Captain Ahoub." He gestured at Emily. "And this is Emily Gravely, one of the organizers of our medical relief effort." That was her cover identity; ostensibly, she was a medical administrator.

Emily smiled at the Chinese officer and held out her hand.

Jing took her hand, but rather than shaking it, he bent and kissed it in the French style. Looking up at her with twinkling eyes, he said, "Ah, yes. One of the angels I've heard so much about. What do you think of Brazil, Miss Gravely?"

"Breathtakingly beautiful," she said, "and appallingly nightmarish, in equal measure."

He cocked his head. Pursing his lips, he said, "Then you have grasped the essence of modern Brazil. A beautiful land, marred by decades of warfare that has gutted entire generations and all but wrecked the country." He smiled. "Still, we'll be bringing all of that to an end shortly. It's amazing what can be accomplished with Chinese discipline."

Lieutenant Commander Jing looked down and gave a perfunctory glance at the package he'd been handed. He nodded at Captain Ahoub. "Sir, your papers are in order. I will not hinder your passage."

Well, that was a relief off Emily's mind. The mission could have easily ended right here.

Jing looked both of them in the eyes, in turn. "But I will humbly advise you not to proceed further. The river beyond this point is not a safe place." He looked away, the smile slipping from his face momentarily to reveal the world-weary countenance of a soldier who'd seen too many bad things. "There are river pirates, territorial warlords and, one hears, bands of predatory child soldiers. Perhaps even, how you say it, the Boogie Man." He turned back to face them. "This Guerra, whose very name means 'War' in Portuguese."

"I take the relief mission where they need to go," Captain Ahoub replied.

The Chinese officer looked inquiringly at Emily.

"Would you say that there are more people in need of medical assistance ahead of us or behind us?"

"Ahead, assuredly," Jing answered, shaking his head sadly.

"Then that is where we are going."

Jing nodded. "I wish you well. It is a fine thing you all do, I just fear for your safety."

07. Back-Channel Communications

War Zone, 23:42
Amazon River, 101 km east of Manaus

Emily snuggled deeper into the bed.

"I was surprised when you knocked on my door." Ahoub nibbled her ear, eliciting a giggle from Emily. "Pleased, mind you, but still surprised."

He was lying next to her with his arm casually draped across her flat stomach and his head next to hers on the pillow. Smiling, she turned her head to look at him. His brown eyes were fixed on her face and his expression was uncharacteristically serious.

In the face of her silence, he caressed her cheek gently with his thumb. Finally, she said, "Just butterflies. The rendezvous is tomorrow." No backing out after tomorrow.

"And you're frightened?"

"Yes, of course," she said. "Who wouldn't be?" Once the mission team left the *Khufu*, they'd be on their own. And if anything went wrong, well, there were a lot of ways to die in a war zone.

"The artwork is that important to you?"

"Yes."

"Important enough for you to risk your life? I mean, you're a curator not a mercenary."

She turned and kissed him lightly. Pulling back a little, she said, "I've loved art, especially paintings, for as long as I can remember. I came by it naturally, I suppose. My father was a museum director and my mother was a graphic artist with a passion for Renaissance paintings. She'd always talk about famous paintings as if they were people, like they spoke to her, made her feel new emotions, showed her the world in different ways. Her favorite painting was the Mona Lisa, so one day I asked if I could see it."

"Oh."

"Yeah. I remember, she got this strange expression on her face. Then she told me that I could see a photo of it, but not the real thing. The real painting had been destroyed in the Paris Flash, when I was just a baby. I recall being devastated, like something beautiful, and profound, had been expunged from the world.

"Maybe it's stupid," Emily said, "but I can't let that happen, losing another important painting. Not when I can do something about it."

"Not stupid," Ahoub said gently. "Brave. Stubborn, for sure."

"Well, that's me. Stubborn is my middle name." She smiled. "What about you? How'd they twist your arm to make you take this mission?"

Ahoub was silent for a moment. At Emily's searching glance, he finally said, "Kushner really underestimated you, didn't he?"

She smiled. "Apparently."

"You know Kushner was Intelligence during the war, right?"

"No, I didn't. I knew he wasn't combat ops, though. Not that he'd ever admit that."

"His contacts got him some photos that, if circulated to the wrong people, could make some very powerful…factions…angry with me. Angry enough to make an example of me, no matter where I am on the river."

"Dare I ask…"

Ahoub reached over and cupped her cheek, then dropped his hand away. "About eight years ago, we were beset by raiders. They thought *Khufu* would be an easy, rich target, but we ripped them apart with the Tempest. By the time the shell casings stopped flying, we discovered that they'd been towing their last conquest." He frowned. "A slaveship. With a hold full of women destined for brothels throughout Brazil and beyond."

"What did you do?"

"We took them under tow. Found a UN peacekeeping encampment to drop them off at."

"How does that—"

"Kushner's got photos of us towing what is obviously a slave transport. Show them to one group of people, I look like a slaver. Show them to the slavers, I look like somebody who stole a lot of valuable merchandise from them. Either way, it's big trouble for me."

"I'm sorry," Emily said.

"Not your fault."

"If I can," she said, "I'll make those photos disappear." She sat up, a determined look on her face. "No matter what, Kushner won't be using anything against you after this, or I'll set the Fuzzy Pandas on him."

"You would do—"

"Of course," Emily responded. "Hell, the honest truth is we shouldn't even be piggybacking on a humanitarian mission like this one. Historically, it's a bad idea. When it comes out, and it *always* comes out eventually, it makes everyone distrust the very people who are trying to make things better."

He gathered her into his arms and held her.

After a short time, Ahoub asked, "Is the artwork really that valuable?"

Emily smiled. "Yeah. Several billion creds. At least."

His eyes widened. "So, a high value target. And highly disposable on the black market?"

"Yeah, if you know what you're doing. Ironically, the Batista's inquiries are what led us to them."

"I don't like it." He shook his head. "So you can't guarantee that you're the only ones that know about the artwork?"

"No." She paused. "In fact, I'm worried about one group in particular. If anybody's going to be a problem, I'd put money down on the Aggies."

"Even worse, then. Could be a free-for-many." He cocked his head. "That's the American expression, right?"

"Free-for-all," Emily corrected.

"Ah, yes. Free-for-all." Ahoub sat up. "You should leave."

She gaped at him. "What?"

"Get some rest. Take a pill if you have to." He paused. "Look, I know this thing we're having is a fling, but I'd like to see you again. If you want to survive this, you need to focus. From now until it's over, no distractions, just…focus. And if it all falls apart, run for your life. I have a contact in Manaus who might be able to help you."

She got up and started putting her clothes on. She heard him get off the bed.

A moment later, he handed her a slip of paper with a name and an address on it. "Memorize it. Then burn it."

"OK," Emily said, heading for the door. She grabbed the doorknob, then turned back to look at him. The light beyond the bed highlighted his chiseled physique.

He said gently, "Stay safe, Em."

"You, too."

"Don't worry about me," Ahoub said, smiling widely. "If I see trouble coming, I'm running."

DAY FOUR

08. Separation

War Zone, 13:07
Amazon River, 95 km east of Manaus

"Kushner wants to talk to you."

Emily stopped giving directions to the staff setting up for their latest stop and turned to face Ester, who looked up at her with big, unblinking eyes. She'd heard that Kushner had finally regained conscious-ness earlier in the morning, but frankly didn't particularly want to talk with him.

She nodded and followed Ester to Kushner's cabin. Gwyn Chambers was waiting for them outside when they arrived.

"Put these on before you go in," the doctor said, handing them all blue surgical masks. "Believe me, you don't want to catch what he's got." After they'd donned the masks, the doctor opened the door for them, but stayed outside. "Try not to tire him out. I'd like my patient to survive this trip."

Kushner was lying on his narrow bunk as they filed in, a bony outline underneath a beige blanket. He was sweating despite the chill of the air conditioning. He'd lost weight since Emily had least seen him and looked at least ten years older.

"There's no way I can go on the mission," Kushner said. Whatever he was going to say next was aborted as he succumbed to an extended bout of coughing.

Ester stepped in smoothly. "He's dictated some instructions he wants you to follow—"

"I don't care what he wants," Emily said flatly. "I'm in charge now. We'll carry out the mission as best we can, but we'll adapt as necessary."

"You'll follow my instructions," Kushner said, almost, but not quite, smiling. "Or face the consequences later." Sick as a dog, but still reveling in confronting the woman who'd been shoved onto his mission by his political enemies.

"You don't get it." Emily smiled with fake sweetness. "All this," she said, gesturing airily. "I don't care about the glory. You can have all the credit. You can even make me the scapegoat if the mission fails. All I want to do is rescue the paintings."

Ester said, "You don't even have any military experience."

Emily chuckled, which was probably a little mean, but it was enervating to not have to tiptoe around Kushner's giant ego. "Neither does Kushner, really. Not tactical, anyway. That's what we have Ghost Team for."

She saw Kushner bridle at that, but he suffered another fit of coughing before he could get a word out. Yes, Kushner had served in the military during the

Time of Troubles, as the historians euphe-mistically called it. So had just about every man, and lots of women, in his age group. He'd even been in combat zones, just never when fighting was actually going on, a fact she'd seen him carefully gloss over in conversations.

Kushner finally recovered from his coughing bout. "You don't have the grit to make the tough decisions—"

Emily snapped, "You mean, like the Clementine recovery, where you abandoned the prize?"

The former mission commander raised his voice, or tried to, but it came out raspy and only slightly louder. "You dare to critique me?"

Ester, ever the lackey, let loose a loud laugh. "You'd need a ladder to come up to his level."

Emily pursed her lips. "Screw you. Both of you. I don't need this bullshit, not right now." She headed for the door; she had to get away before she lost her temper.

Kushner said, "Cross me, and you still think that job at the Metropolitan is going to be waiting for you?"

With the door half open, Emily turned back to look at him. "Are you threatening me?" She cocked her head and frowned. "Aren't the Monumentalists a volunteer organization? Hell of a way to treat a volunteer."

She left the room.

War Zone, 14:46
Amazon River, 84 km east of Manaus

"Hey, Ophelia," Emily said, climbing down into *Paladin's* interior. She was pleased to see that Ophelia was the only one in the APC.

"Hey, yourself," Ophelia responded, turning around and smiling. "What's up?"

Emily sat down at the fire control station, across from Ophelia's seat. "I've got something kind of confidential for you." Ophelia arched an eyebrow. "Ahoub gave me a contact in Manaus, in case everything goes bad."

"Oh."

"I'm not sure I see any real scenario where we'd need it, but I think Ghost Team should have it, too. I just…don't want it to be…common knowledge. Not unless it's needed."

"Kind of like: In case of emergency, break glass?"

"Yeah. Like that."

"I can do that."

War Zone, 23:38
Amazon River, 68 km east of Manaus

Sanford and three other members of the *artistes* were already gathered by the still closed door of the cargo hold when Emily arrived, all with hefty black duffel bags carrying their clothes and other belongings. The surprise was that Ester was with them.

As soon as the diminutive woman spotted Emily, she started forward, an angry and determined look on her face. “Why did you tell them they might not be coming back to the ship?”

“First of all,” Emily said mildly. “I don’t answer to you.” She cocked her head and looked down at Ester. “Second, if anybody’s on to us at all, they’ll be expecting us to smuggle the artwork out on the *Khufu*. It’s the obvious choice. I don’t like being obvious.”

“But Steven said—”

“He’s not in charge anymore.”

Ester insisted, “That doesn’t give you the right to change the plan.”

Emily gawked at her. “Um, yes, it does.” It seemed to her that Kushner’s assistant was having a little difficulty processing the changed circumstances.

She heard the door open and looked over to see Travis beckoning them all into the hold. They filed past the mercenary, Ester tagging behind them. The group advanced about five meters and then, almost as if via some shared unconscious impulse, stopped and spread out to look at the APC glistening under the spotlights. It looked sleek and dangerous, especially with its main gun starkly silhouetted.

She was gratified to see that they’d changed the *Paladin’s* coloring back to its default jungle camouflage pattern.

While they were collectively studying their next mode of transport, she managed to catch Sanford’s eye. Under her withering glare, he gave her a look of chagrin and a modest shrug.

Fair enough. Even Sanford probably had some difficulties handling someone like Ester. She'd probably forgive him for letting her tag along sometime in the next century. Maybe.

Laney emerged from the open personnel compartment at the back of the APC and waved at them. At the same time, she heard footsteps and low voices behind her as more people walked into the hold. Turning, she found Captain Ahoub accompanied by Miller and her last artiste, who was plaintively apologizing for having overslept.

"The gang's all here," Travis said, closing the door. "Time to get this rodeo started."

While Laney helped get everyone settled into the APC, Emily followed Ahoub over to a metal cabinet on the wall of the hold.

"Are you ready?" he asked.

She shrugged. "As ready as I'll ever be."

He chuckled.

Turning, he pressed his thumb against a marked square on the cabinet. There was a hum as it opened and a two-handed control rig unfolded itself from inside the compartment. Ahoub grabbed the controls. Moments later, what Emily had assumed were steel beams along the ceiling of the hold started moving and Emily realized she was looking at a cargo gantry. As she watched, a rectangular lift harness settled into place a few meters above the APC.

Four cables descended from the harness. Travis took each one in turn and attached it to hooks on the underside of the APC.

"Time for you to go, Em," Ahoub said softly. "And good luck. Remember, I want to see you again after all this is done."

"I know," Emily said, grinning. She added more softly, "Me, too." Using her body to block the view from *Paladin*, she reached over and held his hand for a moment, before turning away.

Walking over to the APC, she found everybody belted into the APC's barebones seats, with their duffels already stored behind some netting. Except for her own bag, which Laney wordlessly took from her and stowed.

The only incongruous note was Ester, belted in next to the others, who looked up at her defiantly. "I'm coming along."

"No, you're not, Ester." She had no skills or experience that Emily needed on the excursion and, frankly, she didn't need the disruption. In a vain attempt to soften the blow, she said, "I appreciate your willingness, but this isn't really for you. I'm sorry." Ester looked away, clearly not intending to move.

Travis said, "Miss Ester, you can either get up or I'll pick you up and remove you."

Ester looked up at the mercenary. Something in his face must have convinced her that he was telling the truth about forcibly removing her. She undid her seatbelt, stood up without a word and stalked away, chin clenched and shoulders stiff with anger.

Travis gave Emily a glance that she couldn't read. As soon as Ester stepped off the APC's ramp, he engaged the controls to close up the APC. Emily quickly sat down and attached her own seatbelt. Moments later, the APC was suspended in the air.

While she couldn't see it, she knew what was happening. Part of the hold was covered by a false floor, one that Ahoub was now sliding out of the way to reveal an underwater hatch just a bit larger than the APC. He'd be opening the hatch momentarily.

As expected, a minute or two later, Emily felt the APC move slightly as Ahoub positioned it over the hatch. She could feel the vehicle swinging from side to side. She figured Ahoub was probably waiting for the swings to dampen out. After another minute or so, they started to descend.

"Our feet are wet," Armel, Ghost Team's APC driver, called out loudly enough to be heard in the personnel compartment.

With a gentle thud, *Paladin* settled on the river bottom at a slight angle. A few seconds later, there was a series of thumps as Armel did something to release the cables.

Paladin started rolling along the bottom, leaving *Khufu* behind them.

DAY FIVE

09. Rendezvous

War Zone, 13:07
Amazon River, 95 km east of Manaus

Gwyn Chambers slipped into her cabin, then knelt to root around in one of her suitcases. She pulled out a smooth, black ovoid about five centimeters long.

Holding the ovoid up to her lips, she said, "Is anybody—"

"We're listening." The voice was in English, but with a Chinese accent.

"They're not here," Gwyn said. "They left the ship sometime in the middle of the night."

"How?"

"I don't know. I didn't see them leave. I know where they're going, though."

"And that is?"

"Manaus. They're recovering some missing artwork. I overheard a conversation."

"Do you have any details on Kushner's timeline?"

"No, but Kushner's not with them," Gwyn said. "He's out of commission. Picked up a nasty bug." She still wondered whether Kushner was just unlucky, which was possible, or whether somebody had deliberately infected him. "His second in command, Emily Gravely, is in charge now."

"Interesting."

"Is…is my brother OK?" Her brother was a human rights activist and had been captured by the Chinese while engaged in illegal activities.

"Yes, of course." There was the barest hint of a chuckle from the speaker. "Gwyn, this is not a Tri-D show. We are civilized people. Would you like to speak with him?"

"Yes, please."

War Zone, 9:31
Amazon River, 42 km east of Manaus

Emily stood behind Ophelia, holding on tightly to the back of Ophelia's chair as Armel piloted *Paladin* along the river bottom. The APC was having no significant problems navigating the muddy terrain, though Armel's talents were clearly on display, but the ride was far from comfortable for the passengers. Despite the steady, powerful flow of the river, a surprising amount of debris collected on the bottom and *Paladin* couldn't always go around it.

"Gregorio, come in," Ophelia said. "Can you read me?" Ghost Team's EWS was relaying a signal through one of her drones, trying to reach the local contact who'd be helping them get into Manaus.

They'd been searching for quite a while. Emily figured he'd done his best to hide overnight. The river was a dangerous place.

"*Oi! Born dia!* " a voice boomed in Portuguese. "*About time you all showed up. I was gettin' real lonesome.*"

Emily smiled, then looked to the side and saw Fang watching her. "Hey, time for the next stage," she said.

"Indeed," Fang replied.

Ophelia and Gregorio Ruiz exchanged GPS coordinates and worked out their respective positions. About thirty minutes later, *Paladin* came to a stop below Gregorio's boat, a dilapidated craft about fifteen meters long anchored beneath several looming trees that overhung the river. Armel positioned them so they could do the personnel transfer on the shoreward side of the boat, under the shelter of the trees to subvert possible satellite observation.

Armel deployed an Egress Tube, Retractable, or ETR; basically, a tube with a built-in ladder and flotation arranged around the opening up top. Laney, in her combat suit, went up the tube first, then Emily and her team followed, one by one. Their contact had hung a rope ladder off the side of his boat, so they were able to get aboard relatively easily.

Finding room to stand on the deck was a bit harder. The deck was covered with wooden boxes, baskets of vegetables, and various odd and ends. It looked like what it really was, a working cargo ship.

Gregorio Ruiz turned out to be a sixtyish, dark-skinned Brazilian with a wide smile, a wizened face and graying hair.

He took one look at Laney in her combat suit, cocked his head, and asked, "How do you pee?"

"You don't even want to know."

He grinned and looked around at his passengers. "So which one of you is Kushner?"

Emily stepped forward. "Kushner got sick, so I'm in charge. I'm Emily Gravely." She held her hand out.

Gregorio shook her hand. "Are you nicer than him?"

"God, I hope so." She laughed. "It'd be hard to be more of a jerk." There was some muttered agreement from the rest of her team, which caused Gregorio to raise an eyebrow.

"Well," he said, stepping back and patting the structure behind him, "this here is your cargo container. We rebuilt the aft section of the deckhouse around it." Emily raised an eyebrow. If that was rebuilt then Gregorio's people had done an excellent job of making the alterations as shabby-looking as the rest of the boat. "Right now, it's full of stuff we're taking to Manaus, just like all the deck cargo."

Emily gave him a quizzical look.

He shrugged. "You can't go to the city with an empty boat and not be noticed." It seemed to Emily that Gregorio had just saved them from one of Kushner's planning mistakes.

War Zone, 11:36
Bang Hai, 238 km east of Manaus

"We found them. Ninety-five percent likelihood, according to the analysts."

"Excellent news."

"They're in a small cargo craft, looks like they're carrying a real cargo to blend in. They'll most likely arrive later this afternoon, sell the cargo and then wait around until they can start their recovery run."

"So, we could intercept them?"

"Yes, sir."

"But we don't have definitive coordinates for where the paintings are?"

"No, sir. We know they're in Manaus, but not exactly where."

"Well, the Monumentalists obviously have a plan. We'll let them get the paintings, then we'll just…take them."

"Shouldn't be a problem, sir." Before his commander could leave, he added, "By the way, we identified their mercs. They call themselves Ghost Team." He put a slightly blurry photo of the team's leader on the screen. "They're led by a deserter from our Special Ops."

"Interesting. Well, then, we shouldn't have any trouble get Special Ops involved, if we need them."

10. INTERFERENCE

War Zone, 13:12
Amazon River, 23 km east of Manaus

Ophelia leaned back in her chair and groaned as something in her back cracked. She tried doing some light stretches to ease her aches and pains. General Dynamics had put a surprising amount of effort into making the APC's chairs comfortable, but no chair was up to the number of hours she spent in front of her screens.

She leaned forward as one of her drones showed three boats approaching from upstream.

"We've got incoming," she said over Ghost Team's encrypted comms channel. "Three boats, decent condition, no markings. Coming downriver toward us. Designating as contact Alpha."

The message went out on Ghost Team's encrypted comms channel. She quickly got an "*Understood, moving into position,*" from Laney and a quiet "*Got it,*" from Emily, who was tied into their network now.

"Looks like the *artistes* have picked up some fleas,"

Travis observed, sitting at the fire control station behind Armel.

"Close up the distance," Fang commanded, "and tell the boat to slow down." The boat had been keeping their speed down to match the APC's slower pace, but they were still about two hundred meters ahead of them. *Paladin* surged forward as Armel complied. The ride got noticeably rougher.

Ophelia relayed the message to Emily on the boat, then got a drone into position to get a closer view of the approaching force. The boats were full of armed men, perhaps twenty in all, carrying rifles, machine guns and pistols. No heavy weaponry that she could see. The boats looked like gasoline/alcohol conversion jobs, probably underpowered but serviceable. They were clearly pirates, and brazen ones at that, to be working so close to Manaus. Either that, or the Batista influence was severely waning in anticipation of the upcoming Chinese push.

Fang looked over at Ophelia. "They must have a spotter. Find him and take him out."

"On it," she said.

"Travis," Fang said. "Prepare to fire antipersonnel rounds."

Travis shot him an over-the-shoulder look to make sure he was serious. "You got it." Antipersonnel rounds were intended to take out combat-suited soldiers en masse. Against wooden boats, the results were going to be ugly.

War Zone, 13:18
Amazon River, 23 km east of Manaus

Emily was in the boat's small bridge with Gregorio when she got the warning from Ghost Team that trouble was in the offing. She relayed Fang's order to slow down to Gregorio, who instantly complied, then sent an alert to her team and made sure they were all safely gathered in the cramped common room behind the craft's small bridge—cramped mostly because of all the space taken up to accommodate their cargo container.

"Three boats, pirates, coming downstream," Emily explained. "Ghost Team's going to take care of them."

Gregorio raised an eyebrow.

Emily shrugged. "Don't ask me, I don't know how they're going to handle this."

Through the bridge's window, Emily saw a shimmering haze moving across the deck, then realized after a moment that it was Laney, dynamic camouflage engaged, taking up a position at the bow. It was hard to tell, but she thought the mercenary may have gone prone on the deck. Assuming she had a weapon deployed, it must have been camouflaged, too.

"*COB, maintain course,*" Ophelia said. COB was her own codename, which Fang had told her meant Commander of Boat. Apparently, Ghost Team had found it humorous to apply the term to a civilian like herself with no naval or other military experience. "*And get your heads down, it's about to get dangerous.*"

Emily knelt. Gregorio looked down at her, got the hint and joined her on the floor, though he did keep a hand on the bottom of the wheel to keep the boat steady on its course. In a sensorium window, she flipped through Ophelia's working list of key drone views until she found one that showed their boat and surrounding area from above.

"*Spotter is down,*" Ophelia said.

Emily watched as the three pirate boats rounded a bend in the river. Two of them sped up when they spotted their target. Emily heard gunfire, realized that the pirates had fired warning shots past their boat.

Beneath the seemingly peaceful water, Travis targeted three brilliant antipersonnel rounds, one at each boat. Each round was effectively a miniature missile with enough built-in smarts to determine the best way to engage its designated target. A primary mandate of their targeting instructions included not damaging a nearby wooden craft designated as "friendly." Designed for both underwater and aerial use, each round determined the amount of propellant that needed to be expended to reach the target and penetrate the hull.

What Emily witnessed was the first two boats simply disintegrating, followed a few seconds later by the third. Splinters of wood, body parts, engine pieces and structural elements flew into the air, accompanied by flame and smoke as the fuel supplies caught fire.

A few lucky survivors suddenly found themselves unexpectedly in the water. Then Emily heard the staccato *boom-boom-boom* of nearby rifle fire, and realized that the men in the water weren't so lucky after all, as Laney targeted them.

A moment later, Ophelia said, "*Alpha force has been squashed. You're clear to proceed, just try to stay away from the debris.*"

Emily stood up and Gregorio followed suit. Where three boats had been, there was only scattered wreckage. Even the fires were burning themselves out.

"*The only good pirate is a dead pirate,*" Laney said, satisfaction in her voice.

Emily had no particular sympathy for pirates who'd undoubtedly harmed a lot of innocent people, but it shocked even her, and she'd witnessed it via drone view, that twenty bloodthirsty pirates could meet a violent end so quickly. It was the very definition of an asymmetric fight, amateurs against seasoned mercenaries with top-of-the-line equipment.

Gregorio watched the wreckage as it drifted downstream past them. He turned to her and said, "I'm glad you're on my side." He shuddered. "I'd hate to end that way."

RECOVERY OP

11. Approach

Cargo Boat, 01:22

A half-moon shone in the dark sky as a decrepit cargo boat, its running lights conspicuously off, chugged its way carefully through the narrow waterways of the *favela* that had grown up where the Amazon encroached on the city of Manaus. Even here, fourteen hundred miles from the coast, the Amazon was a tidal river; it was the high tide that had made the boat's surreptitious course possible, and also bounded its use as an escape route.

In the narrower places, the fifteen-meter-long craft almost touched the ramshackle buildings and walkways. A determined resident could have stepped onto the boat, had they not been discouraged by the men stationed on either side of the boat with machine guns.

Inside the boat, the brightly-lit bridge provided a stark contrast to the boat's external appearance, the illumination invisible from outside thanks to the recently installed one-way windows. Emily sat next to

Gregorio, who was helping them navigate their way as discreetly as possible to the warehouse district that was their destination. She was wearing a headset with an attached mic and frowning at the foldout screen in front of her.

"Left up ahead. Then slow down some more 'cause the next turn is going to be a squeaker."

Gregorio nodded. "What's this all about, anyway?" Turning, he gave her a gap-toothed grin. "If you're allowed to tell me." He'd been very well paid, so technically she didn't have to tell him squat. In addition to money, his deal had also included getting his extended family out of war-torn Brazil. On the other hand, the mission was in progress and the need for operational security was past.

Emily smiled back at him. "Artwork."

Gregorio raised his eyebrows. "Artwork?" He turned away to concentrate on navigating the "squeaker" that Emily had mentioned, his hands moving the steering wheel in minute increments.

On her screen, Emily looked at an aerial view from the drone that Ophelia had stationed above them. Thanks to Gregorio's expert handling, the boat made the turn with about a foot to spare on each side.

In her ear phones, Ophelia said, "*Boat One, continue down the channel. Ghost Team is almost in place.*" The drone operator was back on *Paladin*, which was submerged just outside of Manaus.

"Paintings," Emily said. "Thirty-two years ago, in 2082, the One World United Art Exhibition was in Brazil when the war started. It disappeared, nobody knew who stole it." She looked over at Gregorio. "Well, it's just surfaced here in Manaus and we're taking it back. Tonight."

"So, you're stealing back your own stolen paintings?"

"Yes."

"I like it."

"*Ghost One is in position.*" She recognized the clipped tones and Chinese accent of Fang Li, the leader of Ghost Team.

Warehouse Complex (Back Gate), 01:23

Laney Sanders, Ghost Three, let the Underwater Personnel Transporter pull her slowly through the murky and badly polluted water. The UPT, or *petey*, was shaped like a three-foot-long missile with a propeller on the back end, safely encased in a wire cage to avoid unfortunate incidents. Laney gripped the handles that extended from each side of the propeller cage. She toggled the petey to a slower speed as she spotted obstacles looming up out of the muck in front of her.

The view wasn't real, of course. It was a com-posite extrapolated from her suit's various sensors, including the stealth sonar rig they'd added for this mission, and projected on her face screen by her suit's AI. Without it, she'd have been swimming blind.

She was moving through the open area of water that separated the rear of the warehouse complex from the rest of the *favela*. Based on the wreckage she was seeing, mostly broken timbers and smashed furniture, the open area had probably been created by simply destroying the homes of any residents who had been unlucky enough to be living too close to the complex. Recent regimes had been brutal.

Whoever owned the warehouses had upgraded the security by adding a ten-foot spiked fence, topped with razorwire, around the entire complex. In their zeal, they'd extended the fence into the water, with the help of an improbable amount of underwater concrete. Of course, they'd included a gate to allow authorized boats access to the loading dock.

She reached the gate just as she heard Fang Li announce that he was in position, followed a moment later by Trav, Ghost Two.

"Ghost Three, in position," she said.

Cargo Boat, 01:24

Emily split her screen into quarters, showing the helmet view of each member of Ghost Team, plus an enhanced overhead view of the complex that Ophelia was providing from her drones. On the overhead view, the three team members were green dots, each one in their designated positions.

Emily's mouth was dry and her stomach felt queasy. This was the one part of the mission over which she had no control and no expertise. It was almost surreal that she was in charge—she was an art historian, not a military commander.

Ophelia said, "*Infrared shows zeds, locations as follows.*"

A bunch of red dots appeared on the strategic view. One looked like it was in the gatehouse at the front of the complex, as expected. Another was in their target warehouse. Then there was a cluster of six red dots in one of the other warehouses, gathered in approximately a circle.

She frowned. That seemed odd. There was supposed to be one guard per building. Why were so many of them in one place?

From Fang Li, allocating objectives: "One, gatehouse, then open backdoor; Two, take the cluster; Three, secure the backdoor then the target."

"Two, cluster, affirmative."

"Three, backdoor and target, affirmative."

Ophelia said, "The weather is still clear."

Emily shook her head and smiled. Ophelia was even worse at military-style radio-speak than she was. That was apparently her way of saying that her eyeballs hadn't detected any threats,

She leaned forward. "Mission is 'go.'" She felt just a little bit helpless, not a comfortable feeling for somebody as detail-oriented as herself. Now it was completely up to Ghost Team.

Fang responded, "Confirmed. Go."

On her screen, the little green dots started moving.

12. Clear & Control

Warehouse Complex (Front Gate), 01:28

Fang Li, Ghost One, walked slowly up to the gatehouse, careful not to move faster than the chameleon capabilities of his suit could compensate for. He was sweating a little. He was walking across a minefield, which was always destined to be nerve-racking, even if the minefield was only activated if the guard on duty detected a threat. Fortunately, the guard not only wasn't looking at his external view screens (which wouldn't have shown anything, anyway), he had his head down and there seemed to be a bluish light shining up on his face from something he was holding. Fang was willing to bet he was playing some sort of electronic game.

The defenses included a regular infrared scan of the area, but his combat suit was currently in anti-infrared mode. He wasn't emitting anything hotter than the ambient temperature. While his suit couldn't store generated heat for long, this was exactly the type of situation for which the feature had been designed.

Fang's sensors indicated no other security mechanisms in play. As far as he could tell, the only significant defense that the stolen cache of paintings had was that, until tonight, nobody outside of a select few in the Batistas had known even remotely where the cache might be. Stolen paintings worth billions of creds, and nothing but security through obscurity. Unbelievable. Even worse, with all the bombing that the city had endured, it was a wonder that the warehouse complex had never been bombed.

Arriving at the guardhouse, Fang pointed his Marauder pistol at the window and blew a hole in the bulletproof glass with an UltraShock round. The guard gave a startled shout, dropped his ancient comms device and tried to stand up. Fang put the barrel of the weapon in the fist-sized hole and hit him with a tranquilizer round. He went down with a strangled scream and was still.

It was the work of seconds to smash the lock on the gatehouse door. He stepped over the comatose guard and looked at the control panel for a moment. Then he opened the back gate of the warehouse complex.

"Ghost One, the zed is down and the back door is open."

Puzzling over the controls again, Fang finally figured out how to turn the minefield on. He smiled. A nice surprise in case any unwelcome guests showed up at the front gate.

Warehouse Complex (Bldg. 4), 01:30

Travis McCloud, Ghost Two, had already infiltrated the complex and was standing outside the warehouse containing the cluster of guards pinpointed by Ophelia's drones. A fourteen-foot spiked fence was not an obstacle for a man in a combat suit.

He'd been waiting for Fang to take out the gatehouse, so that his own activities couldn't possibly alert the gatehouse guard and spoil Ghost One's stealthy approach. As soon as he heard that Fang had achieved his objectives, he entered the unlocked door of the warehouse.

Inside, the floor space was organized with wide floor-to-ceiling shelves separated by narrow aisles. Travis could see a yellow glow beyond all the shelving. He padded quietly down an aisle.

The guards were sitting about fifteen feet away at a makeshift table composed of a wide piece of plywood sitting on top of two sawhorses. They were playing some sort of card game.

Travis strolled around the corner, pistol up. One of the card players looked startled; he must have noticed a ripple of movement. He shot that guard first, then methodically shot the other guards. Accuracy was almost always better than speed. Only one even came close to getting his firearm out of its holster.

Warehouse Complex (Back Gate), 01:32

Laney swam to one side as the massive steel gate, the backdoor as Fang had called it, began to open. She waited until the gate was fully open, then triggered the ring-like packages she'd installed around the immense hinges.

Her screen dampened the brightness as chemicals mixed and flash-welded the hinges into position. Even through her suit, she felt a flash of heat as the steel melted together. Fang had told her before the mission that he liked to make sure his escape routes stayed open. Laney kind of agreed with his logic.

"Backdoor is locked open."

Laney engaged the petey and headed for the muddy shore next to the dock. A moment later she turned it off, let go, and allowed the device's momentum to drive it a foot or so up onto the mud. She waited for a short interval to see if anybody started shooting in her general direction, though she didn't think that was likely. Still, in her experience, haste was a waste, unless you really needed it. She stood up in the now-thigh-deep water and trudged onto shore.

"*Cluster is down. It was six guards playing cards.*" Well, that was seven guards, including the one Fang had taken out, that would be sleeping until about noon tomorrow. How come Trav got most of the fun?

Her heads-up display showed her that stealth mode was engaging now that she'd left the water. You had to love the tech. Of course, she noted upon looking down, it didn't do much for muddy footprints.

She walked to the target warehouse's side door. Her display showed the guard as being somewhere on the other side of the building, so she grabbed the knob and turned it. She wasn't overly surprised to find it unlocked.

She stalked through a wide area filled with wooden boxes that looked suspiciously like they might hold paintings. Not exactly unexpected, but nice to see, nonetheless.

It turned out that her guard was in the bathroom.

She rolled her eyes.

After a short time, she heard a toilet flush. A moment later, a man emerged from the bathroom and she shot him with a tranquilizer round before he had a chance to even notice her.

"Target is secure," she said. "Bring in the *artistes.*"

All her missions should be this easy.

13. First Contact

Warehouse Complex (Bldg. 6), 01:42

Emily jogged up to the warehouse's main entrance, now wide open, followed at a slower pace by her two art historians and the other volunteers with their rolling carts. A figure in a gray military combat suit stood by the door waiting for them. Too short to be Trav and too thin to be Fang, it had to be Laney.

As she drew abreast of the figure, her ident-ification was confirmed when the fighter gave her a quick curtsy. She thought the suits looked vaguely unsettling, mostly due to their opaque facemasks.

Emily stopped next to Laney. "Well, the hard work can start now."

"Yeah, right," Laney drawled, accentuating her deep southern American accent. "You keep thinkin' that."

Emily laughed.

She spent the next ten minutes getting everybody organized. The first three boxes they opened were paintings, but they looked like local Brazilian artwork. Valuable, but not what they were looking for. They set those to one side.

There were still a lot of boxes to look through, but the potential for disappointment was palpable. What if their information was wrong? They'd found paintings, and she'd bet her life savings that they were all stolen. But what if none of them were the stolen artwork they were hoping for?

Sanford, the more difficult and persnickety of her two art historians, called out, "We got one." She saw smiles break out on everyone's faces. Not a dry mission after all.

She rushed over to where Sanford was standing next to an empty box. It had three relatively small paintings in it, packed in the most dreadfully unprofessional way. Sanford carefully pulled out the middle one for her inspection.

"It's a Degas," he said, "from our list. It's *The Dancers*."

She high-fived him, then had to high-five some of the other workers that had come over to see the Monet, too.

Finally, she had to cut the impromptu celebration short. She stood on a chair and shouted, "All right, folks. We've got work to do. We can celebrate later." She paused. "And I've got a slight change of plans. No more inspections. We're just taking all of the paintings, including the Brazilian ones. So, let's get this show rolling."

When she stepped down from the chair, Sanford approached her. "All of them? Seriously?"

She'd figured he'd be the one to complain about her

little change. He'd complained about so many other things already on this mission. She thought it was a good change, though. With this one adjustment, they not only saved the Brazilian paintings too, but they also reduced the time they needed to be in the warehouse. Listening to Ghost Team's activities on comms had reinforced for her that what they were doing was dangerous. She'd known that before, of course, but now she understood it for real.

"Yes, all of them. They're all stolen. And Brazil has a heritage that's worth preserving, too."

He looked at her intently, pursed his lips and nodded. "Good call." He turned around and walked away.

She spurred everybody on until there was a steady stream of boxes flowing back to the boat. Once they got a rhythm going, she was able to get a handle on how fast they were getting the job done, which was faster than her pre-mission estimates. By her calculation, it was going to take nearly an hour to get all of the boxes moved.

She walked over to Laney, still on station just inside the door.

"Most of the guards were playing cards, right?"

"Yes," Laney replied.

"How come this building's guard wasn't playing cards?"

"I don't know." Laney paused. "You're thinking he might have stayed here because he was expecting company tonight?"

"Yeah." Emily bit her lip, a bad habit that came out

whenever she was stressed. "But it might just be me being nervous."

"In my experience, a little paranoia is a good thing."

"OK. If you don't think I'm crazy, then…" Emily keyed her mic. "Ophelia, we need a weather check. I've got a theory that our local guard might, emphasize might, have been expecting company sometime tonight."

Hawk APC, 02:08

Carlitos Paiva leaned back in his seat, rolled his eyes and tried to get comfortable, always a challenge while wearing a combat suit. On the encrypted command channel, relayed to his implants by the helmet resting on the floor of the APC next to his feet, General Diego had launched into yet another of his extended rants.

"Yes, we're still in transit," Carlitos Paiva said into the hand-held mic, trying to hide his irritation. He was the *expert*; you paid him to get stuff done, not to be micromanaged. "We'll be on station in thirty."

Paiva glanced at the wide, curved screen in front of him. An aerial drone view showed his convoy moving through the twisting, narrow streets of the *favela*. Not for the first time, he marveled at the stupidity of putting a warehouse complex in the section of the city with the worst roads, not to mention that half of the damn area was typically underwater. On the other hand, an area as devoid of useful infrastructure as the *favela* hadn't been pummeled by the extensive bombing that opposition forces, mostly their Chinese allies, had delivered to the rest of the city.

He had two troop carriers, followed by an eighteen-wheeler for cargo, plus a trailing gun truck. And his own Russian surplus APC in the fourth position—sleek, black and dangerous-looking. All to pick up his employer's retirement package, a billion-plus creds worth of stolen paintings, and provide security for it.

"You know how important this is. Don't fail me." General Diego terminated the call with a click. The tension in his employer's voice was obvious to Paiva; the man might be a fat, corrupt, womanizing slob but you had to give him some credit: he focused on details like nobody's business. He was probably the main reason the Batistas still held the city of Manaus.

Sadly, the man's compatriots were nowhere near as effective, which mostly explained why their faction was being pushed back by the Chinese-backed Nacionalistas. The fact that the rest of them generally ignored Paiva's military advice probably had a lot to do with it, too. Why hire a military advisor if you're not going to listen to him?

He turned toward Raynald, a thin, balding man perched like some maniacal spider in front of a wall of aerial views, real-time charts and windows with arcane technical gibberish scrolling past. "Anything? Our employer is getting nervous."

"Nah. Looks good. The drones aren't picking up anything interesting."

"Push the perimeter, please." Paiva scratched his

scalp under his close-cropped black hair and grimaced. "I don't want any surprises."

"OK, boss."

Warehouse Complex (Bldg. 6), 02:16

Emily looked around with satisfaction. The inside of the warehouse appeared to be in total chaos, but it was actually an organized, functional maelstrom of activity. Basically, she'd orchestrated an assembly line, with several men moving crates into a staging area by the door, where another team of laborers would pick them up and carry them to the boat. Her two art historians were in the boat arranging the boxes in storage as they arrived.

And Ghost Team, of course, was stationed outside to watch for trouble.

To her surprise, despite the precarious nature of their situation, she was enjoying herself. It felt like she was really accomplishing something here. Maybe it wasn't rescuing the Mona Lisa, but it was still something.

"*Problem,*" Ophelia said. "*Unknown drone just entered our ops space. I went to passive on that side of my detection envelope and low profile on everything else. Don't know if I was spotted.*"

Emily didn't need to be a military genius to realize this was bad. First, someone was probably coming here, just as she'd feared. Second, drones weren't regular issue for Batista military units. So this unit was better equipped, and potentially better run, than regular Brazilian troops.

Fang said, "*Get a Midnight Special on station.*" Emily wasn't going to second-guess her combat specialist, but an electro-magnetic pulse seemed a little extreme, even the mini-EMP that Ghost Team had brought along. And it was going to take at least a few minutes to get here; *Paladin* was outside the city.

"*Roger that,*" Ophelia responded. "*Kind of expensive, though.*"

"*Ain't expensive, if you need it,*" Travis, Ghost Two, commented, chuckling. "*Plus, we can just add it to our bill.*"

"*Cut the chatter,*" Fang commanded. "*COB, recommend speeding up the recovery.*"

"Agreed." Emily looked around at all the activity and estimated the number of boxes still left in the warehouse. "Twenty minutes, minimum." Even at that, they were going to have to cut some serious corners.

There had always been risk associated with their mission, but now the enormity of her responsibilities hit home. These were her people. Hers. It was her job to make sure everyone got home safe. And that included Ghost Team, too.

Fang again. "*Ghost Two, seed the land approach as defined in Plan B, Option Two.*"

"*Boy, howdy, this is gonna be fun.*"

She turned and watched her crew working for a moment, all of them unaware of the complication headed their way.

"Listen up," she shouted. "We need to speed things up! I need everybody moving boxes NOW!"

14. First Strike

Hawk APC, 02:23

"Hey, Boss," Raynald called out. "Thought I saw something, but now it's gone."

Paiva cocked his head. Frowning, he considered his drone tech. He'd worked with Raynald for a long time. And if his tech thought he'd seen something, however briefly, then it was time to start worrying.

He didn't like surprises.

"Speculate, please."

"Felt like we just brushed up against somebody else's sensor envelope."

Paiva's eyebrows went up. "Somebody else with drones? Like ours?"

"Yeah." Even Sheffield, the APC's driver, looked up at that.

Their drones were state-of-the-art: six-centimeter, air-propelled globes filled with sophisticated electronics and sensors. Paiva knew this, both because he paid the bills, and because he regularly navigated the labyrinthine back channels necessary to procure the top-shelf mil-grade gear. The Batistas had been through too many years of war, and were too cash-strapped, to have that kind of gear. Which left either the Chinese or a third party. Either was very bad news.

"Well," he said, "That's not good." Keying his mic to the general convoy channel: "Pick up the pace, we may have a problem at our destination."

He placed a call to the gatehouse of the warehouse complex. There was no answer.

"Ray…"

"Already on it, boss. I'm pushing our perimeter out and I've released more—"

There was a flash, most of Raynald's screens went blank and the drone tech started cursing in a way Paiva hadn't heard from him in years. At the same time, Sheffield slammed on the brakes as the cargo vehicle in front of him coasted to a stop.

Still muttering under his breath, Raynald swiveled his chair around. He took a few seconds to compose himself. "We got hit with a mini-EMP. I just lost most of my drones."

Paiva whistled. Somebody had some *nice* toys.

Sheffield glanced over his Shoulder. "The cargo truck is down, too."

Well, that was going to put a crimp in their pickup schedule. *Memo to self: don't let General Diego requisition commercial vehicles for a mission again.*

Somebody had also just made a *lot* of noise. Not particularly dangerous to people, the mini-EMP had probably just fried everything electronic for a block around them. Paiva suspected he'd be hearing from his employer again pretty soon.

The drones were combat-hardened as much as possible, but there was only so much you could do with a tiny, glorified instrument package that needed to float in the air. Close proximity to a mini-EMP wasn't survivable, though some on the opposite edge of the perimeter had survived. They carried more, but it was a finite and expensive supply.

Paiva made a snap judgment that this wasn't a full-on ambush, just a delaying tactic from a small force that had somehow beaten them to the warehouse complex. If he was wrong, he'd find out very soon.

"Squad One, dismount your team and take cover," Paiva said. Regular troop comms had been knocked out, but his own mercenaries were unaffected. He had three of his combat-suited soldiers with the first troop carrier, plus two more with the second team. "Squad Two, retreat to Black Orchard Crossing, dismount and deploy to interdict any possible water egress by a large boat from the warehouse complex." Splitting his forces made him uncomfortable, but Squad One could interdict a land escape while Squad Two could close the back door if their adversaries were planning to escape by water. "Sheffield, get us to the water, most expedient path."

Paiva felt the motion as the APC pivoted, then surged into a side street.

"Incoming," Raynald interrupted. "Targeting the cargo—"

There was a muffled *whoof* as the eighteen-wheeler behind them exploded. Pieces of wreckage clattered down on top of the APC.

"Ray, more drones, please," Paiva said drily. "We need visuals on these jokers. And send the gun truck to a good vantage point." Paiva keyed his mic. "Hawk Two, did the driver get out?"

"*Hawk Two here. The driver is with me.*"

"Excellent." Squad One now had thirteen troopers, counting the driver, plus three of his mercs. "Make your way to the complex. Secure the package, or confirm that it's gone AWOL."

"*Will do, Hawk Two out.*"

His opposition had taken out an empty cargo truck, rather than a temporarily exposed troop carrier. As he'd thought, not a full-on ambush. Just more delaying tactics on the part of someone who didn't want to kill anybody if they could avoid it.

Fortunately, he didn't have the same qualms about killing.

Sheffield piped up, "Somebody needs an ass-kicking."

Paiva bared his teeth in a predatory grin. "You got that right." Nothing like a little opposition to liven up an otherwise boring day. He was looking forward to teaching these asswipes what it meant to run up against some serious mercenaries.

Warehouse Complex (Bldg. 6), 02:24

Emily heard a distant boom at same time as she heard a lengthy crackle from her headset. That must have been the "Midnight Special" that Fang had mentioned on comms.

Looking around to find Laney, she spotted the soldier already jogging in her direction.

As Laney came to a stop next to her, Emily said, "What just happened?"

"We dropped a mini-EMP on a column of vehicles, maybe ten blocks away. Including two troop carriers and a gun truck. All told, maybe thirty-odd soldiers plus odds and sods." Laney paused. "And a team of mercs, it looks like. This shit's getting serious. We've got to be out of here in five minutes."

Suddenly, the EMP didn't seem like such overkill after all.

Emily turned and started shouting out orders. Laney pitched in to help with some of the heavy lifting, as did Emily as soon as she got things moving faster. That had to be on Fang's orders.

"Five minutes," Laney called out. "We're done."

Busy helping the others, the time had gone even faster than Emily had realized. Looking around, she quickly spotted at least a dozen boxes still left. She saw some of the other laborers come to the same conclusion as they stopped working and looked around.

Emily bowed to the inevitable. "All right everybody, let's get out of here."

"Beggin' your pardon," one of the laborers said, a Frenchman from Bordeaux. "But we're not leaving anything behind." He gestured at the remaining boxes. "This is our world's heritage."

The other workers nodded in agreement, then went

back to moving boxes. Emily looked over at Laney. "Do whatever you have to. Get us another five minutes." She couldn't help it. She was proud of her workers.

She smiled humorlessly as Laney threw up her hands in aggravation. Then the soldier stood still for a moment, probably relaying the unwelcome news to Ghost One.

"Make it happen, Emily," Laney said. "It's going to be tight. I've got to join the others." She turned and ran out of the warehouse in a blur of augmented speed.

15. Fighting Retreat

Favela (Landbound), 02:30

Fang Li, Ghost One, lay prone on the roof of a decrepit two-story dwelling, stealth mode engaged, and watched Ophelia's feed as his enemies flanked him on his left side. They had what looked like a slightly over-strength squad, augmented by a small number of mercenaries with similar gear to his own.

"*You've got three mercs to deal with,*" Ophelia said. "*They weren't chameleon when they exited the troop carrier.*"

"Ghost Team," Fang said, "gloves off. Let's buy the *artistes* some more time."

They'd given their pursuers two warnings, the mini-EMP and the cargo truck. Apparently that hadn't been enough to discourage them, so the bastards had earned what was going to happen next.

Fang focused his attention on the scope view of his Samson X4 Rifle Launcher, a heavily customized Mexican weapon. He triggered a burst as one of his pursuers, a regular Brazilian trooper, emerged from cover and darted across the street.

The three explosive rounds automatically diverged in flight to bracket his target's position. The triptych of explosions shredded the soldier while Fang rolled away to avoid the inevitable backlash.

Return fire pounded the building, then an explosion took out the area where Fang had been lying. By then, though, Fang was already dropping into the alley behind the building.

"*Electrified one merc,*" Ghost Two said. The entire evolution had used Fang as bait to flush out and incapacitate at least one of the mercs stiffening up the opposing force. He'd used a "Buzz" grenade, which lit the target up with a ridiculous amount of voltage and essentially turned a combat suit into a useless piece of junk.

"*And I got two more troopers,*" added Laney.

Fang smiled grimly and jogged down the alley to the next holding position he'd selected. Rearguard actions were *so* much fun. Not.

Hawk APC, 02:33

"Hawk Three's been bricked, boss," Raynald said, looking back at Paiva, who raised an eyebrow in surprise. Paiva knew of that kind of tech, but hadn't yet managed to get his hands on any of it. It meant they'd just lost a very expensive combat suit, plus Hawk Three would probably be unconscious for a few hours or so. "Plus three of the regulars are gone. Whoever these jokers are, they're good."

Paiva gave him a grim look. "Let's get a jammer up, mess with their comms."

An icon popped into the bottom of his view field indicating that General Diego was trying to get hold of Paiva on the special communication channel Raynald had set up for him. Unsurprising, given the mini-EMP. Paiva ignored it. He was busy and he didn't need management oversight right now.

"Squad One," Paiva said, keying his mic. "Keep up the close pursuit by whatever means available." That would keep the pressure on whoever was acting as rearguard for the art thieves, and also make it harder for them to rejoin their compatriots. "Squad Two, ETA?"

"*Hawk Four, we're on station. Dismounting now.*" Good. They were now below the thieves. By heading east, they'd be in a position to interdict their escape routes.

"Spread out. Stop any boat you see. And be aware that the opposing mercs of their rearguard are top-notch; they may try escaping underwater individually." He would have, if he were in their position.

He was hopeful that he'd be able to mousetrap his enemy's fighters between his two squads. It was lucky his mercs had been embedded with the regulars—the EMP had fried all of the electronics the Brazilians had, including their supposedly hardened communi-cation gear. Even Squad Two's truck had lost its electronics and was running at about fifty-percent fuel efficiency.

As for the thieves back at the warehouse, Paiva was almost certain they'd try to escape by water. They'd need a sizable cargo boat to carry all of the loot.

By Paiva's rough reckoning, it was going to be a close-run thing to get Squad Two, his blocking force, in place before the boat passed. It all depended on when the thieves left the warehouse, if they hadn't done so already.

Still, if they failed to block the getaway boat, they might be able to get themselves some hostages to use as leverage if they could subdue the rearguard. And Paiva had some ideas on how to catch that boat, no matter what.

He changed the comms channel and answered General Diego's call. "Paiva here." He ignored the general's ranting, then cut in when the man relented long enough to take a breath. "We've got a problem. Someone's trying to steal the package. I need choppers and more troops and I need them now."

Paiva didn't like to have his nose bloodied, and he tended to hit back a *lot* harder than he'd been hit. It was past time for some payback.

Warehouse Complex, 02:42

Laney, Ghost Three, fired her Marauder pistol, then scooted back around the corner of the warehouse to avoid the return fire, which chewed up the cinderblock and peppered her with concrete chips. Being outnumbered was not fun.

Not for the first time, she thought it might be time for a safer career. The problem, as always, was that this one paid so well, as long as you survived. She was just another export from a fractured and declining America, a well-trained but unemployed soldier with no real marketable skills except those demanded by the mercenary trade.

She heard a large explosion, undoubtedly one of Ghost Team's pursuers encountering the minefield in front of the gate. A little bit of insurance that Fang had set up when he took the gatehouse. She took the opportunity to pop off a few more shots.

Safely under cover again, she said, "Ghost Three, anybody there?" She'd hoped the relatively close proximity to her comrades would allow her signal to punch through the jamming, but no such luck. Whoever the enemy was, they were well-equipped. Definitely not a regular Batista unit.

She began moving back to the alternate zone Fang had designated right before the jamming started. The front minefield and the current firing positions of Ghost Team should subtly direct the enemy counter-clockwise around the complex to the next logical spot where they could blow the fence and get in. Right where Ghost Two had earlier set up his own minefield.

"*Ophelia here, comms are back, I took out the jammer drone.*" Laney could hear the satisfaction in the tech's voice. Couldn't ask for a better tech.

"*Ghost Three,*" Fang said, "*move to zones as planned, harry our pursuers, then exfiltrate at all possible speed.*

16. Casting Off

Warehouse Complex (Bldg. 6), 02:45

Emily pounded up the boat ramp, her arms aching from holding up her end of a pine box containing at least five or six medium-sized paintings. The Frenchman was handling the other end; he showed her a crazed grin and wild eyes as he backed up the ramp so quickly it was difficult for her to keep up. It sounded like there was a herd of buffalo on her heels as the rest of the workers rushed aboard with the last remaining boxes.

She heard the *pop-pop-pop* of gunfire somewhere behind them followed a moment later by a loud explosion. Then more gunfire.

"Get us untied!" Emily yelled, before she realized that Gregorio was already releasing the ropes holding the stern of the boat to the dock's piling.

Another man took over her load, and he and the Frenchman darted away with the box. She hurried toward the bridge as the stern started drifting away from the dock; there was a loud splash as the boarding ramp fell into the water.

Another laborer had untied the bow. Gregorio darted into the bridge right behind her. Emily settled into her seat and reached for her headset as Gregorio took the controls.

"COB here. What's the situation?"

"*The bad guys just ran into our minefield on the other side of the warehouse complex,*" Ophelia said. "*They are not happy with us.*"

"I bet."

The boat's engine was already idling; now that she was still, Emily could feel the thrum of the oversized engines through the deck. The vibration combined with the butterflies in her stomach to make her queasy.

They'd gotten the paintings, but they already had armed opposition after them. Now that the possibility of danger had become the actuality, Emily was scared, both for herself and all the people on the mission. But excited, too, which rather surprised her.

Fang broke into the command channel. "*COB, don't worry about Ghost Team. We'll cover your back trail and then self-extract.*"

"COB confirms Ghost Team self-extraction." Fang clearly thought things were getting really ugly. Emily found herself in agreement with his assess-ment, and wasn't happy that much of it was her fault, attributable to the delays in moving all the boxes. "Ghost Team, good luck and Godspeed."

Gregorio flashed her a smile and then gunned the boat away from the dock. No need to wait for Ghost Team now.

"All the things I've smuggled in my time," he said, expertly maneuvering the boat through the gate, "and this isn't even really illegal." He shook his head.

Emily laughed. "Well, that won't keep the wrong people from shooting at us." As if to punctuate her words, she heard more sustained gunfire and another explosion in the distance.

Ophelia updated Emily on the overall situation while Gregorio maneuvered the boat at frightening speed into the narrow channels of the *favela.*

Hawk APC, 02:45

"I've got the boat," Raynald announced, putting it on the screen. It was still tied up, though it looked like the stern was swinging away from the dock. The screen suddenly went blank and Raynald started cursing.

"Trouble?" Paiva asked mildly.

"Hunter/Killer swarm," he said in an exasperated tone. "They just took out my closest eyeballs." He put a still shot of the boat back up on Paiva's screen. "I just sent this out to the squads, this is what we'll be looking for." He shook his head sadly. "You gotta get me some better toys, boss."

"*Hawk Two here. The warehouse is empty. Repeat, the warehouse is empty. We also found the guard. He was tranquilized.*" The sound of gunfire could be heard in the background.

Paiva quirked his lips up in a grim smile. "Well, at least we know who we're dealing with now." The

Chinese didn't use tranquilizers and neither did the various Brazilian factions. He looked around the cramped cabin of the APC, where Raynald and Sheffield were both looking at him expectantly. "Monumentalists."

Raynald nodded. "Makes sense. If General Diego put out some feelers about selling any of the art on the international black market, their hackers could have gotten wind of it."

Sheffield glanced back at Paiva over his shoulder. "What are Monumentalists?" Ever the professional driver, he returned his attention to navigating the APC through the narrow side streets.

Paiva stared at him. Sheffield was a great driver, but not a whiz at current events.

Raynald saved him the trouble of answering. "They recover priceless artwork stolen during the world's conflicts. Been around in one form or another for a couple centuries." He grimaced. "Basically, a bunch of well-funded do-gooders who are about to steal our mission bonuses from us."

Sheffield growled, "Not on my watch."

The APC lurched as Sheffield braked sharply. Paiva looked up at the main screen and saw that they'd came to a stop about twenty meters from some ramshackle housing. The street was a dead end, and too narrow to turn around in easily.

"The water's on the other side of that shack," Sheffield said apologetically. I need to find another route."

"No time," Paiva responded. "Go through it."

Sheffield looked at him with wide eyes. "APC vs. shack—the APC wins every time."

The driver shrugged. He revved the engine and smashed through the building, broken boards and debris flying everywhere. The front end of the APC splashed down into the water and momentum carried them beyond the wreckage of the dwelling. Paiva couldn't tell if anybody had been in the building, or not. He didn't much care, either. You got used to collateral damage after a while.

The APC floated, just as it was designed to do. There was a rumble as Sheffield withdrew the wheels into their compartments. As soon as the transformation to boat mode was complete, Sheffield hit the throttle and the APC took off in pursuit of the Monumentalists.

It wasn't the fastest boat around, but Paiva figured it was probably faster than the cargo boat they were chasing. The Russians built a good product.

ESCAPE

17. A New Plan

Warehouse Complex, Near Back Gate, 02:49

Bullets tunneled through the water past Laney, slowing rapidly due to the resistance, as the petey pulled her into the depths of the man-made lagoon around the warehouse complex. One of her pursuers, probably the merc, had been using explosive flechette rounds. She was dazed and her head was still ringing from the buffeting she'd taken from the explosive impacts, but at least she hadn't let go of the petey. Luckily, her suit was only slightly damaged, at least according to her bleary view of her heads-up display.

She heard a hiss and accompanying sting as the suit injected her with something to help her cope with the situation. The fog clouding her thought processes began to clear, enough for her to realize she was in deep trouble. Got to love those combat drugs. You might die, but at least your mind will be clear.

Ophelia's voice penetrated her rapidly evaporating semi-stupor. "*Ghost Three! Get out of there! Enemy APC incoming!*"

She dove for cover on the debris-covered bottom, then she felt pain, a lot of pain, as everything around her exploded and the world went black.

Hawk APC, 02:50

"Got one!" Raynald exulted, throwing his hands up in the air.

One of the screens showed the view of the lagoon behind them; water was still falling from the missile strike.

Paiva smiled grimly. In his experience, there was no such thing as overkill.

Squad One could pursue the other two mercs from the enemy's rearguard. His quarry was the boat. And they couldn't be more than a few minutes behind it.

Cargo Boat, 02:53

"Ghost Three is flatline."

Emily hung her head, tears in her eyes. She was in command of the mission. Ghost Three was a casualty, her first. And it was her fault. God, she'd liked Laney, and now she was dead.

Gregorio looked over at her with concern, understanding that something bad had just happened. "What's wrong?"

"Laney's dead."

He crossed his heart. "It's like smuggling," he said gently. "Which I've done a lot of in my time." He paused to swing the boat through a tight turn. "You accept the risks when you take the job. We all did."

"Yeah, but—"

"Now your job is to see us through this," he said firmly. "You light a candle for Laney later."

She looked at him, seeing iron where before she'd seen just an uneducated local. Suddenly she could envision Gregorio as the patriarch doing whatever it took to keep his extended family safe through decades of vicious warfare.

She nodded, then keyed the mic. "How are we looking?"

"*Not good,*" Ophelia said. "*The enemy APC functions as a boat, and they're catching up. We're inbound to help out, but they'll intercept first.*"

"Understood," Emily said, studying the overhead view on her screen. "Ghost Team, I'm sorry about Laney. Now, I need you to intercept and slow down the enemy APC, or the mission's a bust." She wiped her eyes. "Unless Fang has a better idea."

"*COB, orders confirmed.*" Fang said. "*Concur with your assessment.*"

She doubted the two remaining Ghost Team fighters had the firepower to stop the APC. She'd probably just sent them to die, too.

Emily glanced over at Gregorio, who was giving her a questioning glance. He'd only heard her end of the conversation.

"Our pursuers are catching up too quickly?" he

asked.

"Yes," Emily said. "They have an APC that floats like a boat, so they're not far behind us. *Paladin's* coming in, but it's slow…" She could picture *Paladin* rolling through the bottom muck of the *favela*, a muddy cloud in its wake.

Gregorio said, "When I was smuggling, sometimes we'd use two boats, a prime and a backup. If we were being chased, we'd do a drop and switch. You make a slight detour, if your pursuers aren't too close. Drop the cargo, then get back on your main route and lead your pursuers away. The backup boat would come in after everybody'd passed, maybe an innocent looking fishing boat or something, pick up the cargo and leisurely leave the area."

Emily tilted her head and considered him. "That…might work. I can see some problems, but…" She keyed the mic. "Ophelia, Fang, we might have a strategy. Let me run something past you."

Favela, 02:56

Fang, Ghost One, pounded down a crowded walkway, dodging around people when he could, but shoving them out of the way when he couldn't. Thanks to the fighting lots of people had been awakened and had come outside to see what was going on. At this speed, stealth made him a discernible blur rather than hiding him outright.

"Need some ideas on their APC," Fang said.

"*It's functioning as a boat, right?*" Trav asked. Ghost Two was running also, but parallel to Fang on another thoroughfare, if you could call these rickety walkways thoroughfares.

"*Yes,*" Ophelia said.

Fang passed a cantina with a roof that extended over the walkway. He grabbed a support pole and used it to round a corner without slowing down. "It's got to have weaknesses we can exploit."

"*Jane's says the Russians make an APC that floats,*" Ophelia said. "*Narrow double keel, it's part of the armor, so you'll have trouble damaging that. It's got a rudder, but that looks hard to damage, too. It's water-propelled. Like a jet engine, sucking water in the front using some turbo-props and then jetting it out the back.*"

"So," Fang said, "we take out the jet and it's dead in the water?"

"*Um, two jets, actually. And filters to keep gunk away from the turboprop.*"

"*I sense a plan here,*" Trav said.

"What about witnesses to the drop-off?" Fang asked.

"*My problem,*" Emily said. "*We'll handle it.*"

For a plan cobbled together on the fly, it wasn't terrible. Except, of course, for the part where he and Ghost Two had to take on an APC.

"Execute," Fang said, checking the overhead drone view on his heads-up.

In a moment, he'd worked out the ambush location and timing with Ophelia. The enemy APC was coming up behind him, still out of sight because of the twists and turns of the waterway. Ghost Two smashed his way through somebody's house and emerged on the walkway on the opposite side of the waterway from him.

At almost the same moment, they both leaped feet-first into the water and looked for sheltered positions amongst the pilings that supported the buildings. The water was about fifteen feet deep.

Clinging to a slick, moss-covered piling, Fang reached over his shoulder and pulled the minelayer, a twin to the one that Ghost Two had used earlier, off his back. One hundred pellet mines in an operator-selectable spray pattern. Ghost Two still had half of his load left; the half he'd deployed previously had cost the enemy another of their hi-tech mercs.

So they had a total of one hundred and fifty pellets to put in the path of the APC. Surely, at least some of those would be sucked into the APC's jet intakes.

Fang keyed in some parameters for the pattern and operation of the mines.

"Go deep, Trav," Fang said. It was probably the only chance either one of them had to survive this.

18. Ambush

Hawk APC, 02:58

On the screen, Paiva observed the enemy boat barreling through the waterways just two blocks ahead of them. It wouldn't be long now.

"Not again," Raynald said, exasperated, as the overhead drone view disappeared from the screen. "They've got some HK's left, too." Hunter-Killer drones, for taking out other drones. Raynald turned toward him. "Boss, we gotta get—"

The warning alarm went off. Paiva heard the sound of metallic impacts against the lower hull.

Raynald said, "Oh shit, we're being attacked," which was something Paiva had already figured out.

Then the APC was engulfed in an explosion that made the hull ring and slammed Paiva against the bulkhead. The nose of the APC surged upward and the whole craft corkscrewed left. There was a crash as the vehicle slammed into the pilings of the buildings that lined the waterway. Then more crashes and heavy thumps, as wreckage fell on them.

Paiva looked over at his tech, safely belted into his seat but still dazed from the explosive concussion. Paiva activated the APC's antipersonnel weaponry himself, which was still mostly operational. Around the circumference of the APC, barrels popped out of their slots. High-speed explosive rounds exploded against every obstacle in the vicinity of the APC, with each round spewing titanium flechettes in a deadly circle.

The effect was if someone had taken a buzz-saw and chopped out the wooden supports for every building within one hundred and fifty meters of the APC. As one, the already rickety structures collapsed into the water, taking an unknown number of people into the water with them.

Depressing the barrels as low as they'd go, Paiva next turned the water immediately around the APC into a churning froth.

The weapons finally silent, Paiva looked over at Sheffield, his driver. "Damage report?"

Sheffield cleared his throat, uncomfortable at giving him bad news. "They took out one of our jets and damaged the other. We've got about seventy-five percent power on the one jet, but we can only use about fifty if we want to go straight. Figure quarter speed, boss."

"Raynald?"

"Attacks from both sides," he answered. "I figure you just took care of both remaining mercs. Meanwhile, they took out two more drones while we were busy."

Cargo Boat, 03:01

As soon as Ophelia announced that it was safe, Gregorio took the boat into a narrow side waterway. While the boat slowed down, Emily ran out onto the deck and made her way to the cramped cabin behind the bridge where the rest of the crew was waiting.

"We're dropping the cargo pod right here, right now," Emily said, as her team gaped at her in surprise.

"What about the plan?" Sanford sputtered.

"This is the new plan, the old one went out the window. *Paladin* is on its way and is going to pick us all up, but we've got to get this done during a narrow window, so move!"

Emily flattened herself against the cabin wall as the men sprang into action, all except Sanford and the other art historian, a Swedish woman.

Remaining seated, Sanford raised his eyebrows and took a puff of his pipe. "I hope you know what you're doing?"

Emily said, "Makin' it up as I go along. I hope the cargo pod's watertight, though."

Sanford laughed. "Me, too."

Emily went back out on deck. The boat was just drifting slowly now. There were people on both sides of the waterway, perhaps twenty in all, watching their activities with curiosity.

Gregorio sauntered out of the bridge, grabbed a handhold and clambered onto the roof of the boat. Standing, legs spread apart and somehow looking like a force of nature, he began speaking to the crowd in

Portuguese. Emily had no idea what he was saying, but she clicked her mic both so that Ophelia could hear and so that it could be recorded for later review.

When she reached the back of the boat, the crew had the fake door open, exposing the wide cargo pod that occupied the back two-thirds of the boat's deckhouse. As she watched, it slid out on its rails, a metal box painted in jungle camouflage colors. It smashed the wooden railings and rolled off the end of the boat, dropping into the water with a mighty splash.

It disappeared into the muddy water as if it had never been. Billions of creds of irreplaceable artwork, just dropped into the polluted water to land in the mud. If this didn't work out, not only would she likely end up dead, but she'd go down in history as the biggest destroyer of artwork since the Nazis in the twentieth century. She wasn't sure which she dreaded more.

As Emily walked back toward the bow, Gregorio climbed down from the roof. A moment later, he'd nudged the boat over to the nearest walkway, which came to about two feet above the boat's railing.

Between her own laborers and eager volunteers from above, they brought the boat to a stop against the walkway.

"Everybody off," Emily shouted. "Let's go!"

Under Hawk APC, 03:06

Fang sprawled in the muck about ten feet under the keel of the enemy APC in a pocket of water undisturbed by the maelstrom of weapons fire from the vehicle above. He had no idea what had happened to Trav or the entire neighborhood around them, but it was undoubtedly bad. In the meantime, he'd turned all his emissions off and was trying to look, as much as possible, like debris simply half embedded in the mud. There was certainly enough real wreckage drifting down around him to augment his subterfuge.

Hawk APC, 03:09

"Get us out of here," Paiva snarled.

The APC shuddered as Sheffield complied by levering the craft back and forth to loosen the wreckage that had fallen on it. There was a sharp jerk as the damaged vehicle finally pulled free, only to immediately bump into more debris floating in the waterway.

While Sheffield navigated the debris field they'd created, Paiva looked over Raynald's shoulder for a sitrep. The escaping boat was visible on one of the screens powering down a main channel, but the view was jerky. An overlay showed the boat's distance from them, about a klick away and moving faster than they could with the damage they'd been dealt.

Pointing at the jerky view, "Is that one of Diego's

choppers?"

"Yeah," Raynald said. "Just got here. The HK's won't be taking that out." HK's were good against eyeballs, but not larger targets. They just didn't have the size for significant firepower.

"So they can stop the boat?"

"Yeah, but I don't trust their accuracy, boss." Raynald gave him an evil grin. "I have a better idea."

19. Scattered Forces

In or Around *La Bomba*, 03:10

Despite being surrounded by her *artistes*, Emily had never felt as alone as she did when the boat disappeared around the corner. She was stranded in the middle of a war zone, with both international mercenaries and Brazilian soldiers actively hunting them. And no pickup anywhere in sight.

She turned and considered Miller, leaning on the weathered railing beside her looking down at the diminishing waves from the departing boat's wake. "We can't stay outside like this," Emily said, "we stick out like a sore thumb."

Miller nodded. "OK, let me see what I can do."

On the journey upriver, she'd compiled a skills matrix for everybody on the mission, including, as much as they'd answer questions, Ghost Team. Miller's first wife—he was now on his fifth, making him a dedicated serial monogamist—had been a Brazilian refugee. He still spoke passable Portuguese.

He spoke to a few of the onlookers, who pointed

further down the walkway. "This way," he called out.

The *artistes* followed him, Sanford and another man each carrying bulky, square paintings that hadn't fit within the now submerged container. Another carried a rolled up painting wrapped in canvas with strings around it, which made Emily cringe a little bit. Hell of a way to carry a priceless painting around.

Miller disappeared into a dark doorway ahead of them, then came out a few seconds later. Smiling, he said, "Local bomb shelter. We have to go in one at a time."

He stood by the door conversing amiably with several of the locals while they took turns going through the door. She studied the building. Just a slap-dash, wooden building on stilts, like everything else in the *favela*. Didn't look safer than the other buildings, despite the words "Bomb Shelter" written in neat block letters above the doorway, beneath a phrase in larger lettering that presumably had once said the same thing in Portuguese. Someone had crudely spray painted "LA BOMBA" over the text.

Miller held the door open for her, then closed it after her when she entered. She found herself in almost total darkness, within what seemed to be a closet-sized foyer. Then she realized there was some yellow light leaking around the irregular edges of the wall in front of her. Reaching out, she touched cloth and realized there was a black curtain in front of her. Pushing through, she found herself standing next to Sanford in what was clearly a bar.

As drinking establishments went, it was a dive. The

tables were long planks laid across upright barrels. The bar was a bunch of large wooden boxes arranged in an L-shape. The shelves behind the bar held bottles, most of which didn't have labels, and ceramic jars. None of the chairs and stools in front of the bar matched. And most of the customers at the tables were sitting on what looked like wooden produce crates. The windows were shuttered; the bar was clearly operating in blackout mode, as if that made a difference with modern weapons.

There were plenty of people, of diverse ages, and most of them were looking at her group with unfeigned curiosity.

She moved to the side as Miller came through behind her. He was followed immediately by several of the locals that Miller had been talking to, who started circulating amongst the crowd and ges-ticulating dramatically.

Miller said, "The Chinese have been bombing nightly, but they pretty much leave the *favela* alone."

"Makes sense," Emily said. "It'd be a waste of ordinance."

"Yeah, well, it makes it hard to sleep. So of lot of these folks'll hang out drinking at night, and work or sleep during the day."

Emily raised her voice, so the group could hear her, and said, "We need to scatter and blend in. Everybody grab a seat somewhere. Make sure you're surrounded by Brazilians. And get the paintings and the guns out of sight."

They looked at her blankly for a moment.

Exasperated, she said, "Go!" The *artistes* scattered.

Once the crowd figured out what they were trying to do, they went out of their way to help. The way Emily figured it, by this point in the war, the locals hated the Batistas and the Chinese-led coalition about equally. None of them needed to be geniuses to realize that neither side cared about them.

Emily walked up to the bar and dropped a few small gold coins on the bar. The bartender, a bald old man with a five-day beard and a paunch, grinned ebulliently and made them disappear.

Drinks were pushed into all of their hands. Miller ended up with a woman sitting in his lap while Sanford ended up sitting with a mob of young men, his painting safely hidden underneath the table. A group of twenty-somethings surrounded Emily at the bar. One of them, strikingly handsome and severely aware of it, casually put his arm around her waist as if she were his girlfriend.

Ambush Site (Underwater), 03:12

As soon as the APC's propeller noise disappeared into the distance, Fang extracted himself from the bottom muck and went looking for Travis. Visibility was effectively zero, so he trudged along the bottom in total darkness—the combat suit and his remaining gear made him somewhat less than buoyant—guided electronically toward Trav's last location.

"Trav?" No answer from Ghost Two. Not good.

"Ophelia?"

He wasn't too surprised when Ophelia didn't answer. With the enemy approaching, she'd probably brought the drone that had been relaying their communications down amongst the buildings to avoid detection and elimination. Incongruously, that had probably made it a casualty of their opposition's response to being ambushed. He was incommunicado until she got another drone on station.

Fang hated to admit it, but whoever their adversaries were, they were good.

And ruthless as well. They clearly couldn't care less about collateral damage.

He reached Ghost Two's location and found a mass of shattered pilings and shredded wooden debris; the remains of the building above had been dropped on Ghost Two's position.

"Trav?"

This time he thought he heard some static, so he climbed around the pile to see if he could get a better signal. The debris shifted and he had to jump to avoid getting his leg trapped between two thick beams. He figured he was getting close to Trav when he started hearing cursing interspersed with the static.

"Ghost Two, state your status."

The cursing stopped. "*Blown up, sir.*"

Inside his helmet, Fang rolled his eyes. Ghost Two couldn't be too badly hurt, not if he still had his sense of humor intact.

They were close enough now that his combat suit was able to handshake with Ghost Two's suit, giving

Fang access to Trav's diagnostics. His suit was pretty banged up. The left arm was usable but unpowered. The right leg had been breached, and Trav was bleeding, but not badly; internal seals were keeping water out of the rest of his suit. His longer distance comms had been scraped off, leaving him with perhaps a twenty-meter communications range. His rifle was damaged and unusable, though he still had his pistol.

"Time for you to stop lying around and get back to work, trooper."

"*OK, but can you get this building off me?*" Ghost Two said. "*I'm trapped under a couple of big beams and I don't have the leverage to move them.*"

The AI in Fang's combat suit helpfully highlighted Ghost Two's precise position. He started pulling debris out of the way.

Ophelia said, "*Ghost One, Ghost Two, check, check.*"

Without stopping his efforts, and breathing heavily with exertion despite the powered assist from the suit, Fang answered, "Ghost One here. Ghost Two is slightly dented, but fine. He's got a comms problem, but my suit can relay for him as long as we're within about twenty meters of each other."

20. Distraction

Cargo Boat, 03:16

Gregorio braced himself as he piloted the boat through a sweeping turn that took it from the main channel through the watery *favela* and into a side channel. The back end swung a little wide and smashed against one of the timbers holding up a walkway. He ignored the damage to the boat; he was planning to abandon the boat as soon as he got past one more turn.

He missed having Emily's connection with Ghost Team—it sure was nice to have their bird's eye view of the area. But he felt he wasn't doing too badly. His years of smuggling experience had given him a feel for the rhythm of this kind of chase.

He hoped he'd muddied his backtrail enough that the enemy couldn't figure out where he'd dropped his passengers, not even when they found this boat abandoned. Two more minutes and he'd step off this boat for the last time and just fade into the local population.

His employers had already gotten his family out of Brazil. He'd hide out for a couple weeks, and then take advantage of the same contacts his family had been given to get out himself. Just a few weeks and he'd be able to see his grandchildren again.

Three miles away, Paiva's gun truck pulled to a halt on a street that provided an elevated view of the *favela*. It was a nice neighborhood, save for a few homes that had been demolished by bombing. The gun swiveled in response to precise, real-time coordinates provided by Raynald's helicopter view and fired a single shot from its mass driver.

At almost fifteen thousand kilometers per hour, the supersonic crash of the shot broke windows throughout the neighborhood. The metallic projectile flashed into a cyan plasma that looked more like a laser bolt than a high-speed projectile. It tunneled through one of the neighborhood homes, obliterating the living room and the family dog. It cut a groove through the roof of a building in the *favela*.

The bolt passed through a crowded tenement, missing a man by seven meters who had just gotten out of bed, but sucking him out of the wide exit hole and depositing him in the water with just a few broken bones and minor burns. It evaporated a couple making love in their tiny but neat home, then smashed through the cabin of the boat.

The shot missed Gregorio by two meters but it didn't matter. At that proximity, his body was disintegrated, sucked out the exit hole and spread over an area of about a hundred meters as a fine red mist. The cabin effectively ceased to exist. The impact drove the boat into the far side of the channel where it crashed into a building, which partially collapsed onto the bow of the boat.

***Paladin*, 03:17**

"Jesus," Ophelia said, wide-eyed. "They just took out the boat."

"What?" Armel exclaimed, without turning around. "How?" He kept his eyes on the screens in front of him.

Navigating *Paladin* underwater through the *favela* had never been part of the plan. It was an improvisation born of necessity. Unlike the opposition's APC, *Paladin* didn't float. It rolled across the bottom on its tracks, like an old-fashioned tank, but more agile. Ophelia knew it was taking all of Armel's attention and skills to make sure they didn't get stuck in the mud, hung up on the junk that littered the bottom, or smash into obstacles, like the pilings that supported the building around them, that would give their presence away.

Keying her mic, Ophelia said, "Ghost Team, the boat has been stopped. Rail gun. Looks like it was the gun truck we saw earlier. While we've been busy, they moved it to an elevated position and blasted us."

"Shit," Armel said. "I prefer my bad guys to be incompetent."

"Me, too," Ophelia said, fervently.

"*Shoulda taken that out when we had the chance,*" Travis drawled. "*I guess we're gonna need to keep our heads down.*"

"*Ghost One, ETA on* Paladin*?*"

"Five minutes," Armel said, chiming in on comms, "but we're going to need your help to get the container attached."

Ophelia cursed. She'd been so worried about coordinating things that she'd forgotten about that. Their testing back on *Khufu* had demonstrated that enhanced strength was needed to make the attachment under field conditions. Plus neither she nor Armel had any underwater gear.

"*Ghost One here, we're on our way.*"

"*Yeah, dented but still in service. Mostly.*"

Favela (Underwater), 03:23

Fang bounded over some twisted pilings, moving through the murky water as if he were in a slow motion movie scene. He and Trav had made their way along the bottom across the wreckage of the surrounding buildings. The combat suits were relatively light, thanks to various composite materials, but only relatively. They still floated like bricks. Swimming wasn't an option, even with the strength augmentation.

"*Ah, the scenic tour,*" Trav said. "*You take me to all the good places, Fang.*"

Fang ignored his chatter, knowing that it was just how Trav kept his spirits up in the thick of the action, and focused on the task at hand. A lot of ramshackle wooden buildings had been dropped into the water when the pilings had been chewed out from underneath them. Those closest to the ambush had been further pulverized by the anti-personnel rounds from the enemy APC. This far from the epicenter, the wreckage was looking considerably less chewed up.

Ophelia said, "*Paladin is on station. Ghost One, Ghost Two, we're waiting on you guys now.*"

Up ahead, Fang spotted some pilings emerging from the murk that had been damaged but not destroyed. They'd finally reached the edge of the damage zone.

"Ghost One here, we're moving. Should be out of the water momentarily."

Time to find a place to climb up.

They'd make better time on the walkways.

21. Fateful Intervention

Favela, 03:25

Hawk Four, the leader of Squad Two, jogged down the walkway, shouldering aside any locals who got in his way. Another mercenary pounded along behind him. Seven Batista soldiers were strung out in their wake, having trouble keeping up with the mercenaries, who were more fit in general and also physically augmented by their combat suits.

"*The boat's been stopped,*" Raynald said. A map appeared on his heads-up display, with the route clearly marked. Raynald was nothing if not efficient. "*Hawk Four, expedite approach before the local scavengers start stealing—*"

A bright light blossomed in the sky above, momentarily turning night into day and cutting off the signal with a crackle. Vision filters compensated for the brightness but couldn't do much about the thunderclap of the aerial explosion, which rolled over the city with near-deafening intensity.

His ears were still ringing as his companion pulled

up alongside him and shouted, "That's new!" The Chinese had been bombing Manaus sporadically for the last two weeks, but not like this.

"EMP," Hawk Four responded. They'd probably be making their final push against Manaus soon.

As the flare of the EMP gradually faded, missiles streaked across the sky. It looked like they were heading for downtown. Anti-missile units opened up, sending distant sparks arcing into the sky. Fiery puffballs appeared in the heavens with staccato pops. Distant explosions, probably missile and bomb strikes, added their rumble to the noise.

He saw a helicopter auto-rotating as it fell from the sky. It disappeared from view behind a building, then an expanding fireball outlined the building in billowing waves of yellow and red.

"We've still got a mission," he shouted. "Secure the boat!"

He sped up, legs blurring with augmented speed. His fellow Hawk matched his lead and they left the unaugmented soldiers in their wake.

La Bomba, 03:26

Despite the shutters on the bar's windows, light suddenly washed in around the edges, startling Emily and the rest of the bar's denizens. It had to have been momentarily brighter than day outside. The light was accompanied by a thunderclap of epic proportions.

Emily heard a crackle in her ear as her headset went

dead and—wait—was it actually warmer than it had been a second ago? And something was wrong with her vision. No, not her vision. Her implants. At the bottom of her view field, she usually had the time and her geographical position displayed. Those were gone.

She looked around the bar. Sanford was on the floor, screaming in pain. He had extensive implants, a whole memory augmentation model, if she recalled correctly. A few of the others were shaking their heads, probably discovering the same thing she'd just found with her own implants.

"Had to be an EMP," Emily said as Miller came up to her.

"Yeah."

"Must be the Chinese."

The Brazilians seemed unaffected; she doubted that any of them had implants. Modern conveniences had fled Brazil long ago.

Favela, 03:30

Hawk Four pounded down the walkway at extreme speed, dodging around doglegs in his path, followed closely by Hawk Five. The walkway turned the corner at an intersection. He crashed through the railing and leaped seven meters across the canal, landing heavily on the opposite walkway. A few boards cracked as he landed but momentum carried him safely past the damage.

He didn't bother to look back as Hawk Five made

the same leap behind him. He sprinted another two hundred meters then turned down a narrower side canal. According to his map, the boat was within five hundred meters, though he couldn't see it yet, due to the twists and turns of the waterway.

A few minutes later, he said, "I see it." He sub-vocalized a command and a zoom window opened up on one side of his helmet view. "Looks like there's people on board."

Behind him, Hawk Five asked, "*Survivors or indigents?*"

"Tell you in a minute."

Somebody saw the mercenaries coming and people started to scatter, heading for the nearest walkway or simply jumping into the water. By then, it was too late. The two mercenaries jumped and landed side-by-side on the stern of the boat, facing the doublewide doors where the stolen paintings had presumably been stored. A stray thought stuck Hawk Four as he landed—it was odd that the back railing was broken when it was the bow that had taken the brunt of the crash. He moved left while his companion went right. Careful not to aim any shots at what they assumed was the boat's cargo compartment, they blasted away with flechette rounds that shredded anybody in sight.

Hawk Four said. "I think they were indigents, but it's hard to tell."

While his companion went left to check the forward section of the boat, Hawk Four walked aft to check the cargo compartment. Throwing open the unlocked doors revealed only empty space beyond.

"I think we got a problem."

22. Tribulations

Paladin / La Bomba, 03:35

"Dammit!" Ophelia exclaimed. "I just lost every-thing to the EMP." Her eyeballs, and even the larger HKs that had previously taken out the enemy's jammer—all gone.

"Awesome," Armel said, shaking his head. "This situation just gets more fun by the minute."

"I'm popping our own jammer," Ophelia said, hands moving rapidly across her screens. "Zeds are spread out, their comms'll be rebooting 'cause of the EMP…let's mess with them some more." There was a popping sound and the jammer was away.

Armel chuckled. "Aren't you glad we included reimbursement for expendables in our contract?"

"Yeah." Ophelia chuckled humorlessly. "Well, we're here, and I can't tell anyone." There was no way Emily's comms survived the EMP. She turned to look at Armel. "Get us close to the walkway and deploy the access tube. I'm going to have to go up and get the *artistes*."

"But—"

"It can't be you," she said. "You have to drive. So, tag, I'm it." She unbuckled her harness.

"All right," he said dubiously, "I hope you know what you're doing." He maneuvered the APC a little closer to the walkway. Then there was a *whooshing* sound from above them as he deployed the ETR.

Ophelia stood up and undogged the hatch in the low ceiling of the vehicle, revealing the ribbed plastic tube with its built-in ladder. A few trickles of water splashed down to the deck. She grunted as she grabbed the first rung of the ladder and laboriously pulled herself up into the tube.

A moment later she was at the surface, holding on to what looked like the inner tube of a truck tire. Fortunately, Armel had positioned her right next to one of the supports for the walkway. She reached out, grabbed a weathered cross-strut, pulled herself out of the tube and clambered up to the walkway.

A few natives looked at her curiously. "Seen any foreigners?" she asked, not really expecting an answer.

An old woman with gray hair said, "In *La Bomba*," and pointed to a doorway about thirty meters away. Ophelia gave her a second look, and realized that the gray was misleading; she was probably in her late thirties.

She jogged down the walkway, pushed through the door and curtain beyond and found herself in a rundown bar. The *artistes* were present, though one of them was lying on the floor, surrounded by Emily, Miller and several others.

"We've got to get moving," Ophelia shouted. "Your ride's here and we can't stay long!"

Emily looked up, startled. She nodded and started giving directions. Two of her team members picked up the supine member of her crew; he must have been a casualty of the EMP, distinctly possible for anyone who had extensive implants.

Ophelia ushered the two carrying their casualty to the door. Three more folks followed them, each carrying a painting, with Emily bringing up the rear and herding people along.

Hawk APC, 03:36

To his left, Raynald started cursing. Paiva looked over at him. "No luck on the drones?" They were going through drones like firecrackers on Cinco de Mayo, first losing a set to the Monumentalists' anti-drone swarm and now another one to the Chinese EMP. Paiva hated being out of contact with his forces, especially since he had two squads spread out trying to intercept the Monumentalists.

"Three problems," Raynald said. "First, we ain't got a gun truck no more, the Chinese killed it. Second, the Monumentalists are jamming us. Finally, the drone launch tube is damaged. I can't release anything."

Paiva sighed heavily. He was becoming decidedly weary of these damned Monumentalists. He had two squads out looking for his foes, and now he couldn't even contact them. "Anything else?" Raynald shook his head. "Can you launch the drones manually?"

"I'll need to pull the whole unit," Raynald said, "But I've got to do it from outside. I've got the tools, but it'll take a while. And I can't do it while…" Trailing off, he pointed at the screen in front of Sheffield, the APC driver.

Paiva watched impatiently as Sheffield attempted to navigate through the debris field. The engine rotors whined angrily as his driver tried to push some timbers out of their path, to no avail, as the APC-turned–boat twisted sideways rather than making forward progress.

Paiva rubbed his forehead, a telltale sign of his frustration. Sheffield was making progress, albeit painstakingly, just not fast enough for his needs. The fundamental problem was that a watercraft, any watercraft, just didn't have the leverage to force its way through the floating wreckage that surrounded them.

"I'm dismounting," Paiva snarled, unhitching the three-point harness holding him in his seat.

Sheffield looked over his shoulder. "Sorry, boss—"

"Not your fault," Paiva said, picking up his helmet. "My orders, my fault. Just get out of this mess as fast as you can." He pulled his helmet on.

"At least we pasted those Monumentalists," Sheffield said.

Paiva nodded curtly, stood up and undogged the hatch on the APC's ceiling, which popped open with a hydraulic hiss. Ignoring the pull-down ladder, he leaped up, grabbed the rim of the hatch and propelled himself to a standing position on the APC's hull.

He grimly considered the bobbing, shifting

quagmire of floating timbers, demolished housing, furniture and bodies that surrounded the APC. Ignoring the collateral damage, to which he was largely inured to by now in his lengthy military career, he simply considered the unstable terrain as an obstacle to be crossed. Choosing a large piece that looked relatively stable, he leapt onto it and began making his way through the wreckage.

Outside La Bomba, 03:39

Emily helped one of her people lift Sanford over the railing, gently passing him to someone else down below, who then slid him into the arms of Miller waiting in the opening of the tube. Ophelia and two other team members stood behind Emily, guarding the extra paintings and watching the struggle to get Sanford down to the *Paladin.*

"Uh, Emily," Ophelia said, "we've got a problem."

Emily turned around and saw a combat-suited mercenary behind them, holding a massive rifle pointed at Ophelia. As she watched, a group of perhaps six Brazilian soldiers filtered down the walkway toward them, guns also aimed in this direction.

"We were so close," Emily said.

"Why don't you ask your guys to climb back up over the railing?" the mercenary said. "Or we can shoot them. Your call."

"All right," Emily said. "You win." Keeping her

hands clearly in view, she turned slightly and called out, "Come on back up, you guys."

One man, the one who'd been passing Sanford down to Miller, climbed slowly back over the railing. There was a burst of gunfire behind him as several of the soldiers fired on Miller and Sanford. Emily leaned forward and saw the tube floating below, Miller well down in the accessway and still holding Sanford in front of him. She didn't see any signs of blood. As she watched, they fell into the APC. She couldn't tell for sure, but somebody may have slammed the hatch behind them.

Emily faced the mercenary. It was disconcerting seeing her face reflected in the shiny surface of the mercenary's helmet. And even more upsetting to see a very large gun pointed directly at her.

"This is Hawk Two," the mercenary said. "Can anyone read me? Squad One has captured the thieves." Apparently, he wasn't having luck getting hold of anyone. Hawk Two gestured at Emily with his weapon. "What do you have down there in the water?"

"A mini-sub," Emily said, figuring that the best lie was the one that contained at least enough truth to be plausible.

"Makes sense," he said. "Tell them to surface now, or we'll start shooting some of your people."

"They won't listen," Emily said. "If you were them and you had the perfect getaway vehicle, would you surface?"

Emily tried not to react as Fang appeared on the roof above Hawk Two. He fired a stubby-looking gun with a large barrel at the enemy mercenary. It hit the mercenary and enveloped his suit in something that looked like an electrical storm. Emily dived away from Hawk Two, then felt her arm get singed by an electrical discharge as she reached out to sweep a rolled-up painting out of the way. The mercenary fell heavily, clearly out of commission, whether unconscious or dead, Emily couldn't tell.

"Down," she yelled as the soldiers fired back at Fang. Ophelia was already down, but her *artistes* hit the deck as well, huddling with fear and trying not to appear like viable targets. Some of the soldiers fell, thanks to Fang's intense return barrage. Then Travis appeared behind the soldiers and caught them in a crossfire.

Half deaf from all the gunfire, Emily had time to realize that the gun battle had only lasted perhaps thirty seconds. All of the combatants except Fang and Travis were down. Where the soldiers had been, blood and body parts were splattered everywhere.

Fang jumped down from the roof, landing next to Emily with a solid thud. "Let's get everybody loaded," he said. "It's time to get the hell out of here."

Ophelia said, "We need one of you guys to hook up the container."

Walking up, Travis said, "It's going to have to be you, Fang. My suit's too damaged." Emily tried hard not to stare. His formerly shiny and pristine combat suit was so dented and scraped up it looked like somebody had run it through a washing machine.

"All right," Fang said. The whole walkway shook as he jumped over the railing and into the water.

23. Action

Favela, 03:42

Paiva was angry. Not only was he out of position, admittedly due to his own perhaps overly enthusiastic suppression fire, but now he was completely cut off from his squads, too. He'd expected comms back by now, but the Monumentalists were jamming.

Hearing gunfire in the distance, he sped up even more.

Somebody was going to very sorry when he arrived.

Favela, 03:45

Fang stood in the mud and glumly contemplated the dilemma before him. The problem was twofold. First, the container and *Paladin* were at slightly different levels. Second, Fang had no leverage; he kept sinking into the mud every time he tried to exert enough force to get the container hitched up.

What he really need was a winch to raise the

container a bit. Well, he had rope with him, in a compartment. Actually a cable. Standard military gear.

"Armel," Fang said. "I want you to swivel the main gun so it's over the container. I'm going to improvise a winch."

"Ghost One, I could use one of those, too," Travis drawled, *"but I typically wait until after the mission."*

Outside La Bomba, 03:46

Emily watched as her last team member, a Swedish woman in her mid-forties, climbed down to the floating tube. Clinging to the pylon, the woman reached out with a foot, hooked the inner tube and pulled it closer. Then she gingerly climbed into the tube. She stopped partway and reached up as Emily hung off the railing and handed the last painting to her, the one that had been rolled up for safekeeping.

Emily straightened up and looked around. It was just her and Travis now, and Fang down in the water working on the connector. Unexpectedly, she was looking the right direction as two more combat-suited mercenaries raced around a corner.

"Travis!" she screamed, and leaped over the railing and into the water. Rounds tore the railing apart where she'd been, sending pieces flying everywhere. She felt a something catch at her arm, and she splashed clumsily into the water.

She came to the surface about two meters from the tube, which should have been an easy swim. Except for the most excruciating pain and the fact that her right arm wasn't working. She almost fainted when she realized there was a foot-long splinter of wood piercing her upper arm.

She gritted her teeth and tried to swim toward the tube, just a simple sidestroke using her other arm. She was dimly aware of copious amounts of gunfire going on above her, but her focus was on her goal. Despite her efforts, the tube was receding from her.

How could that be? And then she realized that the tide was running out, carrying her away faster than she could swim.

Paladin, 03:48

Ophelia cursed. She'd launched a few more eyeballs as soon as she got back inside *Paladin*, but it had been too late to detect the enemy mercenaries. Now Travis was fighting two enemies with a damaged suit, and *Paladin* was vulnerable to enemy assault if they got past Travis—the hatch was still open. The sound of gunfire could be heard distinctly throughout the vehicle.

"*Uh, I could use some help here!*" Travis said, breathing heavily.

"*I'm coming up,*" Fang said.

Ophelia started to speak, but Armel cut her off. "Negative, Ghost One, I'ma take care of this."

She turned and looked at him, then realized he was accessing *Paladin's* fire controls. It wasn't his primary duty, but he could operate fire control from his console when he had to.

Jesus, firing at close range. She looked back at her drone view. It looked like Emily was in trouble, but still floating; more importantly, she was a safe distance from his likely blast zone. She moved an eyeball to give Armel a better view of the battlespace. Hidden from the view of the combatants, but not from her tiny drone, the APC's main gun elevated until it came out of the water underneath the walkway.

As the two mercenaries advanced on Travis' position, it fired once. A cyan bolt flashed and the screen went momentarily white. As the brightness dissipated and the scene gradually reappeared, ten feet of walkway around the blast was simply missing, as was the front of the building adjacent to the blast. The perimeter of the blast area was on fire. The two attacking mercenaries were nowhere to be seen.

"*Goddamit, I think you singed my eyebrows!*" Ghost Two bellowed.

Outside La Bomba, 03:55

Paiva followed the smoke, a highly visible beacon in infrared view, to the scene of the battle. Part of the walkway was still burning. The decrepit buildings had been so badly peppered by gunfire that they looked like they had the new chickenpox HX. Hawk Two was sprawled about five meters from the fire. He'd been bricked like Hawk Three had been earlier, but someone had uncoupled his helmet so he wouldn't suffocate inside the dead suit.

A bunch of dead Batista soldiers littered the walkway on the other side of the fire. Probably the rest of Squad One.

"Hey, boss," Raynald said. "The jamming stopped." Paiva translated that to mean that their opponents didn't think they needed jamming anymore and had probably retrieved the jammer for later use if necessary. "Got some eyeballs coming your way, too."

"Good," Paiva said. "The Monumentalists have managed to break contact."

"Shit, boss. And, uh, I'm not seein' vital—"

"Two is bricked. I think Four and Five are gone." It had been more than two years since he'd lost a fighter. Casualties were the worst part of this line of work, even though he knew it was an inevitable consequence of the mercenary trade.

"Oh, hell."

"I expect they're going to try to escape via the river. Let's see if we can head them off."

"On it."

Paiva hated failing at a mission.

He knew he had a crack team, and they'd traded blows with the Monumentalists like two heavyweight boxers in a world title match. And they'd lost.

At least for now.

24. Exfiltration

Paladin, 04:21

Emily came to gradually, becoming increasingly annoyed at the way *Khufu* was rolling in the waves of the Amazon River. After a while, she realized that there were people looking down at her and the ceiling above didn't look remotely like her cabin aboard the *Khufu*.

Well, let's see. That must mean she was aboard the *Paladin*. Those weren't waves; they were rolling along the uneven bottom. She was alive, so clearly she hadn't drowned. She could kind of feel her arm, but it seemed numb. She turned her head gradually. Yup, bandages.

"Where are we?" she croaked.

"Still in the *favela*," Miller replied.

"They lookin' for us?"

"You bet your bottom dollar," Travis said.

"I know how to get out," she said tiredly. She closed her eyes for a minute, felt herself start to drift off. Forced them open again. Travis bent down over her and she whispered into his ear. She closed her eyes again. "We just…" Her voice faded out and her head lolled to one side as she passed out again.

Travis looked up at the concerned faces around Emily. "That's crazy," he said, then smiled. "It's so dumb, it might just work."

Paladin, 06:37

Dawn rose over a city shrouded in the smoke of the nighttime bombing. Some wooden buildings were still on fire and would continue burning until the late morning tropical rainfall quenched them.

Helicopters noisily criss-crossed the sky over the dark waters of the Rio Negro and the *favela* while armed soldiers filtered through the narrow walkways of the shantytown. They peered under walkways and buildings, used long poles or electronic devices to probe the canals, all searching for any traces of the mysterious quarry they'd been told to find.

With all official attention drawn to the beehive of activity of the river side of the *favela*, *Paladin* rolled ashore on the far side of the *favela*, sporting the drab olive color and markings of an official Batista military vehicle and pulling what looked like an eight-meter-long truck trailer in jungle camouflage colors.

Its exposure was about five seconds. If anybody associated with the Batistas had noticed a vehicle coming out of the water, well, that would have been noteworthy. But after it was no longer in the water, after it had turned onto a road, it was just another official military vehicle, albeit a strange-looking one.

And the further from the *favela* it got, the less noteworthy it was.

Inside *Paladin* an hour later, after Miller, their only Portuguese speaker, had helped them bullshit their way through a checkpoint to get out of the city, Travis looked at Fang and Ophelia, in turn. “I can’t believe this worked.”

Khufu, 09:45

Ester leaned over Kushner’s bed and shook his shoulder. His eyes snapped open. “Any word?” he croaked.

“Nothing,” Ester replied. They knew that all hell had broken loose last night, thanks to the Chinese bombing. And that a full-scale EMP had gone off. “But I’ve got something else to show you.”

She pulled out a flexi and folded it open so Kushner could see it. “I acquired a password to Ahoub’s surveillance system.” She smiled with a certain amount of satisfaction. “Looked over someone’s shoulder while they were typing it.”

“Old school,” he said, “but effective.”

She pressed a button on the screen. “This is January fourteenth, when you sent Emily to get tea.” The screen showed her walking with the tray in her hands, on her way back to Kushner’s cabin and the ongoing strategy session. But first, she stopped in front of her own cabin and went in. A moment later, she came out and continued on to Kushner’s cabin.

"You may recall," Ester continued, "that when she came back, she made a point of personally fixing you a cup of tea."

Kushner clenched his teeth and looked up at her. "You're saying she infected me deliberately." His eyes were glittering with anger.

"Yes," she said. "I think so."

"That bitch! I'll destroy her." Kushner started coughing, painful hacking coughs that shook his frame. When they subsided, he said, "She'll never work in the art field again, never. I'll see to that."

War Zone, 10:19
Bang Hai, 238 km east of Manaus

"What do you mean, you can't find them?"

"Just that, sir. They've disappeared. The Batistas have forces all over the *favela* and the river looking for them."

"The Batistas? How are they involved?"

"There was some sort of running battle. We think the Monumentalists got the artwork, but were interrupted by a mercenary group called the Hawks. They work for a General Diego, of the Batistas, and were probably commissioned to transport the artwork to the buyer."

"So, the Monumentalists have the artwork? And we don't know where they are?"

"Yes, sir."

Favela, 11:41

Manuel was in his narrow bed, a grandiose name for what was really just a cot, napping through the heat of the mid-day, when he heard the scratching at his backdoor. Groaning, he sat up, ignoring the aches and pains as much as he could. Getting old was a burden, though it surely beat the alternatives.

He slipped his feet into some sandals. He remembered living in far finer places than this hovel in the *favela*, where one could actually walk on the floors without risking splinters. But that was before the Batistas and his fall from grace.

He shuffled his way slowly to the backdoor and opened it. A foreign woman was huddled in the doorway, blond and blue-eyed and surprisingly muscular. One side of her face was bruised, black and blue from her neck to her temple. She wore a hodgepodge of clothes, probably stolen, he noted, and she was dirt-covered and splattered with what looked like blood.

She was holding her side, clearly in pain, and breathing shallowly, as if breathing hurt. Maybe broken ribs, that would be consistent with what he was seeing.

"Are you…are you Manuel Barbosa?" she asked.

"I used to be," he said. "Now I'm just an old man living in the *favela*."

"Anton Ahoub…if there was trouble…I…" she said haltingly.

"Ah." The old man smiled. "Of course I'll help you." Ahoub had saved both of his granddaughters from slavers. A side effect of his fall from grace; his enemies had taken his family, too, except for the two girls that Ahoub had rescued. He bent down and, despite the pain in his back, lifted her up and helped her hobble into his meager home.

"I'm Laney," she said. "I should…warn you…" She sagged down onto his bed. "They're looking for me."

"The Batistas?"

"Yeah."

Manuel smiled. Even better. Two birds with one stone. Repay Ahoub and stick it to the Batistas. It was shaping up to be a lovely day.

SALVAGE MISSION, PART 9

An anti-grav gurney was waiting at the airlock to the *Oxcart.* Together they placed the body of the Curator, Kate Walton, on the pallet with care.

"She knew the entire time she was doomed," Carter said. "She doomed herself to starvation. Just to make sure this art survived. Knowing she would not."

"That is a different kind of brave."

"Guys, I just got an estimate back from the Oklahoma Salvage front office," Pope said. They could hear the smile in her voice. "Even though it's not our usual kind of salvage, they found an auction house that is eager to handle it. The auction estimate for the paintings and sculptures alone is 1.4 billion credits."

Quinn and Carter looked at each other.

"There's more," Pope stated in awe. "If they

confirm that the body and stories are real. A set of original stories by Kate Walton. The log files and recordings of her writing them from Lex as proof of provenance are… is…"

"Are what?" Quinn and Carter asked at the same time.

"Priceless."

ABOUT THE AUTHORS

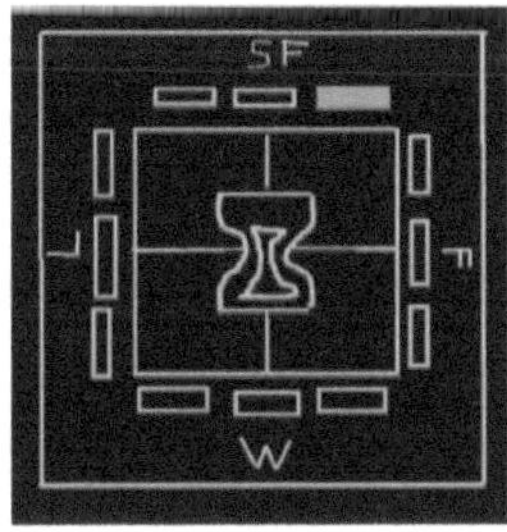

The authors are all members of the *Hourlings*, a writing group based in the Northern Virginia area of the United States. For more information about the activities of the Hourlings, its anthologies, and the publications of its various members, see the group's Facebook page at:

https://www.facebook.com/Hourlings

TR Dillon is a writer who lives and works in the Washington, D.C. metropolitan area. He can be reached at trdillon@trdillon.net.

Peter Dube Jr is known for his poetry, art, and love of role-playing games. His most recent publication is *Elysium: The Shimmering City* and his illustrations can be found in *The Gift* by D.J. Piper. Originally from New Hampshire, he is a military spouse and therefore travels. He can be reached at peter.dubejr@gmail.com.

Elizabeth Hayes writes *Lord of the Rings* (LOTR) fanfiction under the pen name Uvatha the Horseman, and is the author of *How to Write Faster: Strategies for Planners and Pantsers.* She holds an engineering degree from Carnegie-Mellon and has spent a career in the space program, which is to say, she knows essentially nothing about writing, yet persists in doing it anyway.

She lives in Northern Virginia with her husband and three children. Given her fascination with medieval reenactment, she rarely sets foot in the real world.

Jeffrey C. "Timehorse" Jacobs is a failed physicist, professional software engineer, and drives an electric car around the Mid-Atlantic region. He assists local writing groups, Doctor Who societies, cosplays, organizes EV events, runs Science Book Clubs and created/produced *Project Kronosphere.* He can be found online at Facebook (TimeHorse) and Twitter (@TimeHorse).

David Keener is an author, editor, artist and public speaker who lives in Northern Virginia with his wife and two, oops, three inordinately large dogs. He writes science fiction, fantasy and mystery but loves the idea of mashing up his favorite genres in new and (hopefully) unexpected ways.

He is the grand instigator behind the *Worlds Enough* anthology series, and co-editor of the first volume, *Fantastic Defenders.* His next anthology will be *Tales From the Forever House*, about a mysterious inn that travels randomly throughout the multiverse.

He frequently speaks at technical conferences and SF/Fantasy conventions, where he often conducts workshops on writing and public speaking. Find out more about him and his books online at Twitter (@keenersaurus) or at his web site:

http://www.davidkeener.org.

S. C. Megale's real first name is Shea–like the butter. Or the stadium in New York, which got knocked down. She was born in 1995 and her first published novel, *This is Not a Love Scene*, will release in 2019 from Macmillan/St. Martin's Press.

Her passions include music, history, the woods, God, men, and humanity, especially if the humans are men. Confined to a wheelchair since the age of two in greater Washington, D.C., Megale defines courage and adventure as her favorite virtues. When not writing, she can be found playing her bamboo flutes, flying in helicopters, accepting the American Presidential nomination, and converting her first name into two initials because it's cliché. For more of Shea's books and to find out what the C in S.C. Megale stands for, please visit www.scmegale.com.

Donna Royston enjoys writing about people who are not quite what they seem. She primarily writes fantasy, often based loosely on real mythologies from around the world. She is also the co-editor of *Fantastic Defenders*, the first volume of the *Worlds Enough* anthology series.

Erica Rue is a reader and writer of science fiction and fantasy, especially YA. Her abandoned biology major and handful of astronomy classes have prepared her well for writing sci-fi. She enjoys learning new words and promptly forgetting them so that she can rediscover them. When she's not writing, she forgets to water her garden, completes every side quest she triggers, and boosts her dog's self-esteem.

Martin Wilsey is a full-time author, hunter, photographer, rabble-rouser, father, camper, friend, marksman, storyteller, truck driver, frightener of children, carnivore, engineer, fool, philosopher, cook, and madman.

In his former life, he was a research scientist for a government-funded think tank. The skills he developed serve him well in researching various aspects within his writing.

He and his wife Brenda live in Virginia with their cats.

ACKNOWLEDGMENTS

A surprisingly large number of people helped with this anthology in one way or another, including the members of the Hourlings Writing Group, the Loudoun County Writers Group and the Reston Writers' Review who were gracious enough to critique many of these stories.

Special thanks to Lawrence Block, who in many ways inspired this anthology about art with his own delightful anthology, *In Sunlight or in Shadow: Stories Inspired by the Paintings of Edward Hopper.*

Finally, kudos to the New York Metropolitan Museum of Art for graciously making digital copies of hundreds of thousands of famous art pieces available rights-free for the benefit of the public.

ARTWORK CREDITS

1. *On a Lee Shore*, by Winslow Homer, 1900. CC0, from the RISD Museum in Providence, RI.

2. *La Calavera de la Catrina*, by Jose Guadalupe Posada, 1912. CC0 from WikiCommons.

3. *Madame de Brayer*, by Gustave Courbet, 1858. CC0 from the Metropolitan Museum of Art.

4. *A Meadow in the Mountains: Le Mas de Saint-Paul*, by Vincent Van Gogh, 1889. Public domain from WikiArt.

5. *Palm Trees at Bordighera*, by Claude Monet, 1884. Public domain from the Wikimedia Foundation.

6. *The Bear Calls Renard to Appear Before the Council of Animals*, by Hendrick van Alcmar, 1650 - 1675. CC0 from the Metropolitan Museum of Art.

7. *Lurking*, by Peter Dube Jr., 2018. Copyright © 2018 Peter Dube Jr. All rights reserved.

8. *The Dancers*, by Edgar Degas, around 1900. CC0 from the Metropolitan Museum of Art.

9. *Hourlings Pin*, by S. C. Megale, 2018. Copyright © 2018 S. C. Megale. All rights reserved.

Five action-packed fantasy novelettes about unlikely heroes defending against deadly, mystical threats.

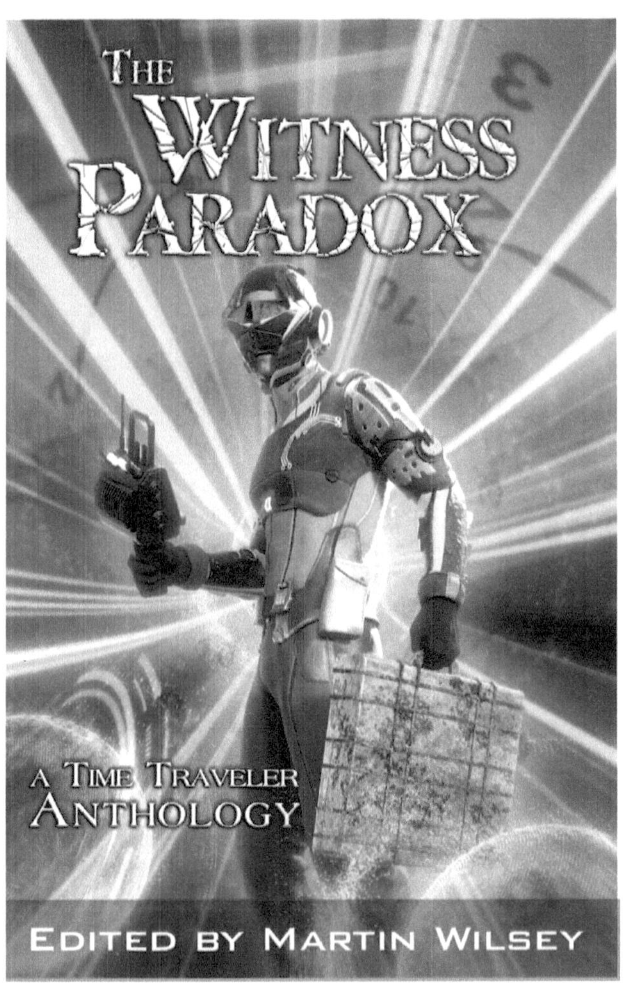

Time travel might be possible…but will it ever be safe?